A FASCINATING STRANGER

Sighing, Clara entered the house and crossed to the stairs. She grasped the elaborate, gold-gilded banister in one hand, lifted her skirts with the other, and climbed to the second level. She pushed open the door to the captain's room. He was utterly alone. He could die at any moment, and no one was there by his side.

Before the doctor had arrived, she had accompanied the footmen who carried Captain Hawke to his room. She had tried to help, but Mrs. Rossi, the housekeeper, had insisted tending a sick man was no place for a Carrington lady.

Clara glanced up and down the hall one last time before slipping silently into the room. No one was about. Captain Hawke's dramatic collapse at dinner, followed by the doctor's house call, had been enough excitement for one evening, and her parents had retired. The house had grown silent, and Clara was free to look in on the patient—or even tend him.

She hardly knew the man, but his strange, dismissive attitude toward her intrigued her. He was nothing like other Englishmen she had met: staid, deferential gentlemen reluctant to express their feelings. Oh, he had made a good enough show of manners during dinner. But when they were alone together, the pretense vanished, replaced by an intriguing and even brutal honesty. He was the most fascinating man she had ever encountered.

A 5TH AVENUE AFFAIR

Tracy Cozzens

ZEBRA BOOKS
KENSINGTON PUBLISHING CORP.
http://www.kensingtonbooks.com

ZEBRA BOOKS are published by

Kensington Publishing Corp.
850 Third Avenue
New York, NY 10022

All Kensington titles, imprints and distributed lines are available at special quantity discounts for bulk purchases for sales promotion, premiums, fund-raising, educational or institutional use.

Special book excerpts or customized printings can also be created to fit specific needs. For details, write or phone the office of the Kensington Special Sales Manager: Kensington Publishing Corp., 850 Third Avenue, New York, NY 10022. Attn. Special Sales Department. Phone: 1-800-221-2647.

Zebra and the Z logo Reg. U.S. Pat. & TM Off.

First Printing: September 2003
10 9 8 7 6 5 4 3 2 1

Printed in the United States of America

For Kellen, who believes in the power of words

Prologue

Central Provinces, India

The stench filled the air, choking him. Charred wood, overlaid with the unspeakable smell of burned flesh, filled his nostrils, and he gagged.

Smoke from the explosion darkened the skies, blotting out the hot Indian sun. Captain Stone Hawke stumbled toward the wreckage that had so recently been his men's barracks. Gone in an instant. Not a soul stirred in the clutter. Even those standing on the veranda outside had been silenced.

Even those standing outside . . .

Chapter 1

New York City, 1895

The rattle of the brass knocker against the front door could not have been less welcome. Clara's legs ached, and she wanted nothing more than to peel off her clothing and curl into bed. The spring rain outside had soaked through her woolen cloak, now dripping a puddle into the iron pan at the base of the walnut coatrack.

Already the grandfather clock in the hall had struck eleven—hardly the time for social calls. She waited one more minute for Edgar, the family butler, to appear, but knew at this late hour he was already abed. Where she should be.

Tonight's benefit had dragged on much too long, with an emphasis on the showy food and gowns and scant attention paid to the downtrodden. There had to be more one could do for the poor, huddled masses mentioned in the inscription on the Statue of Liberty in the harbor.

As if God had heard her thoughts, she swung open the heavy door to find a bedraggled fellow standing on the stoop. He hunched over, clutching a thin mackintosh against his lean frame. A flat-topped derby shadowed his face, and a worn leather satchel rested at his feet.

"Good evening," Clara said, on guard from the man's disreputable appearance. Perhaps he had the wrong address.

He removed his derby. The outdoor electric lights, installed the previous year, illuminated a sharp-planed face under dark beard stubble. She guessed him to be less than thirty. A strained, haunted look in his eyes spurred concern in Clara. Perhaps he was a vagabond who had heard of her good deeds and was seeking assistance.

She could give him the address of a relatively clean and well-run flophouse that would house him while he searched for honest employment. At this late hour, she dare not escort him there. She couldn't be gone past the time her parents would return from their soiree, or her mother would fret—and Clara's freedom would be curtailed for at least a week while her charity cases suffered the consequences.

The visitor glanced about, as if worried he was somewhere he ought not to be. "The Carringtons. Do they live here?"

He spoke with an English accent. Recently off the boat, perhaps, and out of work? "Yes, this is the Carrington residence."

Relief flickered in his brown eyes, the color of

aged bronze. Turning, he waved to a hackney cab that waited on the street. With a jingle of its harness, the two-wheeled hack disappeared into the night mists, its tail lanterns swaying.

"Perhaps you should have asked him to wait," she said. "It's too late for me to help you now. If you will return in the morning—"

His brow furrowed. "The letter. You must have received the letter."

Clara stared at him in confusion. "I'm sorry. I don't know of any letter. Perhaps my father . . ." He hardly looked like a business associate of her father's, but she could think of no other explanation.

"Nate." He sucked in a sharp breath that dissolved in a coughing fit. Clara reached out to him to offer comfort if she could, but he held up his hand. "Nathaniel Savidge, I mean."

"Pauline's husband? Did you travel from India, then?"

He nodded. Clara had already swung the door wide to allow him entrance. Her sister Pauline had sent him. That was all she needed to know. "Please, come in. You must get out of the cold. We'll get a nice fire going."

She strode toward the east hall, but he didn't follow. He stood in the front hall in his dripping coat, his satchel in one hand, his folded umbrella in the other. Craning his neck, he peered up and around, turning in a circle to take in the mansion's interior. Above their heads, a three-tiered electric chandelier burned brightly, suspended from a French-carved twenty-five-foot ceiling. A pair of winding staircases flanked a front hall large enough to serve as a ballroom. On the landing above, a long gallery displayed her family's collection of pastoral landscapes by now-dead European artists.

His gawking seemed to make him dizzy. He swayed and stumbled back a few steps, his legs threatening to give out.

Clara watched him carefully, worried he might succumb to his obvious fatigue before she could see him settled. No longer hunched in the rain, the man had straightened to his full six-foot height. Rapier cheekbones accentuated piercing eyes that appeared strangely glazed, as if he weren't quite in his right mind. He wasn't dangerous, was he? No, not if Pauline had sent him.

Still, Clara's eyes darted to the in-house telephone on a hall table. She gauged the distance to it, in case any trouble should follow on the heels of her charity. Her recent, clandestine visit to the tenements and sweatshops of lower Manhattan had taught her to be on alert in unfamiliar situations—and with unfamiliar people.

A shudder racked the man's body, and his knees bent. "Sir?"

He straightened and glanced at the umbrella he still held, as if he had no idea what to do with it.

Clara stepped forward and gently pulled the limp umbrella from his hand. At least two of the struts had snapped from the wind. No wonder the poor fellow was soaked through. She dropped it in the gold-rimmed umbrella stand.

"That brolly is a lost cause," he said, finally coming alive again. He glanced at his feet. "I'm dripping on your fine carpet. Turkish, I'd wager."

"I—I wouldn't know. My mother. She oversees the decorating."

"Take all this for granted, do you?" he asked wryly, his gaze flashing pointedly to her.

"I find more fulfilling things to think about than worldly goods," she said with a touch of diffidence. Nevertheless, it often embarrassed her how much her family possessed. Her mother was engaged in an ongoing quest to compete with the Astors, Vanderbilts, and Rockefellers. Certainly the Carringtons' wealth matched theirs, even if their position in society wasn't as well established. Mrs. Carrington made certain their home boasted only the finest furnishings. From the practical—such as the triple-lacquered teakwood table that held the house telephone—to the purely decorative.

Clara followed the visitor's gaze to the stained-glass window above the door. It had been imported by the house's architect from a Bavarian castle. Her visitor probably felt he had entered a museum.

He looked at her skeptically, clearly not believing her protestations.

"The carpet might survive if you remove your sodden coat," she said bluntly. She felt strange filling the role of butler, but the servants were abed. She didn't mind tending to some of his needs. Her curiosity aroused, she wanted to learn more about this mysterious stranger from a distant land.

"Of course." His fingers shaking, he struggled to undo his coat buttons. He took so long at the simple task that Clara had to fight not to step forward and help him as one would a child. She had

14 *Tracy Cozzens*

no desire to be on the receiving end of another searing gaze.

When he had finally shed his mackintosh, Clara saw that he wore sand-colored trousers accented with a side stripe. His faded red jacket reminded her of a soldier's uniform. It bore no insignia, but spots of unfaded fabric seemed to indicate that patches had been removed. How odd.

Clara hung his dripping coat in the armoire inset in the wall. "The parlor is this way. If you'll follow me."

His scuffed, worn boots thumped on the inlaid marquetry floor behind her as she led him down the hall. A coal-fed boiler in the basement warmed the first floor during the day and the bedrooms at night. But the air had grown chill since then. Without asking for permission, the stranger fell into a chair just inside the parlor door.

His sallow complexion began to alarm her. He seemed ill. Certainly the chill, damp spring weather would do nobody any good. "Tea. You look as if you could use a cup."

He nodded weakly, and Clara, finally admitting she needed a helping hand, rang the bellpull to the parlor maid's quarters. While she waited for the maid to arrive, she sat across from the man. "You know the marquess?"

He looked at her blankly. "Marquess? I hardly travel in those circles."

"But you said you know Pauline and her husband."

"Yes."

She restated the obvious. "Then you know him,

the marquess." Goodness, it was like talking to a child.

"Who, exactly, are you referring to?"

"Nathaniel Savidge."

He looked at her blankly, and Clara began to wonder if he was touched in the head. "Lord Nathaniel Savidge, the marquess of Bathurst."

His eyes widened in comprehension. "Nate is a marquess?"

She nodded as he absorbed the information. Then a rough bark of laughter exploded from his lungs, ending in a coughing fit. When he had it under control, he said, "That scoundrel. He never said. Not one word."

Clara found herself smiling. It was just like Nate and Pauline not to mention his illustrious status. They preferred the jungles, where Nate had established his reputation as a great hunter. The last she heard, the couple was living simply in a small Himalayan village.

"Well," he said, "whoever my friend really is, my coming here was entirely his idea. Has a fool notion being out of the country will be good for me. Since I'm no longer in the army."

"The British Army, in India."

He sighed. "He should have explained all this, in the letter."

"Which never arrived, to my knowledge," Clara said ruefully. "But that doesn't matter. Of course you may stay here, as long as you like."

Lucy, Clara's personal maid, appeared in the doorway. She wore a wrinkled gray uniform and a grumpy expression. "Sally was too lazy to get up.

She said I should come and put you to bed." She spotted the visitor. Her eyes widened; then she asked with elaborate diffidence, "Excuse me, Miss Clara. You rang?"

Clara bit her lip in dismay at Lucy's unseemly revelations over servant disputes—and how they all still viewed her as a child. "Lucy, I'm sorry. I know it's late. But we have a visitor. He needs a spot of tea, and can you please build a fire in the grate?"

"That's the butler's job," Lucy whispered none too softly in her thick Irish brogue. "And tea would be the cook's!"

"Lucy, I need your help. Don't be difficult." Lucy lacked the habitual deference of the forty other servants employed at the Fifth Avenue residence. Clara had rescued the sixteen-year-old from the streets and convinced Mrs. Carrington to allow her into the family's employ. Unwilling to train an inexperienced servant, her mother had made her Clara's personal maid, which had been both a blessing and a curse. Barely twenty herself, Clara felt close to Lucy, but being friends inappropriately blurred the line between employer and staff.

"Ain't it a little late to be entertainin' gentlemen callers?" Lucy asked saucily.

"Lucy," Clara chastised. "He's a guest of the family from overseas. He'll need a guest bedroom."

"I ain't been told of no people comin' today," Lucy protested. "Your mum never said—"

"There was a bit of a mix-up, but he's still an honored visitor and you must treat him as such."

Her eyes grew wide. "Wha's his name?"

"He's—" Clara froze. She had been so intent on helping the man, she hadn't bothered to learn his name. How embarrassing. "Excuse me, sir," she said, turning toward him.

His eyes now closed, his chest rose and fell with the even breathing of sleep.

Clara stepped forward, hand extended, intending to shake him awake. Then she thought better of it. He looked utterly exhausted, his booted feet splayed, his hands limp on the chair arms. His face, now relaxed, reminded her of a painting she had seen of the archangel Michael, filled with suffering and ecstasy—and, now, blessed peace.

Lucy cocked her head, her eyes bright with interest as she studied the sleeping man. "He's awfully handsome, ain't he, with that cap o' brown curls? Makes a girl want to brush it back into place."

"There will be no brushing, Lucy," Clara said sternly. Her uncharacteristic anger instantly banished Lucy's smile. Clara sighed, annoyed that Lucy's typical flirtatious banter should bother her.

"Where do you want me to put him? In the east wing, or at the back of the house? By the look of 'im, he ain't so important. I could put 'im in my room," she said with a sly, dimpled smile. "If you don't even know who he is—"

"That's enough, Lucy," Clara snapped. "Why don't you go back to bed. I'll take care of our guest myself."

"Yes'm."

Chastened, Lucy wasted no time excusing herself, leaving Clara alone with the sleeping man. Though she didn't know his story—or even his name—tomorrow would be soon enough for such answers. Lifting a blanket from a cedar chest, she shook it out and gently covered him. He didn't stir.

Removing her shoes, she sat on the sofa opposite him. Curling her feet under her, she watched him sleep, wondering who he was and why he had come.

"Who in the world . . . ? Clara? Clara Anne!"

The furious female voice jolted Stone and he came awake with a start. Through bleary eyes, he peered up at a svelte, well-dressed matron with gray-touched black hair and a decidedly angry demeanor.

Chapter 2

"Mother! I'm sorry. I must have fallen asleep." Stone's attention was immediately pulled to the young lady who had spoken, the girl who had let him in the night before. The bright morning light slipping through the lace-curtained parlor windows revealed a delicate creature with honey gold hair, garbed in a well-tailored dress of fine fabric. She stretched gracefully, her extended arms pulling her burgundy bodice tight against her round breasts, a startling contrast to her fashionably wide leg-o'-mutton sleeves. She hid a healthy yawn behind a fine-fingered hand that had never known a day of hard labor.

"Your shoes." Reaching down, the matron lifted a pair of white leather boots from the floor and held them out to her daughter. "You're in your stocking feet!" Her eyes shifted warily to Stone. Finding her daughter sleeping in the same room as a strange man could hardly be a mother's wish, even if they were both fully dressed.

"I was going to go to bed after he woke up. When I saw him situated, I mean," she rushed to explain. "He's our guest."

"Is he, now? Perhaps you should start by introducing me to him," the matron said.

The girl looked from her mother to him, panic building in her guileless blue eyes. Gorgeous eyes, Stone suddenly decided. As welcoming as a still mountain lake.

He couldn't help rushing to her aid. Pushing to his feet, he gave a small bow, hoping her mother might be impressed by such formalities. "Captain Stone Hawke, ma'am. I am a friend of your daughter's husband, Nathaniel Savidge of Naintal, India. Lord Nathaniel, that is. The marquess." His eyes met the young lady's in silent remembrance of last night's stunning revelation.

"I am quite aware who Pauline is married to," Mrs. Carrington said. "I welcome any friend of her husband's. I would, however, like to know your business here in New York." Her eyes flicked again to her daughter, and Stone wondered if she imagined he had come all this way to woo the girl. As if he had any energy for something of that nature.

"Nate—Lord Bathurst—he wrote about my circumstances in a letter," Stone explained. "The post being what it is, I apparently arrived before it did. My ship landed last night and I came straight here."

"I see. And you plan to stay . . ." she prompted.

"Not long. That is, I hadn't planned . . ."

"I see," she repeated, not bothering to hide her

skepticism. She turned to her daughter and spoke with rapid, clipped words. "Clara, if you would come here, please."

Shooting him a look of apology, the young lady followed her mother through a pair of doors into what looked like a library.

The girl's concern over his feelings surprised him. After all, he was nothing to her. At least he now knew her name. Clara. It fit her. Soft and gentle, sweet and trusting. Filled with all the false optimism of youth. Then again, why wouldn't such a pampered flower be optimistic? She had no worries in her life, nothing to challenge her spirit or forge her soul. Or twist it and cut it and turn it into something sad and dark and desolate.

"Clara, he's an army captain! They're known for drinking and gambling, and consorting with all sorts of undesirables. And there's no telling what sort of family he comes from." The closed doors failed to muffle Mrs. Carrington's strident voice.

"He needs us." Stone strained to hear Clara's calm yet firm response. Despite his better nature, he rose and moved closer to the door to hear more of her defense of him.

"So he says. We have received no letter from your sister. He carried no letter of introduction, nothing to prove his story is true. He could be anyone, seeking to ingratiate himself with our family and take advantage of us. Everyone in the city knows our family is connected to the great houses of England. Most of England knows."

"He was living in India," Clara pointed out. Stone smiled at her unassailable logic.

"What is India but an extension of England—if he even came from there? All we have is his word that he knows your sister."

"He is an officer. His word ought to be trusted."

"Oh, Clara, you are so naive! You must be careful not to be taken advantage of."

"No one is taking advantage of me. He is in dire straits and needs my help. He looked so weak last night, I feared he would faint on the stoop."

Stone winced at Clara's all-too-accurate description of him. He was worthless. As a soldier. As a man. His strength deserting him, he collapsed into a blue settee by the door.

Not surprisingly, Mrs. Carrington didn't share her daughter's concern for him. "You never did understand the importance of keeping up proper appearances and cultivating worthwhile relationships. You ought to be putting your energies toward finding a suitable husband, not taking on yet another lost soul to rehabilitate. Suitable gentlemen are anxious to court you, yet you hardly spare them the time of day."

Clara's voice was filled with righteous intensity. The chit probably truly believed her minuscule efforts meant something. "How can I when so many people need my help?"

Stone heard Mrs. Carrington sigh. "Why you persist in spending so much time on charity projects is beyond me. One or two worthy causes is sufficient for a well-bred lady, but you've taken on a dozen! Besides, taking care of the poor is not your place."

"Then, whose is it?" After a moment, her voice

lowered, filled with passionate intensity. "Mother, please. Barely a mile from here, people are living in tumbledown tenements in horrid conditions, without water or heat or light—"

"How would you know that?" Suspicion filled Mrs. Carrington's voice.

"I've seen their plight, Mother, with my own eyes."

"You *what*? I never gave you permission to venture into such neighborhoods. You could have been attacked, or Lord knows what else!"

"I wasn't attacked. Lucy came with me for protection. She knows—"

"She is hardly a proper chaperon. I'm not even convinced she's a suitable lady's maid. But I do know for certain that—that *captain* in there is hardly a proper influence for you. Lord knows if he is even telling the truth about knowing your sister."

"You can't think he's lying," Clara said. It astounded Stone that the possibility had never occurred to her. "You don't even know him."

"He's so—unkempt," her mother said.

Stone shifted on the chair, realizing he had collapsed into the velvet settee as if it were a cracked leather chair in the officer's club. He must look a state, unshaven, his jacket unbuttoned, his sleeves frayed. If he had known the sort of home they lived in, he would never have come. He *should* never have come.

"Mother, look around you! God has given us so much. How can you not believe it is right to share what we have?"

"If you had your way, you would throw open our

doors to every bedraggled, wretched, filthy criminal in the city, putting us out of house and home."

Criminal, Stone thought, a sick feeling churning in the pit of his stomach. *She thinks I'm a criminal.*

"Oh, Mother," Clara said, her voice heavy with irony. "We are so far from such a state, it's ridiculous to say such a thing. We have at least a dozen guest rooms. You can't honestly think Captain Hawke showed up here without an invitation, can you?" Her voice turned pleading, and Stone pictured her laying her delicate hand on her mother's arm in gentle supplication. "Can you, Mother? You know we must open our home to him. Otherwise, when the letter does arrive . . ." She let her words trail off. Stone guessed Clara was playing on her mother's need to impress her son-in-law, an English marquess.

He didn't wait to learn the outcome of the conversation.

He shoved to his feet. The sudden motion triggered an unholy chill that racked his muscles from deep inside. Forcibly restraining his shaking limbs, he swayed, riding out the wave of dizziness until his equilibrium returned. Then he stepped into the front hall, grasped his satchel and coat, and quietly let himself out of the imposing mansion.

Miss Clara had stated her thoughts plainly enough. He was a charity case—nothing more, nothing less.

Stone's thoughts were pulled into the depths of his whiskey, reflecting the hazy, smoke-filled light in the seedy tavern. The memory of better days danced before his mind's eye. Younger days, naive days, when he believed he owned the world. He used to pride himself on his manliness, his ability to protect tender damsels, the Miss Claras of the world.

How far he had fallen, and all due to his own foolishness. *No, not a fool. That's far too generous. Another word describes you much more accurately.*

At least his body no longer seemed to be warring with his will as it had last night, when he'd stumbled from the gangway of the small P&O ship. His first night's sleep on land after three weeks at sea also helped, even though he'd spent it in a chair instead of a bed. The three-week-long sea voyage had done him no earthly good. He was a soldier, not a sailor. In his heart, he always would be a soldier, no matter what the army said about his fitness for duty.

Late last night, he had struggled to make his way from the docks to the door of the Carringtons' shockingly huge mansion, his head aching, his eyes bleary. He had expected a narrow brownstone, not this European-styled edifice at 675 Fifth Avenue, on New York City's most exclusive street. The entire boulevard was lined with similar palaces—replicas of French chateaux beside Florentine palazzos. The cab driver who delivered him here called this the most magnificent street in the world, and Stone was inclined to agree.

Neither Nate nor his wife had explained her family's true standing. How humiliating, to appear on the doorstep of such an obscenely wealthy home dressed in his retired uniform, and carrying his old army satchel and nothing else. Everything he owned was in that bag, now tucked securely under his feet.

No wonder he was nothing in Mrs. Carrington's eyes. And he had too much pride to be a burden to any family, well-to-do or otherwise.

His pride. At least he still had a little of that left.

He took a final drag on his ciggie, then mashed the butt into a tin ashtray on the bar. That slim remnant of pride would prevent him from ever submitting to the tender mercies of the prim and beneficent Clara Carrington.

Squeezing his eyes shut against the incessant pounding in his head, he took another sip of whiskey, relishing the heat trickling down his throat and through his body.

He sighed as his muscles slowly began to relax. He had spent his last thought on Miss Clara. After all, he would never see her again.

"Oo-ee, lookee here. Don't usually see her like in the Bowery," the grizzled man beside him said. "Hope she's not one o' them do-gooders lookin' to rain down hellfire and brimstone."

Stone followed his gaze to the door—and choked on his mouthful of whiskey. He erupted in a coughing fit, drawing the attention of Miss Clara Carrington. She had tracked him here. Nothing else could explain why she was gracing this seedy establishment with her Fifth Avenue refinement. Though the tavern hosted a handful of female customers, they were of a much different ilk than the sweet young Clara. Despite this—or perhaps because of it—hoots and suggestive invitations filled the air.

She ignored them all. Her sky-blue eyes centered

on him alone, sending a secret thrill through him. Her delicate features set in a determined expression, she began to make her way over to his end of the bar. A brawny footman in full livery, complete with top hat and polished boots, followed behind her like a personal guard.

She had tidied up since her night sleeping on the parlor room sofa, so close to him. She had changed into a dress and jacket matching the blue of her eyes, with a fluffy white jabot at her neck and a pert hat on her head. She wore her golden tresses in a loose, layered chignon with curls placed around her face just so.

And she had bothered to find him. His dismay at having been so easily located warred with his admiration for her determined interest in a complete stranger. Yet he had no intention of allowing her to talk him into anything. *Put her off. Make certain she knows how little you care for her charity. How little you need it—or her.*

She stopped directly in front of him. Before she could utter a word, he lifted his whiskey glass to her in a toast. "Drink?"

"Whiskey, at this time of day?"

"I felt like it. So sorry it offends your delicate sensibilities."

She nodded in a knowing manner that irritated him no end. "*That* is your problem. There are missions and other helpful situations I can direct you to, but first you must swear off the demon drink."

"I am not a drunk." The nerve of the girl! "I came in here to get away from you."

"It didn't work, did it?" Snatching the glass from

his hand, she set it on the bar, then knelt down and grasped the handles of his satchel. "You are returning home with me."

His satchel, sad as it was, contained everything he owned in the world. He leaped to his feet and grabbed the handles. She didn't relinquish her hold, forcing the side of his hand to press against hers. Even through her glove, he was aware of her softness, of her pure *femaleness*. "Release my bag."

"I will not. Pauline sent you to us. I won't turn you out into the street." She tugged on the bag.

Amused despite himself, he tugged back, but not hard enough to dislodge her hold. Instead, the movement brought them closer, so close he could smell her fragrance—spring lavender, that's what she reminded him of. Like the lavender that bloomed in the Cotswolds, where he had grown up.

He hated that this girl made him think such ridiculous things. "You're daft. I don't need you and your pretty manners."

"*I'll* come home with you," his bar mate piped up. When he smiled, only three tobacco-stained teeth were visible.

Rather than cringe as he would have expected, Clara smiled gently at the man. "Not today."

She turned her stern gaze to Stone. Once again he was struck by her arresting blue eyes accented by thick brown lashes and thin, wing-shaped eyebrows. "You disappeared without taking your leave of us. I can only surmise you overheard certain . . . concerns of my mother's."

"I merely realized I had no need of your generous hospitality," he said with a wry twist to his lips.

Her eyes flamed. "You have somewhere else to

go, then? Or is it that your pride is too big to fit in my home?" Her delicately featured oval face with its small, pointed chin gave her the appearance of a fragile damsel. Despite that, her determined, angry demeanor drew the attention of everyone in the seedy establishment, and all conversation stilled.

"Impertinent chit," he growled. "I'm quite capable of taking care of myself."

"Then, tell me, where are you planning to go?"

"That is none of your concern. Let go of my bag before I rip it from your delicate, milk-soft hand."

Her eyes widened in disbelief. "You mean to insult me."

"You would be right." Enough of this game. He yanked his satchel toward him. To his shock, she still didn't release her hold. Instead, she gave in to the force and fell against his chest. Instinctively, his free hand wrapped around her to steady her.

Their surprise embrace caused the fascinated clientele to hoot and shout their approval. A shock swept through him and his dizziness returned in a rush. He swayed back, pushing her away. As he regained his balance, he caught her footman glaring daggers at him over her shoulder. The man looked as if he wanted to call Stone out with pistols at dawn.

Damn. Stone knew her reputation wouldn't stand much more of this. The girl should never have set foot in here. She ought not even to be in this part of town.

Making a decision, he grasped her elbow and steered her toward the door, his satchel in his other hand and her servant taking up the rear.

"You have no compunction against making a

scene, do you?" he bit out, hoping her brush with indecent company might have at least knocked sense into her.

"There wouldn't have been a scene if you had simply come with me in the beginning."

On the street, he swung to face her. "How did you find me?"

"How do you think?" she said, gesturing to the yellow enameled landau with glass windows sitting by the curb, harnessed to a team of four matching black horses.

Stone groaned. He had accepted a lift from the carriage driver as the man left to make his rounds, leaving calling cards all over the city—and leaving him on the street where Clara had found him. His gaze narrowed on his betrayer, a young footman in livery matching that of Clara's bodyguard. The man ignored him as he swung open the carriage door.

Clara turned to her bodyguard. "Manfred, place his bag aboard."

Manfred glowered toward Stone. "But, Miss Clara, your mother—she wouldn't approve."

"Nonsense. He's coming home with us." She crossed her arms and stared at the man, who was at least twice her size. "*Now*, Manfred."

With a heavy sigh, the brawny footman grasped Stone's satchel and swung it up behind the driver's seat. In chagrin, Stone watched his bag disappear.

"Dinner will be served at eight," Clara said. "Who knows? Cook might be serving a meal that complements whiskey."

Turning, she accepted the footman's extended hand and climbed inside.

Stone hesitated only a moment. He felt like he

was being kidnapped, but he no longer had the strength to fight her. After all, he could always leave later—after that luncheon she promised.

Despite himself, the prospect of a hot meal, followed by a solid rest between warm sheets, appealed to him. Reining in his pride, he followed Clara aboard the carriage.

He sank into the blue velvet carriage seat across from her, his arteries humming from the whiskey's warmth. A familiar shadow of dizziness lurked at the corners of his eyes, threatening to overtake him.

Desperate to fight it back, he focused on the pair of white-gloved hands clasped so primly in the lap of the girl across from him.

If he were a romantic instead of a hardheaded realist, he would blame his light-headedness on the lovely Miss Carrington. After all, she had managed to throw him thoroughly off balance.

She thought the problem was strong drink. What an easy answer that would be!

He could no longer hold his liquor as he had when he frequented the Officers' Club in the Nagpur cantonment. Gone were the days when he returned from the field to find respite in the company of his fellow officers, sharing drinks and swapping stories. *Such a loss* . . . Memory of his fellow officers—and of the men entrusted to his care—stabbed like a knife in his gut.

He realized his female companion was giving him a strange look, probably noticing how lost in thought he had been—probably thinking he'd imbibed too freely of the tavern's wares.

He may be a lot of things, but a lush was not one of them. "I'm not a drunk."

Her eyes remained wary, silently studying him. "Good. Then your presence in my home should pose no difficulties."

"You don't really think your sister would send you a drunk to tend, do you?"

Her eyes flicked over him, from his tousled head to his worn army boots. "What did she send me, then?"

"A man in need of a good rest."

"You've been sick."

He declined to answer, merely laid his head back against the carriage seat. He knew he looked a wreck. He had thought he no longer cared.

Now, however, with the lady across from him looking shiny as a new penny in her crisp blue dress, he wished he made a better impression. He straightened his back and gave a swift tug to the hem of his jacket, then realized he had left his shirt collar unfastened. He'd removed the stickpin while relaxing in the tavern. Alone. He pulled it from his pocket.

He waited for the woman's attention to turn from him to the window. Furtively he reached up and fumbled with the stickpin, attempting to insert it through the collar. His hands chose that moment to commence their infernal shaking, making the task ridiculously difficult.

"Here." The next thing he knew, Miss Carrington had slipped beside him on the carriage bench. After removing her gloves, she leaned close and pulled together the ends of his limp collar.

He shoved her hands away. "I am quite capable of dressing myself."

"I'm sure that you are, but your hands are shaking." She leaned close again, filling his nostrils with her sweet floral scent.

Again he shoved her away. "I am not a blasted invalid!"

She stared hard at him, unfazed by his outburst. "You're being ridiculous. Collars are difficult even when using a mirror, which you are currently lacking." She yanked the ends of the collar so tightly together, they began to choke him. She managed to fasten the stickpin in place before completely cutting off his air supply, thank God.

For a breathless moment, she remained close to him, her peach-colored lips a breath away. He could move just a bit closer, and they would be kissing. He had no reason to want such a thing, no desire to be intimate with this girl. No desire except a desperation he only now acknowledged not to be so blasted alone.

Without thinking further, he leaned toward her.

Chapter 3

As the mysterious captain moved closer, Clara instinctively sat back, putting a much more respectable distance between them. Had he intended to kiss her? She had almost welcomed such intimacy! For a moment, she had been dangerously captivated by his haunting eyes, which seemed to beg for relief from some unnamed torment.

The man would laugh derisively at her silly notions—if he knew how to laugh at all. She took satisfaction in having gotten her way with the intractable fellow as far as his collar was concerned.

Until he spoke again.

"You seem to have experience dressing strange men," he commented, his tone suggestive.

"Anyone can fasten a collar. Besides"—she gave him what she hoped he'd see as a reassuring smile—"you're not a stranger. You're a friend of my sister's."

"I hardly know her."

She shrugged her shoulders. "But you know her husband."

A pensive frown crossed his face as he toyed with the hat in his lap, his fingers sliding along the worn brim. "And if I lied about that?"

"I know you didn't."

"If I had, you would have no reason to keep me about."

"Don't be silly." She wondered what his concern was. She had already made it quite clear that he was a welcome guest. Goodness, she had come across town to bring him home! She explained softly, "You need help, which my family and I can provide. Mother has agreed to open our home to you for as long as you need."

"It's all about *need*, then, is it?" His voice sounded dark and dangerous. "For a man like me."

She grew wary. "What do you mean?"

"You know exactly what I mean. I'm not of your set." His tone was so brittle and cold, Clara half expected the carriage windows to crack. She drew her bolero jacket tighter across her chest.

"Yes, indeed, you're quite the little do-gooder," he continued, relentless. "I imagine you take great pride in your simple basket charity, thinking you're somehow making a difference. Let me guess—you donate to the poor at Christmastime; you ladle soup in soup kitchens. Perhaps you even visit shut-ins. How utterly typical. All the while imagining your efforts are appreciated by those lesser beings you deign to shine your countenance upon."

Clara stiffened. She prided herself on her patience and understanding, but this fellow managed to strain her temper in the worst way. "Your condemnation of me is cruel and unwarranted. You're a friend of the family—that is, of my sister's. That's why you're our guest. Besides, you don't even know me."

He leaned forward suddenly and grasped her bare hands between his. The inappropriate flesh-to-flesh contact shocked her entire body. "Then, tell me, little miss. Do you honestly expect your mother to welcome me—looking as I do now—to your family dinner table? Is that what you think? Or have you even thought that far ahead?" His grip was surprisingly powerful, despite his weakened and inebriated condition.

His penetrating eyes bore into hers, right through the pretense of polite society and down to where she truly lived. Her eyes swept over his face, rough with beard stubble, his eyes bloodshot, his hair uncombed and ragged against a collar badly in need of starch.

As for the rest of his clothes . . . it made her ill to acknowledge how right he was. Her mother would frown upon a guest dressed in such a threadbare jacket and stained trousers at her dinner table.

She pried her hands free. "We'll clean you up, of course."

He sat back with a smug smile. "That's what I thought."

"Don't tell me you want to remain all . . ." She flipped her hand toward him.

"All . . .?" he asked curiously.

"In need of a shave, and unpressed. Surely you wouldn't find taking care of those things such an imposition before dinner."

"I suppose not. But my clothing—"

"You will be welcomed," she said, a hard edge to her voice.

Despite her pronouncement, she wondered if her parents would truly welcome this man. Wondered if she herself could ever learn to like him. Wondered if he could ever learn to like himself.

"He's cut his face. Blood is dripping everywhere."

Clara looked up from the dinner table, where she was overseeing a housemaid's placement settings to make certain the captain was put next to her. She wanted the fellow to feel at least a little comfortable, and thought her somewhat familiar presence might help, if anything could.

Lucy had already helped Clara dress and prepared her hair in an upsweep with a sprig of baby's breath at the crown. Now the redhead stood wringing her hands, her freckled face bright with panic.

Despite knowing how Lucy exaggerated, Clara couldn't help worrying about their guest. Lifting her full dinner skirt in both hands, she followed Lucy down the hall to the guest room occupied by the captain. When her father had commissioned this mansion, he had insisted every bedroom be equipped with its own bath. Hawke's room was no exception.

"I was bringin' him extra towels, just as you told me," Lucy said. "Then I saw the blood. His hands are shakin' so, he can't shave for cuttin' his skin to ribbons."

Clara cringed. This was one time she didn't appreciate Lucy's colorful language.

Lucy led Clara to the door connecting to the bath. Stone stood before the wooden stand holding a porcelain basin, pressing a cloth to his neck. Brass taps above the basin provided both hot and cold water. The innovative household plumbing system freed the servants from carrying water up the stairs.

Stone's back muscles drew taut under his cotton undershirt, the muscles in his shoulders flexing as he applied the cloth. Clara's face heated. She ought not to be in the presence of a man not properly dressed. He wasn't even wearing suspenders!

Then again, she reasoned, he was a man in need—even if he wouldn't admit it. And she had long ago learned to ignore social convention when it came to aiding those in need.

Stone spotted her in the mirror over his shoulder. His penetrating eyes narrowed slightly; then he straightened with a sigh and turned to face her with a cold expression. Shaving cream streaked down his neck, dampening his undershirt and drawing her gaze to curls of dark hair escaping from the neckline.

He pulled the cloth away. Immediately blood welled up from a ragged gash on the underside of his chin.

His eyes hardened as he looked at her. "Come to watch the show? See how a grown man has lost the ability to shave his own face?" Turning back to the mirror, he wiped at the cut, then tossed the cloth away and picked up the razor from the basin's edge.

Shaking off the excess water, he lifted the sharp blade to his lotion-covered cheek. His hand trembled, sending the razor vibrating against his skin.

He could cut his neck attempting this. "Please," she said. "Lucy will finish for you."

"Me?" Lucy squeaked. "I ain't never shaved nobody. I'd turn his face into sausage."

"It would seem he's managing that quite well himself," Clara said.

He faced her with a scowl. "Why don't *you* shave me, then?" He stepped closer and held out the handle of the razor to her.

Never one to turn down a challenge, she snatched the implement from him before fully considering what it would mean.

Lucy wasted no time leaving Clara to the task. "Very well, miss, I'll go back to m' chores, then." She curtsied, then hurried from the room.

Clara watched her maid leave, the wooden handle of the razor heavy in her hand. The captain stood before her, his half-shaven face twisted in a smirk.

He was laughing at her, with the merciless silence of a man who cared nothing for her lady's position. His enjoyment of her situation set fire to her determination.

The best way to handle this potentially dangerous fellow was to be commanding, to take control. Though she had only begun her forays into the wider, dangerous city in the past month, she had quickly learned that only the very young and very old accepted help without question. Just last week, a fellow too far into his cups had needed a generous dose of prodding before she managed to escort him to the mission. Well, she decided, the captain hadn't protested her shaving him, so she would simply behave as though he looked forward to the experience.

She pulled a padded rail chair from the wall and set it in the center of the room, under the light that hung from the ceiling. "Please, sit."

He studied her with mocking eyes. Her breath caught in her throat. What if he simply refused? Somehow she doubted Captain Stone would be as easy to convince as that drunk had been.

Her worry proved unnecessary. With a sigh, he sank into the chair, his weight causing it to squeak. Crossing to the porcelain sink, she set down the razor and turned the tap, releasing a dribble of water into the lather cup. Swirling the brush around, she created a thick, creamy lather. She knew how to do that much, at least. Turning back to him, she filled the brush with as much lather as it could hold, then began spreading it on the scraggly bearded patches where lather had dripped away.

A huge glob landed on his mouth. He scrunched up his face and spit the lather away. "By God, woman, are you trying to drown me in the stuff?"

She swiped the brush across his lips, trying to rectify her mistake and only managing to thicken the layer along his lower jaw. A few globs fell onto his lap, staining his trousers.

Lurching up, he grabbed a towel off the edge of the sink basin and wiped the lather from his mouth and trousers. Shooting her an annoyed look, he fell back into the chair.

She grasped the razor, her pulse beating in her ears. His fidgeting did nothing to steady her nerves.

"Sit still," she commanded.

"I am still, now," he said, planting his feet flat on the floor and bracing his hands on the chair arms. "You know what you're doing, right?"

"Of course. Relax, and I'll have you spruced up in no time."

He swallowed, his Adam's apple bobbing under his stubbly chin. Standing behind him, she pressed her fingertips to the edge of his jaw and tilted his head back.

The crown of his head touched her stomach, startling her. She fought the urge to jerk away. Once again she was made conscious of the inappropriateness of this situation. She should have asked Manfred or one of the other male servants to do this task. But she hadn't wanted to embarrass the captain further by discussing his disability with others. Stepping closer, she allowed his head to press into her belly.

His dark eyes slid up to meet hers, not quite trusting. Yet he was submitting to her ministrations. She gave him a reassuring smile, but no echo of her smile was returned. If anything, he looked resigned to his fate in her hands.

The razor she held caught the light from above and flashed it back at her, reminding her how sharp and dangerous the tool could be. She swallowed in a suddenly dry throat and adjusted her grip on the handle. Her hand trembled slightly, betraying her nerves.

Calm yourself. You can do this. She adjusted her grip, and shoved aside all thoughts of who this man was, of the way his gaze bored into her. All she allowed herself to think of was the task at hand.

Starting at the base of his throat, she slid the blade against his skin, lifting away lather and flecks of black hair as she did so. She rinsed off the blade in the sink, then drew another path through the lather, beside the first. The skin of his neck was slowly revealed, smoother than she had expected. Pleased with her success, she soon finished with his neck and under his jaw and moved on to his cheeks. He helped her where necessary, stretching his facial muscles to provide a smooth canvas for her to work.

His eyes followed the careful sweep of the razor as she brought it under the hollow of his cheekbone. She had never seen a man with such pronounced cheekbones. Perhaps they stood out more than usual because he was malnourished. Thank goodness she had found him and brought him home, were he could be properly fed.

Knowing her unsure motions made him nervous, she tried to distract him with conversation. "Is this your first visit to New York?" she asked, wondering if the question sounded as silly and stilted to him as it did to her. Beneath her hand, the blade made a soft scritching sound, carrying away more of the stubble.

He only grunted in response. She supposed he wasn't in a position to answer.

She returned her concentration to her task. The soothing rhythm absorbed her. The tan, even texture of his skin fascinated her. Skin not unlike her own. Though male, it felt so silky when shaved. With great care, she maneuvered around the small gash beneath his chin. Then, with a final arc of her wrist, she removed the last bit of stubble from his upper lip.

"There." She lowered the razor and took a step back.

Before she could study her achievement, he

snatched a towel from the rack and buried his face
in it. He scoured his face and neck, then lowered
the towel. He tossed it over the edge of the basin
and studied his reflection in the mirror.

Clara waited while he angled his face this way
and that, perusing her handiwork. She felt inordinately proud of herself. She hadn't cut him, despite her lack of experience. Certainly she had
done a far better job than he had been able to.

He turned to face her. A broad smile spread over
his face, transforming his usually dour countenance.
With those sharp cheekbones over a square, strong
chin, he appeared the classic aristocrat, despite his
state of undress. And that smile—good Lord, it lit
up the room, burning her silly pride out of her.
Stunned by the power of his countenance, her
breath jammed in her throat, and her heart
thrummed against her rib cage like a caged bird.

"You managed not to slice open my throat. Not
bad for a woman." He rubbed his cheek.

Annoyed, she stepped forward and snatched
the towel from his hand. "I did a far sight better
than you did."

"After the gruel served aboard ship, I would do
anything for a properly cooked meal."

"The food was as bad as all that?" Her travels
with her family in first class had meant full-course
gourmet meals and sometimes dining at the captain's table.

"Perhaps I would have found it filling, if not
tasty, if I had managed to keep it down."

"That's not uncommon for those aboard ship."

He didn't respond.

He must be suffering from something more

than mal de mer, she decided. She hesitated, longing to learn his situation but not wanting to pry. Finally, she asked directly, her voice low with concern, "What is it you have?"

"Swamp fever."

"Excuse me?"

"Malaria. Courtesy of the Indian jungle."

"And you feel ill now?"

He sighed. "I have been fighting off a fresh bout of ague since before we docked. I had chalked it up to the boat—a bit of wishful thinking on my part."

She gave him a smile meant to reassure. "Your health will improve, now that you're back on land."

He squeezed the padded chair arms until his knuckles turned white. Clara could feel the frustration pouring off him in waves. "I know better," he muttered. "The sickness is in my blood, like a curse."

Yearning to help, she touched her palm to his forehead to check for fever. "Perhaps we should call the doctor—"

With shocking suddenness, he gripped her wrist so tightly she gasped from the pain. He shoved her away and shot to his feet, his lanky six-foot frame towering over her in the close quarters of the bath. His eyes flashed dark and brittle under the bright electric lights. "Your attempt to play nursemaid is misplaced. Don't lower yourself. Your help is no more required than it is appreciated."

She stared up at him, appalled at his coldness and lack of appreciation for her generosity. "I have already helped you. I just shaved your face!"

His lips twisted into an alarmingly suggestive

smile. Inexplicably, his expression caused her pulse to accelerate. "Apparently the task intrigued you. Certainly it's nothing you couldn't have ordered one of your servants to do—a fellow who knows how to accomplish the task with a more deft hand, I'll warrant." He stroked at his cheek as if she had left it coated in stubble. She could see no evidence of such a thing.

Clara stared at him, her rational mind fighting to conquer the quivering frustration he had engendered in her. *He's sick. You've known sick people before. They're not rational.*

Just as her reaction to him wasn't rational. She wanted to argue with him, to put him in his place, to tell him exactly how wrong he was about her— even as she knew how foolish it would make her look. So she resisted in silence.

Turning, he strode toward the door. Clara bit her lip, fighting a surge of tears at his ill-mannered, even brutal reaction toward her generosity. Playing nursemaid? That's what he thought of her genuine concern? How dare he!

Crossing into his bedroom, he swung open the door to the hall, indicating she should take her leave. Holding her chin high, she crossed to the door he pointedly held open for her, her skirts rustling against her legs. Before she reached it, she passed the armoire, its door open, his single clean tweed jacket on a hanger.

She was almost through the door when he spoke again, causing her to stop right beside him. The intimate timbre of his voice made her nerves buzz with awareness. "My wardrobe. It's rather limited. As appearances matter to your highbrow kin, you might put those charitable impulses toward a worthy endeavor and have your servants find me a proper dinner jacket."

She stared boldly into his handsome face, far too close for comfort. Yet she couldn't step back, not without seeming weak. "I appreciate your desire to appear presentable," she said stiffly, determined not to appear shaken by his nearness. "I am sure we can find a suitable jacket for you. I'll have one of the *servants* provide you with one." She exited with as much aplomb as she could muster.

Without even a thank-you, he firmly shut the door behind her.

Chapter 4

Stone slammed the door behind the charitable Miss Carrington, relieved to finally be out of her presence. She had a face like an angel, and a disposition to match.

To his chagrin, part of him enjoyed her attentions. The part that had no pride left, the part that accepted he could hardly take care of himself.

It made him ill to realize how the lady viewed him. No self-respecting young woman would allow herself alone in a bathroom with a fellow not her husband—unless he were very young, or very old.

Or very sick.

Worse, he had allowed her to shave him. *Shave* him, as if he were an invalid incapable of the simplest task!

Aren't you? Damn near.

His musings led him back into the bathroom. He stood in the doorway and took a good look around. This single room was almost the size of his parents' cottage in the Cotswolds. Vivid red walls were trimmed in gold crown moldings, and beneath his feet was a marble tile floor. Against one wall, a porcelain tub rested on clawed feet, the latest in indoor amenities for a fully plumbed house. His gaze flitted over the water closet in one corner. Back at the cantonment, he and the soldiers had still gone out back to take care of business.

He didn't belong here, any more than he had belonged in India.

Kicking aside the chair he'd sat in for his shave, he studied his image in the mirror above the basin, shocked at how gaunt he looked, how unhealthy. His complexion was so sallow. At least he looked presentable for the family dinner table. Despite his insults, she had done a remarkably careful job. Though she had taken too damned long at it. Every movement of her wrist, every scrape of the blade across his skin, had drawn her near, bathing him in her sweet scent.

As she groomed him, he had succumbed to a blissful, numb state of relaxation. Through lowered eyelids, he had studied her as she worked, reveling in her tender touches as a lover might.

Under her spell, he had noticed a tiny crease form above her right wing-shaped eyebrow the color of sable. Enjoyed the way a stray tendril from her coiffure had tickled her silky earlobe. Watched her full Cupid's-bow lips turn down at the corners in studied concentration. Which led him to wonder if she had ever been kissed by a man.

That mystery sparked his fantasies as he imagined touching her in inappropriate ways. The thoughts spinning through his fever-weakened mind would have shocked her to the soles of her slippered feet, if he revealed them.

Certainly similar thoughts about him hadn't crossed her mind, not once. How galling. In the army, he had regularly drawn the interested gazes of ladies at the cantonment. Now this young, inexperienced thing saw him as nothing but an opportunity to relieve her charitable impulses.

How far you have fallen, he silently told his reflection. And the illness was only the outward manifestation of an inner death.

He fingered the sharp blade of the razor she had left by the basin. He should have thrown himself overboard, let the sea finish him. Even now . . .

Grasping the razor handle, he lifted the implement to his neck and pressed it very slowly against the pulse throbbing below his jaw. *One good slice and this would end, as it should have months ago.*

His hand shook and he dropped the blade. It clattered against the porcelain sink, then fell to the tile floor. He gripped the edges of the basin, bracing himself with stiff arms as a violent shudder racked his body.

So weak. Too weak to get well; too weak to end his pain. What a prime example of manhood he was.

Disgusted with himself, he picked up the razor, tossed it in the basin, and left the bathroom.

"Do you think he will be presentable?"

Mrs. Carrington approached Clara, who waited at the foot of the stairs, anxious for Captain Hawke to make his appearance for dinner.

It annoyed her that her mother put into such direct words her own concerns. "I lent him a coat of Father's."

"That's a start, I suppose. Still, there's no telling if his manners are up to snuff."

Clara sighed in exasperation. One would think their guest was from the lowest dregs of society rather than a respectable army officer in genuine need. "He will be fine, Mother. You needn't worry."

Mrs. Carrington gave her a skeptical look before turning her attention to the housekeeper, who was waiting for her approval on the floral arrangements now gracing the dining room.

Clara wandered back through the adjoining parlor, then into the front hall, just as the man in question began to descend the sweeping staircase.

Clara instantly realized she was no judge of men's clothing. The black jacket she had lent him—from her father's own collection and borrowed under protest from his personal butler—hung loosely at the waist. His wrists extended past the sleeves. And the herringbone tweed clashed with his army trousers.

Still, he was presentable—clean and sharp. When he stepped off the final step, placing himself before her, she revised her opinion. More than presentable. Dashing, even.

His coal-dark eyes flicked over her face. "Do I pass muster, princess?"

Without thinking, she reached up and straightened the turned-down collar of his shirt so that the points would align. After the minor adjustment, her fingers lingered on his chest. He pulled in a rattling breath, and she felt him quiver under her palm.

"No," he growled, his eyes igniting with fierce pride. He grasped her wrist, his grip as strong and impervious as a steel band. With insistent pressure, he pulled her the final inches to him. "I don't appreciate it," he said, his jaw tense and his eyes sparking with disdain. "So don't do it."

Clara's lips parted, but she could think of nothing to say. His familiar touch mortified her, along with her own too-familiar behavior toward him. She had touched him as if he were her own father—or husband.

Desperate to be free of him, she twisted her wrist. At her resistance, he instantly released her.

"A shame your mother hasn't trained you better."

"I didn't think—"

"Oh, I know your thoughts all too well, Miss Carrington."

Clara regained a measure of composure. "I meant no harm. You ought not to be so touchy when people mean you well. Nevertheless, I promise not to touch you again." She rubbed at her wrist, which still felt the imprint of his hand. "As long as you promise not to touch me."

He stepped back and nodded. "Point taken. My apologies, miss. It won't happen again."

Inexplicably, his certainty annoyed her. The sardonic twist to his lips silently mocked her, and despite her knowledge that he was a man in pain, a man in need, she couldn't keep from feeling highly vexed by his attitude.

She stiffened her lips and gave him a cool stare. "Of that, you can be sure."

From the other end of the wide, high front hall, the large front door slammed. Mr. Richard Carrington entered, followed by a man she had never seen before. Immediately Edgar appeared to take their hats and coats and ask his traditional question, "Good evening, sir. Did you have a very good day?"

"Very good, Edgar, Very good. Consolidated two more railroads under Altantic-Southern." Her father was garbed as usual in his three-piece business suit. His neatly barbered handlebar mustache held only a hint of gray.

"Ah, a profitable day, then," Edgar said with a smile.

"Before long, we'll control every rail line in the Eastern states, eh, Gerald?" He turned to his companion with a smile. "God willing and the Mississippi don't rise."

The man named Gerald laughed heartily at his quixotic comment—too heartily, Clara decided, but her father seemed to appreciate his audience of one. Under his thick cap of light brown curls, Gerald's pale eyes were hidden behind wire-rim glasses. His open face struck her as guileless. Handsome in a comfortable, homey way.

"This is our humble homestead," her father said, making a sweeping gesture to encompass the interior of their grand home. Clara rolled her eyes at her father's vast understatement. He had hired the city's most renowned architect to design their home in the style of a French chateau.

"Magnificent, sir. Simply magnificent." The young man gazed about with an awe similar to the captain's, but his praise was far more effusive. "Breath-taking. A monument to your achievements in stone!"

His gaze landed on Clara and Captain Stone. "And this"—he took a step toward her—"this lovely lady. Is this Miss Clara?"

"Ah! Clara, come here. This is someone I want you to meet."

"I have someone I want you to meet as well," Clara said. She took a step toward her father, but the captain didn't follow. She fiercely gestured him to come along as she crossed the thirty feet to where her father stood.

Her father glanced past her to the captain. "Indeed. I believe I know who this is. Captain Hawke, is it?"

"That's right." The captain held out his hand and they shook. "Good to meet you, Mr. Carrington. Thank you for your hospitality."

"You're welcome." His gaze skimmed over the coat the captain wore, and he frowned—probably in recognition. As she expected, he said nothing, not in front of his guest.

Turning his attention from Stone, he slapped a hand on Gerald's shoulder. "Clara, meet Mr. Gerald Burnby, an associate at the firm. My right-hand man, eh, Gerald? A brilliant fellow, with a sterling future ahead of him."

"You flatter me far too highly, sir." Indeed, the fellow looked flustered, his face starting to color.

"It's nice to meet you," Clara said, extending her hand.

He grasped it and bowed low over it. "Miss Carrington. I've heard so much about you. I can't tell you what an honor it is to finally meet you. Really, Miss Carrington. You're so much more lovely—that is, lovelier," he stammered, "than I—than I imagined."

"Thank you," Clara said, shooting a glance at her own guest. The captain looked bored beyond belief by her admirer's effusive praise.

"Gerald is joining us for dinner," Mr. Carrington said. "We're late, I know." He bowed his head and said conspiratorially to Clara, "Don't worry, pumpkin. I'll explain to your mum. Bringing Gerald to meet you is bound to placate her."

Embarrassed, Clara lowered her own voice and turned away from both their guests. "You brought him here to meet me? Father!"

"Don't look so surprised. Nothing wrong in a father looking to his daughter's interests."

He turned away from her and ushered Mr. Burnby through the twin doors to the parlor, then into the dining room beyond. Had the fellow seriously been taken with her, Clara wondered, or had he merely wanted to impress her father? She never knew when her father introduced her to potential beaux. Why did her father choose this, of all nights, to bring home Mr. Burnby? She wasn't sure she could focus on making proper small talk with the gentleman, not under the captain's sardonic gaze.

"What a charming fellow," Captain Hawke said from behind her. "How kind of your father to find him for you."

Clara turned and studied him. His words sounded polite enough, but the tone in them left no doubt he was goading her. "I'm quite capable of finding my own men," she shot back, then realized how inappropriate her words sounded. Lifting her chin, she grasped her full skirts in her hands and headed for the dining room, leaving the man she had "found" to follow on his own.

By the end of the first course of the ten-course feast, Captain Hawke began to wish he hadn't taken up the offer of a free meal.

Oh, it wasn't the food. That was easily the finest he had ever eaten, from the imported Bordeaux to the light bouillabaisse and oysters on the half shell. Nor did the prompt attentiveness of the servants leave any doubt that he was being treated as well as a member of their own class would be. A footman of his very own, in blue satin breeches and long tails, stood behind his chair, making sure his wineglass remained full and the desired amount of sauce was ladled onto his roast beef.

Nor was it necessarily the company, though he could have wished for a more relaxed atmosphere in which to dine. He felt like he was in a museum. The room was immense. Baccarat crystal chandeliers hung from twenty-foot-high ceilings supported by alabaster columns with bronze capitals. Fine objets d'art rested on pedestals about the room, below paintings by the old masters. If any occasion called for him to display an officer's manners, this was it.

To his dismay, his personal nemesis had decided tonight was the perfect time to make its ugly presence known. Every bone in his body felt as if it were being twisted by an unseen hand. His skin felt clammy. His stomach rebelled at the smell of the food.

His fingers shook as he attempted to slice through the thinnest part of the roast beef on his plate. He tore off a ragged piece covered in gravy, thankful the sauce disguised how poorly he had wielded the implement.

But he smiled and forced himself to take one bite, then another. He wasn't going to appear weak before these people, before *her*. He was tired of being weak and helpless. He was a gentleman, damn it, and he intended to behave like one.

He expected her to want to get far away from him after his contemptuous treatment of her. Looking at her now, as pretty as a Dresden figurine in her ivory satin dinner gown, guilt engulfed him. She was the picture of gentleness of spirit, a kindness and compassion one could only possess if one had never experienced the world, experienced pain and loss.

To his surprise, Miss Carrington had seated him beside her at the fourteen-foot-long mahogany table. Her fawning admirer sat directly across from her. Her parents, of course, took up seats at each end.

He noted her parents' avid interest in the meaningless conversation between the two young people, looking desperately for any sparks that might signal a matrimonial conflagration.

When the fifth course, succulent quail in cream sauce, was set before them, her father finally turned his attention to him. The bombastic tycoon's penetrating eyes bore into him. "Well, then, Captain Hawke, is it? You are a friend of Lord Bathurst's, is that right?"

"I consider him my friend, yes. And his wife. Your daughter."

He nodded, a curious look on his face. "I see. It was her idea that you should come to New York, then?"

"To be honest, I can't quite recall where the suggestion originated. It was during a conversation shortly after I left the army." Left the army. That was a polite way of putting it. *Was relieved of his command* was nearer the truth. His inability to shake this blasted illness was the official reason, but the truth was much darker. He had lost his ability to command.

"I hope you weren't relying too heavily on Pauline's judgment to plan your affairs," he said with a smile. "She's caused us more than a little concern with her schemes."

"Her harum-scarum schemes," Mrs. Carrington chimed in. "My gray hair is due to her, and her alone."

"Don't be silly, Mother," Clara said. "You worry about all of us. Lately you seem inordinately worried about me."

"Of course I worry! What with the stories the servants are telling me about your secret trips into lower Manhattan." She glanced toward Gerald Burnby and forced a smile to her face. "But we shall discuss this at a more appropriate time and place."

Heavy silence fell on the table. Stone felt ridiculously uncomfortable, considering he neither knew nor intended to know these people very well. If they hadn't had a mutual acquaintance in his friend Nate—Lord Bathurst, of all people—their paths would never have crossed. "You have two daughters, then?" he finally asked, to break the silence more than from a genuine curiosity.

"Five."

"Five?" Burnby said, his eyes lighting up. "You have five girls?"

"Three married off, two to go," Mr. Carrington said with a grin. "If we can find good men willing to take them off our hands."

"The eldest is now a countess," Mrs. Carrington began to elaborate, clearly filled with pride at her matchmaking successes. "Lily, our second, wasn't quite so successful, but her husband is a high-ranking government official in England. Then, Pauly, of course, is a marchioness. I could only dream that Clara might do as well."

Stone's gaze slid to Clara, who was turning a light shade of pink under her parents' observations. Poor girl, she looked utterly mortified. "I can't conceive of that being difficult," he said mildly. "As pretty as Miss Carrington is."

Her startled gaze shot up to meet his; her lips parted in delicate surprise. She hadn't been so stunned when Burnby had flattered her. He wondered if she actually cared what he thought. More likely, she was surprised to find that her charity case had manners. He couldn't completely blame her for thinking little of him. He had insulted her, been chill to her, cut her to the quick. He preferred it that way to having her imagine anything honorable or worthy about him.

Her father continued, "The youngest is at Bryn Mawr."

"Indeed? Whatever for?" Burnby asked.

"A curious thing for a girl, but Meryl insisted," Mr. Carrington said. "She has in mind helping me in the family business someday."

Burnby huffed a laugh. "A girl? At Atlantic-Southern Railroads? Not seriously."

"Seriously." The discussion seemed to make Mr. Carrington uncomfortable. Probably out of a desire to change the subject more than genuine curiosity, he turned his attention to Stone once more. "I'm told you are a captain in the British Army."

"I was," he murmured.

"Clara tells me you have health problems," Mrs. Carrington piped up, "and that's what has brought you all the way across the sea to stay with us."

"Lord Bathurst thought a change of scene—any place but the fetid air of central India—would do me good. I am inclined to agree with him."

"That's awfully unfortunate," Burnby said, leaning back with a sigh as if a weight had been lifted. As if he had decided Stone was no competition for Clara's attentions. "To be deprived of one's chosen career. Most dreadful fate, I say."

Mrs. Carrington continued to study Stone suspiciously, probably imagining all sorts of plagues a lesser being might bring into her palatial home. "What sort of illness?"

"A touch of malaria, is all. Quite common for those who work in the tropics. I'm already recovering. I am determined to get back on my feet in short order, and out of your hair." Despite his claim, the heat filled his veins, the air thick in his lungs. His collar clung to his sweat-dampened neck, the fever once again pushing to the fore.

"Your staying here is no imposition. Really," Clara said firmly.

His gaze slid to meet hers. "Are you quite sure of that, Miss Carrington?"

"Quite sure." She shot him a rebellious look. "We're going to Newport in a few weeks. You must accompany us. The seaside will do your constitution a world of good. And the sunshine might brighten your outlook," she added under her breath.

Mrs. Carrington frowned at this suggestion, and Stone thought the lady hoped he would be gone before he invaded the family vacation.

"That's an excellent suggestion, Miss Carrington," Burnby said. "You are so good-hearted. After all, there's nothing like a good dose of sea air to cure all bodily ills."

"Thank you, Mr. Burnby." Clara gave him an appreciative smile.

"I hadn't planned on staying that long," he said flatly, glad to interrupt their flirting. "Already I am feeling better. I see no reason I should impose on you past a couple of days, until I can find a more . . . suitable situation. Perhaps one where I am doing something more than relying on the goodwill of strangers."

"You are welcome to stay," Clara said.

"No, I think I should leave. Tonight. I have no desire to interfere with your life, Miss Carrington. And it's quite obvious you have other concerns to tend to."

"Don't be ridiculous."

As she continued to protest, the wineglass he held began to appear fuzzy around the edges. He moved to set it down, but it slipped, struck the side of his plate, and cracked, splashing wine across the tablecloth and into his lap. Without thinking, he attempted to right the broken glass. Pain cut into him as a shard embedded in his palm.

Lurching to his feet, he pressed his cut hand into his napkin. The blood soaked through the white linen. He staggered back from the table, knowing he was making a mess, a scene, proving how unsuitable he was to be dining with such a wealthy family.

Wrong decision. Standing on his feet, he struggled for balance, the room swimming around him in lurching waves. He fought to find a lifeline, a landmark in the blur, and settled on Miss Carrington's concerned face beside him. She reached for him, her hand sliding along his arm. He swayed and tried to reclaim his seat. Before he could, his legs buckled beneath him. He struck his chair and knocked it over, then collapsed amid a clatter of silverware and china. He landed hard on the carpet on all fours, like a dog. Pain sliced through his palm in a fresh wave, adding an unneeded shock to his weakened body. His gut convulsed, sending the dinner he had so carefully consumed burning upward through his throat and onto the carpet before him.

A dog . . . He was as sick as a dog, right in the middle of the fancy imported carpet before the marble fireplace. Humiliation battled with his pain, his need to give in to the blackness that teased the edges of his vision. The blackness promised the greater comfort, and he allowed it to overtake him.

Chapter 5

After what seemed hours, Doctor Thackery entered the parlor, where the family waited.

"He's resting, though he is still in the grip of fever. I put a few stitches in his hand, and I have dosed him with quinine." He set his black leather bag on the credenza against the wall. "That should reduce his fever."

"So, it is malaria?" Clara asked, gripping a pillow she held on her lap.

"Nothing contagious, I hope," her mother said. "No diphtheria or—or white plague?" she asked, a trace of fear on her face over the most insidious inner-city disease.

The doctor smoothed his white mustachios. "No sign of tuberculosis. I am something of an expert on contagious diseases, and I am quite sure of my diagnosis." As he discoursed, he unhooked his stethoscope from his ears, folded it, and stored it in his black bag. "Malaria is ravaging the British Army in India. I've heard close to one-third of the men have taken ill at one time or another. This man's paroxysm is among the worst I've seen. It is quite apparent to my highly trained eye that he has been neglecting a healthful regimen. He is highly dehydrated. Do your best to encourage him to drink."

"Drink?" Clara stared at him, imagining pouring the captain whiskey after whiskey, until he fell into a drunken stupor, just like some of the fellows who appeared at the mission where she volunteered.

A smile flickered across his face. "As all men know, alcohol has many cleansing properties, if imbibed in moderation. Also feed him, of course. Give him weak broth to begin with. After that, soft food, anything he might be able to keep down."

He accepted a handshake from her father, said his good-byes, then followed Edgar out to the front hall. The ever-attentive butler had appeared with the doctor's hat and coat at just the right moment. The doctor placed his bowler on his head, shrugged on his coat, and headed out the door, black bag in hand.

Clara hurried after the doctor and followed him out the front door. "Doctor Thackery."

He was halfway down the path to the street. He turned around and looked at her. "Miss Clara?"

Clara lifted her skirts and strode up to him. "There has to be more we can do."

He shrugged. "Do whatever you can to keep him comfortable. To be frank, at this point it's out

of our hands. I've seen less afflicted patients succumb."

"Good Lord." His matter-of-fact pronouncement chilled her worse than the night air prickling
her bare forearms. She wrapped her arms about
herself.

Dr. Thackery frowned. "I was under the impression you scarcely know the fellow, that he appeared
only yesterday on your doorstep."

She forced her head to move, her voice to work.
"Yes, but—but if he should . . ." She couldn't voice
that terrible, fatal word.

Thackery patted her arm. "It is never easy. One
must put his faith in God in such an instance." He
turned again to leave.

"How—how long, before we know?"

The doctor furrowed his brow and glanced toward his carriage, where Manfred held the door
for him. He sighed impatiently. "If he survives this
bout, the fever should break in a day or so. After
that, regular doses of quinine will mitigate symp-
toms of further paroxysms, but will not prevent a
recurrence. Only time will rid his body of the disease, though a healthy outlook may help." He removed his glasses and began polishing them with a
handkerchief. "I'm surprised he wasn't already taking quinine. Most soldiers regularly imbibe a gin
and tonic as a matter of habit."

"Is there anything else?"

"I left instructions with your housekeeper. You
needn't be so concerned. He is merely one fellow,
and from what your parents say, not a very important one."

"Indulge me," she insisted, her voice chilling along with the night air.

The doctor relented, probably imagining Clara's interest to be nothing but a young girl's fancy—or her folly. "I suppose you might encourage him to build up his strength. That way, when the next bout comes, he will be better able to fight it." He turned his back on her, ending the conversation. Passing his black bag to Manfred, he climbed into the carriage.

Clara watched the landau rattle down the broad sweep of Fifth Avenue, frustrated that the city's finest physician had no better answers, no better news. She leaned against an Italian marble column supporting the portico above the door and stared at the stars. They weren't easy to see past the bright electric streetlights lining the avenue.

Die . . . Captain Hawke could very well die. He was so young, not that much older than she. In the prime of life, one might say. Tired, embattled by some inner demon, yes. But hardly ready to die.

Or was he? Why hadn't he been taking quinine, and why had he allowed his physical condition to deteriorate so badly?

Sighing, she entered the house and crossed to the stairs. She grasped the elaborate, gold-gilded banister in one hand, lifted her skirts with the other, and climbed to the second level. She pushed open the door to the captain's room. He was utterly alone. He could die at any moment, and no one was there by his side.

Before the doctor had arrived, she had accompanied the footmen who carried Captain Hawke to his room. She had tried to help, but Mrs. Rossi, the housekeeper, had insisted tending a sick man was no place for a Carrington lady.

Clara glanced up and down the hall one last time before slipping silently into the room. No one was about. Captain Hawke's dramatic collapse at dinner, followed by the doctor's house call, had been enough excitement for one evening, and her parents had retired. The house had grown silent, and Clara was free to look in on the patient—or even tend him.

She hardly knew the man, but his strange, dismissive attitude toward her intrigued her. He was nothing like other Englishmen she had met: staid, deferential gentlemen reluctant to express their feelings. Oh, he had made a good enough show of manners during dinner. But when they were alone together, the pretense vanished, replaced by an intriguing and even brutal honesty. He was the most fascinating man she had ever encountered.

Street light filtering through the curtains revealed the shadowy four-poster bed. A small nightstand held evidence of the doctor's earlier attempt to make his patient more comfortable—a ewer with water, several cloths, the bottle of quinine, a glass, and a spoon.

Closing the door behind her, Clara crossed to his bedside. She turned the key-shaped switch on the electric Tiffany lamp resting on the nightstand. The golden glow revealed a face tight with pain she couldn't begin to imagine. Beads of sweat dotted his brow, plastering tendrils of hair to his forehead and temples. His unusually high cheekbones appeared even more prominent than usual, casting his cheeks in shadow. Mere hours before, she had shaved that face. If Mrs. Rossi learned of that, Clara would never hear the end of it. She had best not let her family know she was here now, in Captain Hawke's room, alone. At night.

Her gaze dropped to his chest, half-covered by a sheet. Dusky curls escaped from the V-shaped neck of the cotton nightshirt that he had been placed in. His bandaged hand, cut on the shattered wineglass, rested outside the sheet.

Even though he was lean to the point of gauntness, corded muscles accentuated his tall frame, so it seemed odd to see him so weak. To think such a young, potentially vital man could die! The thought terrified her.

Not if I can help it. Resolve filled her. Feeling decisive, and more than a little rebellious, she reached for a cloth and soaked it in the tepid water, then wrung it out. She had tended sick children at bedside during her charity rounds, but never a man. Such intimacy had been deemed too unseemly. But a man's life was at stake.

Very carefully she sat on the edge of his bed. Leaning over, she patted his forehead with brisk, gentle touches.

A moan burst from him. Startled, she jerked away. His eyes snapped open and he looked right at her. She began to blush, until his glassy-eyed gaze and confused burst of words told her he didn't even see her.

"My penny!" he cried out. "Where is my penny?" He sounded so pitiful, so lost.

Filled with longing to comfort him, Clara leaned over him and stroked his brow as gently as she could. His skin felt clammy and so very hot, like the fireplace screen when she drew too close to the roaring flames within.

"Penny," he gasped. Was he imagining himself as a child, playing with coins? Or some event from his more recent past?

Unsure, Clara fell back on the usual reassuring words. "It's all right. You're safe here. You'll be well and then things will look much brighter."

"Don't," he groaned in a hoarse voice. He gripped her forearm, his eyes frightening, wild. "Don't go there. Don't."

The desperation in his voice shocked her. The fever racking his body had burned away his usual bravado and anger, replacing it with an emotional pain that hurt to hear. She felt strangely close to him, yet almost voyeuristic in seeing him so exposed, his walls now gone.

Her heart ached in response. Before she was aware of it, tears had dampened her cheeks. Yet she didn't even understand why. "I won't. I'll stay right here, by your side," she said, patting his shoulder, wishing she could do more.

"Oh, God, no." Taking his hand from her arm, he wiped it on his chest in jerky strokes, over and over again, knocking his sheet below his waist. Thank goodness his nightshirt continued to protect his modesty. Still, Clara flushed to think only a thin layer of fabric hid him from her. "The blood. I can't get it off."

His fever dream, memory, nightmare—whatever it might be—had him in an unrelenting grip.

She stroked his brow, murmured sounds she hoped would soothe him. "Shh, Captain, everything is going to be all right."

"Penny?" he mumbled. "Where?"

His eyes focused on her for one long second, and she felt he was with her, there in the room, instead of in his fever dream. "Forgive me."

His voice shattered, cracking with emotion, the pain he expressed as palpable as a touch. She felt desperate to help him, but could think of nothing but useless words.

She squeezed his hand in hers. "Captain, please. You're sick. You need to rest, restore your—" Before she could finish her plea, he lifted his arms and wrapped them around her. He fell back against his pillows, taking her with him.

His secure hold surprised her with its strength. Still, she could have pried herself free, if she desired to.

Instead, she found herself allowing the scandalous embrace. Though she didn't pull away, she couldn't relax, unaccustomed as she was to being held by a man. Her senses overwhelmed her. The touch of his silken nightshirt under her palms, hot and damp with his perspiration; his male scent, mysterious and compelling; the arms holding her— powerful yet gentle, insistent with the raw need to find solace. All of it spun her into another place entirely from the sickbed, into a place she'd never ventured with any man, sick or well, a languid, secret region of fevered dreams only a woman could have. A curious longing filled her, a desperation not to let go, to allow him to continue holding her, to be held like this forever. "Everything will be well," she soothed, wondering if her platitudes were helping at all.

Forever didn't last. It changed as soon as she spoke, into something far more potent.

"Forgive me," he murmured, his voice a raw whisper in her ear. "Please forgive me." His lips traced her earlobe.

Clara gasped in shock at the intimate sensation.

"Penny, forgive me."

A woman, then. He was remembering a woman. . . . Yet despite knowing he sought comfort from another woman, Clara couldn't bring herself to pull away from his unexpected attentions.

She remained still, shocked to her core as his lips burned against her tender throat, stroking, kissing, touching as only a lover should. She fisted her hands in the smooth Egyptian cotton of his nightshirt, bracing herself as shafts of physical pleasure danced through her.

For one wild, irrational moment, she wished she were his Penny, if that was her name. She wished he were truly pouring out his need and desire on her, and not on a dream.

Yet he wasn't, and she ought not to allow this to continue. She began to push away from his hold.

He resisted with more strength than she imagined a sick man could possess. His arms tightened securely about her hips in a familiar fashion, and he pressed her entire length against his. Her feet left the floor and she found herself lying almost fully beside him. His hand dropped from her hips.

Relieved, she pulled in a breath and slowly began to release it. Her relief ended in a burst of shock. She gasped as his hand closed around her breast, cupping her through her dress and corset.

Chapter 6

The captain's touch scorched her through, as if he had transmitted his own burning fever directly into her bloodstream. Desperately striving to retrieve her senses, Clara scrambled away from him and back onto her feet. Her gaze flew to his face, looking for some sign he was aware of what he'd done, aware of her.

He had closed his eyes. His lips slightly parted. The hand—that dastardly hand that had touched her *there*—hung suspended in the air for a long, slow heartbeat, then dropped lifeless to the sheet. His head rolled to the side as his fever dream passed, and with it, any further efforts to touch her. She doubted he was even aware that she stood beside him, quaking in her handmade Italian leather shoes.

She remained standing there, her pulse returning to normal only after a very long while, staring down at this strange man who had done such naughty things to her. His chest began rising and falling evenly, and she knew he had fallen into a deep sleep.

Turning off the bedside light, she backed out of the room, never taking her eyes off the man in the bed.

Central Provinces, India

"Psst. Witherspoon."

The blond, sturdy young officer turned toward Stone and peered into the shadows. "Captain!"

Stone watched the approach of his friend with a measure of relief. He was one of the few who understood his doubts about his upcoming nuptials.

Lieutenant Peter Witherspoon smiled broadly and strolled into the alley toward him. "I didn't see you there. You're not at the club?"

Stone gave an insolent shrug. "Can't do it. Miss Flynn . . ."

"Ah." Witherspoon nodded. "Avoiding her again, I see."

Stone lit a cigarette. "Yesterday she was talking about a cottage in the Cotswolds, where we would move as soon as I quit the army. Not a day too soon, for her. Today she was naming our *grand*children."

Witherspoon winced. "You haven't said your vows yet. Why is she in such a hurry to grow old?"

"Nearest I can suss out is that she senses my reticence. Thinks she'll change that by giving me the long view."

Witherspoon shook his head. "Women are such silly things."

"Want to hear the worst of it?" He took a drag on his cigarette and blew out a stream of smoke. "Penny's hoping I'll resign my commission, become a shop owner or something back in bloody old England."

"I say, if she wanted to marry one of those average blokes, what is she doing here, fishing for a mate?"

"I've told her I'm a career officer. Seems she doesn't understand what that means."

"Or she doesn't care. Heads up. She's coming this way."

Stone jerked around and saw her strolling down the lane, all lace and ruffles, her dark hair tidy under a jaunty straw hat. Her boots clicked on the wood of the boardwalk lining the shops along the cantonment's main boulevard.

To his relief, she crossed the street away from him before she passed the alley. God, he was such a coward! He wasn't looking forward to seeing her face crumple into tears when he told her. Knowing her, she wouldn't take it well. What woman would? She would cry, perhaps rail, possibly slap his face. He had strategized the best place for breaking with her—the cantonment club. There, before the eyes of her peers, she would be much less likely to create a scene. Image meant a great deal to her, as it did to most well-bred young ladies.

"You could catch up with her," Witherspoon said from beside him. "If you wanted to."

"Later." He wasn't ready to face her, not yet. Tomorrow, perhaps. Dropping his ciggie, he ground it into the fine dust of the Central Plains with his boot heel. *Just as she intended to grind out my dreams,*

*my spirit. I may have wanted to bed the chit, but I refuse
to pay that steep a price. . . .*

Witherspoon leaned around the edge of the
building. "She's heading toward your men's barracks. No question she's looking for you."

"Fine. Let her look."

"You aren't going to say anything to her? Not
even to put her off?"

Stone shook his head. "I can't. I can't *pretend* anymore. I'm worn out."

"I'll go, then. Tell her you're unavailable. It seems
the polite thing to do."

Stone grimaced at his friend's censorious comment. Witherspoon had always been the better
gentleman. "Fine," he said, his lips tight. "Entertain
her. Spend all night with her if you like. It makes
no difference to me."

"All right, then." Witherspoon nodded, then
headed toward Stone's fiancée. Stone hung back
in the shadows. A minute passed, then another.
Then his curiosity got the better of him. Leaning
around the corner, he watched Witherspoon talking to Penny, hat in hand, his face turning a light
shade of pink.

Perhaps he fancied her. Unfortunately for Witherspoon, he already knew Penelope Flynn thought
little of his friend—in his own mind, another mark
against her. Witherspoon wasn't dashing enough
for her to parade on her arm, apparently.

God, how he hated her shallow thoughts. Why
had it taken so long for him to see that about her?
Damn a stuffy English society that kept him from
spending enough time with her alone to truly
know her—the good and the bad.

Tomorrow I'll tell her, he decided right then. He couldn't stand this skulking about, not anymore. He was man enough to break it with her. He would do it. Tomorrow—

The explosion rent the air from the direction of the barracks. The earth shook out from underneath him and he landed hard in the earth, dust and blood filling his mouth. The reverberations had just begun to die away when he pulled himself to his knees, his fingers exploring where his teeth had cut his upper lip.

What on earth . . . ?

An attack, and I'm unarmed. Pulling to his feet, he hurried around the corner—and into hell.

New York City

"Clara." Her mother rose amid a protesting crinkle of petticoats and whalebone stays. She tapped a folded piece of paper against her palm. "It has arrived after all."

"What, Mother?" Clara asked, only mildly interested. No doubt her mother had received yet another invitation to a social event Clara would have to attend.

"The letter from Pauline, about your—that is, the captain. Our ill guest."

"Oh!" Clara's steps quickened, her interest piqued.

"Poor man, suffering so." Mrs. Carrington clucked her tongue sympathetically as she perused the letter, her reading glasses perched on her nose. "It seems many of the soldiers under his command died in an explosion. What a dreadful blow."

Her stomach ill at the thought of so much suffering, Clara sat on a sofa and pulled a petit-point throw pillow onto her lap. "What happened?"

"Pauline doesn't say. You know how poor she is about her correspondence. I am left to read between the lines."

"What do you gather between these lines?" Clara extended her hand, and her mother passed her the letter. She accepted the letter, eager to read about her guest, hoping for some clues to what demons plagued him. The note was disappointingly brief. She gleaned no more than her mother had already revealed. No hint as to how the explosion occurred, or why, or what role the captain had played in the battle. If it had happened in battle.

"I wish she had written more."

"We're lucky we even received this letter. Pauline is so delinquent in her correspondence. This letter was late arriving as it is."

"Yes, since Captain Hawke is already here," Clara said, her eyes straying to the ceiling as she thought of the man abed upstairs.

Her mother sighed. "Well, I can't say I'm not embarrassed."

"You, Mother?" Clara looked in surprise at the ever-confident Mrs. Carrington, who almost never doubted her decisions or views.

"I was suspicious of the fellow. You were not. It seems you were a better judge of character—in this case."

"One must always strive to look beneath the surface to determine an individual's worth," Clara said, reveling in her small victory—and the opportunity to press her viewpoint of the worth of all individuals, regardless of station.

Her mother's eyes narrowed. "I am always ready to admit when I've made an error, Clara. That does not mean I give you leave to mingle with people of his class, or with him, for that matter."

Clara stiffened imperceptibly, praying her mother hadn't somehow learned about her visit last night to the captain's bedroom—and her shocking experience in his arms.

She hadn't yet dared to check on their guest this morning. He had made her feel so many outrageous things, and filled her mind with dangerous thoughts no proper lady should have. Even now, recalling how he'd held her, how he'd touched her, set her entire body atingle, from her tightly corseted breasts to her stockinged feet.

She slid a furtive glance toward her mother, certain there must be some outward manifestation of her unusual feelings, but her mother seemed oblivious. Mrs. Carrington continued to lecture her along the usual theme: how Clara should throw her energies into her social obligations, rather than charitable ones. Clara stopped listening, pondering the too-brief letter and what might have happened to the captain's regiment.

His men had died. On top of that, a dread illness threatened to rob *him* of life as well. The captain seemed determined to join them, considering what the doctor had said about his poor health. What horrors from his past haunted him, causing his spirit to suffer so, banishing hope?

He shouldn't be left to suffer, all alone, with no

one to aid him through this difficult time. No one to offer succor and relief for his tortured spirit—except her. He did have her.

Conviction filled her. He desperately needed help, for the mind as well as the body. And no one was more suited to the task than she.

The scent of lavender wafted across Stone's nose, making it twitch and dragging him back to the world of the living.

His tongue stuck to the roof of his mouth, and his throat scratched. His skin felt clammy with dried perspiration, a residue of his fever. God, he needed a bath.

The lavender teased his nose again. He knew that scent. The image of Clara's face formed behind his eyelids. Was she here, in his room with him?

He cracked open his eyes. Late-afternoon sun slid through the nearly closed curtains on the right wall of the posh guest room he had been given, a far cry from the rustic bungalow he had shared with Witherspoon in Nagpur.

Don't think about India. With great effort, he shoved down the memories and focused instead on the woman puttering about the room. A much more pleasant harbor for his thoughts.

She placed a clean spoon on the bedside table, arranging it precisely beside the bottle of quinine the doctor had left.

Her frame, slender to the point of delicacy, was gowned in a day dress the color of old roses. The shade brought out the natural glow of her cheeks.

So healthy, so vital. And she was wasting that vitality by a sick man's bed. Foolish girl.

Her skirts rustled against the edge of his bed, close to his hand. Extending his finger, he let her movements draw the expensive silk against his skin. His gaze, parallel to her gently rounded hips, slowly slid upward. Her waist, cinched in by a corset, appeared so tiny. Her rib cage flared upward to a small bosom beneath at least three layers of stays and cloth, carefully constructed to hide all but her natural upswell. Heat flashed through his groin, making him harden instantly. His entire body tensed in surprise. Where had that reaction come from? Yes, the girl was comely, but her demure attire shouldn't spark such a blatant physical reaction.

So he reasoned. Yet he couldn't keep from enjoying the sight of her feminine form, so graceful and innocent. His mind, so recently racked by fever, began to drift along fanciful trails. He longed to bask in her presence, to allow her purity to wash over him, her lavender scent to obliterate the stink of charred wood and burned flesh that scarred his nostrils.

Knowing he couldn't touch her, his gaze lingered on the bits of flesh he could see—her delicate wrists and hands, the column of her neck from her ruffled collar to her upswept golden hair, her angelic face limned by muted sunlight.

She looked toward him and caught his gaze on her. Immediately she dropped her eyes, returning her attention to arranging the spoon and bottle—again. Why such shyness? She had always been bold with him before.

"Mr. Stone. I mean, Captain Hawke. You're awake. How do you feel?" Her sky-blue eyes slid over slowly, tentatively, to meet his.

And she smiled. The gentle kindness in her eyes nearly undid him. God, he was so weak, that a woman's attentions should affect him so. Odd, how pleasantly she gazed upon him, considering that at their last encounter he had passed out in his own vomit.

He groaned, humiliation hot in his chest. "Sitting vigil by a dead man's bed? Don't you have some soiree to attend?"

"You're not dead."

"Might as well be. God, deliver me from well-meaning ladies."

Her eyes sparked. "That's a rude thing to say."

"What are you doing here?" he murmured.

"I live here," she said with a perfectly straight face.

"Not in this bedroom, you don't."

"Our dinner guests don't usually collapse during the fifth course." Her voice softened. "I was worried about you."

Worry again. He was so tired of the pity. "A wasted emotion. You're neglecting that fellow, Burn-me whatever—"

"Mr. Gerald Burnby is long gone."

He was almost afraid to ask. "What day is it?"

"You were delirious for more than a day, then asleep many hours. Tonight is two days since you . . . since dinner."

That bad this time? His head dropped onto the pillow.

She continued to linger by his bed, smoothing

his sheet, adjusting his pillow, her hands flitting like twin butterflies seeking a place to rest.

"Who is Penny?"

Her words were so soft, so surprising, he had to concentrate before he could answer. "She's . . . She was a woman I knew," he said, not wanting to discuss it.

"I gathered that."

He frowned. "How do you know about her?"

"While you were ill, you fell into a delirium. You said her name. You don't remember, do you?" She sounded almost hopeful.

He shook his head, though it intensified the dull throb of his headache. "You were here? By my bedside?"

"I came to check on you. You were quite distraught."

"The fever talking, of course," he said coldly, hoping to head off any more questions. He failed.

She smoothed her skirt under her and sat on the edge of his bed, near his hip. "My sister's letter arrived. She explained that your regiment—that there was an explosion . . ." She clasped her hands in her lap. "I'm here, if you want to talk about it. I'm a very good listener."

"I'm sure you are," he said, infusing his words with condescending patience. "Your garden club friends no doubt benefit from your willingness to listen to their all-important gossip."

She frowned, her hands knotted so hard her knuckles were white. "There is no need to be rude."

"There is every need. I and my business are no business of yours."

"You ought to make it somebody's. Unless I'm

mistaken, you have no one. Everyone needs some-one to talk to."

"And you, in your infinite worldly experience, fancy yourself the perfect person for me to pour out my heart to."

Color began creeping up her face, making her usually serene eyes glitter with passion. Ooh, he'd angered her now. A sense of victory filled him, though he knew it made him a right bastard to want to hurt the girl.

"You are despicable. But I suppose you take plea-sure in that."

"Bloody right, I do."

Her small hands balled into fists, and he won-dered how far he could push her, whether she would actually strike him despite his weakened state. The prospect wasn't entirely bleak. In fact, he rather enjoyed the image of her flailing her lit-tle arms against him. Her anger infused her face with a vivacious glow. To his mortification, his body reacted at the thought as it had before. He glanced down to be certain the duvet was positioned to hide the evidence of his arousal.

Shifting uncomfortably, he muttered, "My life is hardly a story for a delicate lady such as you. Surely you're late for a tea party or garden club meeting," he said, his voice dripping with sarcasm.

"And *my* life is hardly a subject with which you should concern *yourself*," she countered calmly. "It's time for your medicine."

Did she really intend to play nurse? God, he hated the idea. "I'm tired of this. I need a bath. Then I want my clothes, and directions to a vermin-free flophouse."

"I'll send for a servant to draw you a bath—"

"I can bathe myself!"

"—but before I do, you need to take this." She grasped the quinine bottle and unscrewed the cap. Taking up the spoon, she poured the medicine into it. "Open up."

He glared at her. "I can do *that* myself, too."

"If I could trust you to, I would. The doctor says you have not been taking proper care of yourself, so please open your mouth." She leaned over him, the spoon hovering before his firmly closed lips. *"Now."*

He continued to glare at her. Nothing could possibly surpass the humiliation of having this young female tend to him as if he were a child. Blast. If he had any strength at all, he'd throw off the blankets and leave this place. Intent on preserving at least a shred of his dignity, he gritted out, "I said, I can do that mys—"

His words were brutally cut off. Tired of waiting, Miss Clara had taken advantage of his open mouth to shove in the spoon. The bitter-tasting medicine trickled down his throat. He began to gag, then cough, but the medicine went down.

Clara stood back, a triumphant look on her face, her angelic features appearing surprisingly devilish. "Very good. I will ring for your bath now." Holding her pointed chin high, she turned and strode from the room, in perfect command of her subordinate in the bed.

Stone stared after her, annoyed beyond bearing that she'd gotten the better of him—this time.

* * *

Fifth Avenue stretched below his window in all its opulent glory. Across the street, numerous windows reflected a vibrant sunset daubed in orange and vermilion. On the street below, footmen in full livery delivered their employers into enameled victorias pulled by matched teams of four. These soon joined other carriages rolling down the wide boulevard as the evening activity began to pick up— the aristocrats heading to dinner engagements, balls, and galas of every sort.

To the right, beyond the corner of East Fifty-ninth, Stone caught glimpses of Central Park, its elm and oak trees vibrant, beckoning.

He had the sudden urge to gather his things and leave the house, to explore the world outside his window. To rejoin the world in some capacity.

His fever had broken in the middle of the night, leaving him restless as the disease once again began to retreat into his bloodstream—until its next attack on his body. And his hand was now healed, the stitches removed, leaving a tender pink scar as a permanent reminder of that humiliating scene at dinner.

Lucy entered the room, letting the heavy door bang shut behind her. Crossing to his side, she leaned down to retrieve the tray from the table before him. "You ain't touched your broth. You won't get well if you don't eat."

"Take it away." He waved his hand without looking at her.

A sound caught his attention from the stoop below and to the right of his window. Leaning out slightly, he saw the family carriage pull up to the stoop, its harness jingling. Manfred, the hulking footman, hopped down and swung open the door.

Mr. Gerald Burnby stepped out, dressed in a tuxedo and top hat. His white-gloved hands carried an ebony cane. He was the very picture of an aristocratic gentleman.

"Overstuffed ponce," Stone muttered. His rational mind told him Gerald was perfectly nice. But he still couldn't stand him.

At his mutterings, Lucy paused. She set the tray back down and peered out the window. "Miss Clara has a gentleman caller," she said, sounding far too gleeful. "That's Mr. Burnby, remember? I just did up her hair. She looks loverly, if I do say so meself. She has to look her very best. Mr. Burnby is takin' her to a ball."

"How kind of him," Stone said dryly.

"Oh, it's not just kindness. He's smitten with her, head o'er heels, I say. He's set her cap for her, he 'as."

Stone found himself drawn to Lucy's homey Irish lilt. "You sound like my family's maid. She was from the Emerald Isle, too."

"Was she, now? Did your family have a very large staff?"

Stone smiled ruefully. "Just the one."

"Ooh. You're barely even middle class, then!" Lucy said. She poked his shoulder. "Fancy that. Yet here y'are, livin' the life of Riley, right in the lap o' luxury. Lucky bloke."

"That's me. One lucky bloke." Stone watched Burnby spend far too long adjusting his jacket hem and smoothing his overcoat before he got his courage together and advanced to the front door, under the high portico roof and out of sight.

A few minutes later, he reemerged with Miss Carrington. Her arm entwined with Burnby's, she stepped down the broad stoop to the carriage. Her silver fox cape added to the finery of her mauve ball gown.

So, the little miss was going to a ball. Again. Every day she left the house for some social event. Her life was as fluffy and useless as that dress she wore.

A shaft of envy pierced him. In another life, he had proudly escorted young ladies to balls, danced with them, flirted with them. Made innocent chits like Miss Clara think their first not-so-innocent thoughts about the opposite sex.

You could again, a small voice tried to convince him. He tried to listen, but the voice couldn't compete with the pain that ravaged his soul.

As if Miss Carrington could read his thoughts and sense his presence, she chose that moment to look up. Their eyes met. Instantly his body caught flame, but this time not from the fever.

A moment later, she turned away, leaving the fire to burn within him untended, unfed.

Lucy picked up the tray again. "Well, they're off. Time for me nap. She'll won't be home until the wee hours, so's I take me rest where I can." She turned to go.

"Lucy, hold off," Stone said, surprising himself as he gestured for her to return. Taking the tray bearing the broth from her, he set it on the table before him and picked up the spoon. If Burn-me was dining in style, the least he could do was take in a few mouthfuls of broth. He might need his strength—in case he ever got the chance to deck him. "Maybe I have an appetite after all."

Chapter 7

Clara knew something was wrong the moment she entered her bedroom suite. Lucy's face appeared pale, accenting the freckles scattered across her nose and cheeks. She stood by Clara's dressing table, nervously shifting her feet, fiddling with a hairbrush. "Praise Mother Mary, you're finally home! I've been frettin' and frettin'!"

Clara began working off her elbow-length kid-skin gloves, the first step in preparing for bed. Her legs ached from endless dancing, her spirit exhausted from an evening spent in small talk and coy flirtation, when her thoughts had gravitated over and over, here to the house, and the captain. She longed to know how he fared, and if the medicine had succeeded in dousing the ague that plagued him.

Right now, however, her maid's concerns took precedence.

"Lucy, what is it?" Clara pressed her hand to her

stomach, where a tense knot of worry had begun to build. She pictured the captain suffering a terrible setback, perhaps even . . . "Something awful has happened," she murmured through a tight throat.

"Erin needs our help somethin' fierce," she burst out. "I told her to stay well away from that Killian fellow, but she had nowhere else to go. Now she's gotten herself into his business. He beats her, and she's too 'fraid to leave him."

Clara's relief that the captain wasn't involved faded in light of Lucy's distress. She knew Lucy had gone to visit relatives while she herself went to the ball. "Erin. She's your—"

"My cousin. She's only thirteen and a half years old! That Killian has had his eye on her for over a year, thinkin' she'd be an asset to his devilish business. The nerve of him."

Clara shivered, knowing Lucy must be referring to that most heinous of institutions, prostitution. She squared her shoulders. "We must rescue her, of course."

Lucy's face transformed instantly. She smiled broadly and gave Clara an indecorous hug. "Thank you, thank you, thank you! We've got to go, right away." She grasped Clara's hand and began to tug her toward the door.

"Now?"

"Before he hurts her worse than he already has. Please, miss."

Lucy's plea tore at Clara's heart. When someone was in need, and Clara had the power to help, she found it impossible to refuse.

* * *

A sigh, a breath, a premonition.

Stone snapped awake with a start. He had fallen asleep in the wing-back chair, some time after the sun had set, after Miss Clara had gone out with her beau.

A sound, that's what had awakened him. He remembered now. Footsteps on the polished oak floor in the hall outside his door—the soft, quick step of women.

The window again drew his attention as he spotted movement on the street below. She appeared just as she had before, wrapped in her fur cloak. This time, however, the flash of red hair from her companion showed him that Lucy was by her side.

Curious, he glanced at the clock on the mantel, saw that it was well past two in the morning. The time for young ladies to return from balls and parties and retire to their beds under the watchful eyes of their maids.

But not Clara, apparently.

Worry began to nag him. He sat up straighter and leaned over the sill, watching the women below. Where was she going at this late hour?

Where *would* a young woman be headed? Only one thought occurred to him. An assignation.

Gerald Burn-me? No, by God, she couldn't be meeting him. Who else? Some other fellow intent on stealing her innocence?

Over his dead body. He jerked to his feet, swayed once before securing his balance on spread feet. Yanking off his robe, he pulled open the armoire opposite the bed, where the household maids had placed his pitiful wardrobe: two pairs of trousers, two shirts, a derby hat, a vest, and two jackets.

No matter the condition of his clothes. They would serve him as well as they always had. He dressed quickly, choosing his former uniform jacket over the herringbone. He might be going into battle, after all.

Reaching for his service-issue satchel stored at the foot of the armoire, he pulled out something that would serve him even better, should the need arise. He checked the chamber of his .455 Webley revolver, also standard issue from the British Army. The weapon was brutally simple but nearly indestructible. With the holster buckled around his waist, the jacket hid its presence. He prayed Clara hadn't done something so foolish that he would have to use it.

The previous two times Clara had ventured into the Lower East End—the other Manhattan—it had at least been daylight.

Though the May evening was mild, Clara tugged her cloak tighter around her, feeling unsafe even inside the hack she had hired at the corner of Fifth Avenue and West Fifty-ninth Street. She wondered for the hundredth time since leaving the safe confines of her family home whether she should have come on this errand. Whether she should have trusted Lucy's judgment. She knew her maid would never harm her, not intentionally. But Lucy was used to the people in her own neighborhood. She understood the life they lived, had shared their burdens.

Clara began to realize the depth of her own inadequacies, her own painful naïveté. She'd grown up in a protected world of silk gowns and china place settings. She knew so little of life!

What did Lucy expect of her? Did she really believe Clara could help her cousin? Yet, she had her family's resources at her disposal, she reminded herself. And a great desire to help. Surely that would see them both through.

The broad sweep of Fifth Avenue soon gave way to narrow, unlit streets where even the moonlight barely penetrated. The electric street lamps were spaced much farther apart, leaving huge pockets of darkness and alleyways in deep shadow.

As the blocks passed her carriage window, the noise transmuted. Joining the lively clip-clop of carriage horses came the pitiful wail of a baby in the night. A woman screamed somewhere in the distance. They entered another neighborhood where, despite the late hour, the air was ripe with sounds—the clatter of frothy ales against barroom counters, the high-pitched wail of a child, a heated argument between a man and a woman.

Accompanying the changes in sight and sound was the smell—the fresh air of Central Park's trees and flowerbeds vanished under a rancid smell of rotting trash, overlaid with manure and urine, possibly that of the carriage horses passing by on the streets, but just as likely to emanate from privies in the tiny yards behind the tenements.

A few more blocks, and the tenements grew even more decrepit, with broken windows and plaster peeling from crumbling brick walls. Lucy told the cabdriver to stop. She jumped out.

Clara sucked in a fortifying breath and followed. She glanced about. The street was little more than an alley, lit more by moonlight than the handful of electric street lamps. Narrow tenement buildings pressed close together, while many of the residents clustered on balconies and in windows, seeking fresh air. The breeze beat against blankets, and clothing pinned to clotheslines stretched between buildings. Outside a pungent Chinese restaurant, a stray dog dug through a pile of refuse. From a brightly lit tavern next door came the sounds of men arguing heatedly, while honky-tonk music spilled into the street.

Clara began to pay the driver, but then thought better of it. They had no other way home, and it could be difficult to find a hansom cab here at this time of night. "Please wait for us. We won't be long," she said.

The cabdriver stroked his unshaven face and grimaced. "T'ain't wise to make me wait, not in this neighborhood."

"We'll only be a few minutes."

"She'll pay double," Lucy chimed in.

The driver sighed, then cast a distrustful glance up and down the street. "You'd best hurry, miss. Best hurry."

Clara nodded. Locking arms with Lucy, she nodded. "Let's go."

Her confidence wasn't improved when she caught Lucy's furtive glance to each side. "She's this way."

Lucy began to lead the way past the Chinese restaurant and the tavern. Already they were drawing attention. A cluster of working men standing outside the tavern began calling out suggestive remarks. Lucy turned and glared at them, shooting back comments in kind.

Grabbing Clara's arm, she hurried her past the men to the next door down. The five-story tenement looked like a hundred others, with crumbling steps and a door of peeling paint hanging open on a broken hinge. Crumbling plaster siding exposed weathered wood and brick.

A pair of young men on the stoop studied them both but focused most of their attention on Clara. One of them fingered a wicked-looking knife. Her blood chilled at the predatory look in their eyes, eyes that stayed riveted to her as they swept past them through the door.

In the narrow hallway inside, a little boy lay sleeping against the wall. Lucy said softly, "His ma kicked him out of their room."

"Why would she—" Clara began.

Lucy's eyes darkened. "She's got a payin' customer, o' course. This way." Lifting her skirts high to avoid the trash that littered the floor, she began to climb the rickety steps to the second floor.

Clara looked up the unlit wooden stairwell that bisected the building. Beyond lay nothing but shadows. She swallowed hard.

Once again she debated the wisdom of accompanying Lucy on this errand. *Think of the innocent little girl,* she reminded herself fiercely. *Think of Erin!*

A door beside her cracked open, pulling her from her thoughts. A pair of weary eyes peered out, transforming to large circles of surprise when they spotted Clara.

Lifting her satin skirt, Clara hurried up the narrow stairs behind Lucy, who had just vanished past the flight above. As she reached the landing, more eyes peeked from behind doors, and whispering began to fill the air. Each floor was identical, with four doors leading to four apartments smaller than her family's least remarkable parlor.

Clara followed Lucy up the next flight—smack into a working brothel.

Half a dozen men, none-too-clean, and some of whom smelled as if they came straight from their jobs at rendering plants or iron foundries, lounged against the scarred wall outside a door that had been painted a garish red.

Lucy glared at all of them, then turned and pounded on the red door. "Killian! Killian, I'm here again. And this time you had best not turn me away."

"A new one. A real class act," Clara heard a man behind her mutter. Someone tugged on her cloak. She jerked about and found herself facing a thick-necked, balding fellow with a barrel chest clad in nothing but a sleeveless undershirt.

"What'll two bits buy me?" he asked with a heated leer.

"Let go of me," she bit out, yanking at her cloak. The man let the silky fur slip through his ham-fisted fingers, but Clara had no illusion that he couldn't have easily kept hold of it—and her—if he resolved to.

Turning her back on him, she moved closer to Lucy, who continued to pound on the door.

The door swung in suddenly. Lucy fell forward a step, almost landing against a stick-thin man in a cheap, threadbare tweed suit. A cigarette dangled from his puffy lips. His eyes raked over first Lucy, then shifted to Clara. Clara felt as if she had been doused in ice water, the man's glare was so cold and mean.

Stepping back, he cocked his head, signaling for the women to enter. Lucy hesitated a moment, then swept past him, head high. Clara pulled in a fortifying breath and forced herself to follow. *Lord, don't let Father learn of this,* she fervently prayed.

Killian shut the door behind them.

Clara scanned the room, empty but for an overstuffed chair with torn ticking and a worn side table. Her gaze flew to one of two closed doors— presumably one led to a kitchen and the other to a bedroom. Groans and cries emanated from behind the thin wall of one door. A tingle of embarrassment wound up Clara's spine, even though she was unclear what she was hearing.

Lucy's face paled. "Where is she? What have you done with her? She's not—"

Killian took a menacing step toward her. "You had best keep your nose out of my bi'ness. You'll scare off the customers, comin' 'round, accusin' me of things I ain't done."

"You took Erin. I saw you drag her from her home this afternoon! Snatched her away from her mother . . ."

Ignoring her tirade, he turned his attention to Clara. "Who is this, your bodyguard?" His narrow black eyes played over Clara in a brutally familiar manner that made her skin crawl. "Kinda spindly. But clean. I like 'em clean."

"She's my friend, a very *good* friend. Her papa is a very powerful man in this city, one o' them industry barons. And if you don't give me Erin, she'll—"

His eyes still on Clara, he snapped, "Her mother sold her to me, you stupid cow."

Lucy's face lost all color, her freckles standing out in stark relief against her pale Irish skin. "She did not. She would never—"

"Got thirteen other brats back home. Won't miss one. But the new one will make me a pretty penny, yes indeedy. Once she's trained to please."

"You're lyin'," Lucy repeated, sounding less sure than before.

He reached for the doorknob. "I've had enough of you. Get out of here." When Lucy refused to budge, he reached out and shoved Lucy's chest, pushing her toward the door.

"Don't you dare touch her." Clara stepped in front of Lucy, thankful her gown hid her quivering knees at facing down this scoundrel. Mustering her courage, she continued, "You bring out the girl, or I'll—"

"You'll what? Send Daddy to deal with me? Go right ahead, missy. I ain't afeard of no man."

"He'll squash you like a bug," Lucy said.

"Let him try." Killian crumpled up his cigarette in his fist and tossed it at Clara. Ashes fell on her satin shoes.

Then his demeanor changed. He slouched against the doorjamb and his tone took on a soft, seductive tenor as his eyes narrowed on Lucy. "You want Erin back pretty bad. Maybe I can make a deal, just for you. Tell you what. I'll let little Erin go."

Hope sprang up in Clara's chest, but Lucy didn't seem very excited at having achieved their goal. "Go on," she said coldly.

"A simple trade," Killian continued. He tapped the ash from his cigarette onto Lucy's feet, his mouth twisting in a taunting smile. "You take her place."

Clara stared at him, aghast. "You—you monster!" Reaching out, she slapped his face, regretting the touch the moment her hand hit his unclean cheek.

"Bitch!" His eyes flaming with hate, he grabbed Clara's elbow and twisted her arm, making her cry out in pain. Her knees nearly gave out, but she managed to fight against him by kicking at his shin.

Lucy screamed and jumped to her rescue, pounding her fists on his back. Reacting quickly, he swung around, threw her off, then punched her in the jaw. Lucy reeled back, landing hard on the wooden floor.

Clara advanced on the man, clueless how to fight him. He had the audacity to grin at her, as if he relished any attack she might launch. Clara had the horrible suspicion he wanted to touch her, and not merely to throw her out of his apartment.

She looked at Lucy, at the blood tricking from the corner of her mouth. If a streetwise girl like Lucy couldn't defend herself, what hope did she have? She had to get Lucy on her feet, get them out of this hellhole.

Crouching by her side, she asked in a breathless rush, "Are you hurt?"

"Clara, no—"

A hand fastened into her hair and yanked her backward. She landed hard on her rump, and her elbows struck the floor. Pain lanced up her arms, and she cried out. Her neat chignon destroyed, loose locks of hair tumbled across her face and shoulders, temporarily blinding her.

Shoving the curtain of hair from her face, she looked up to see Killian straddling her hips, a lascivious grin on his face. Leaning over her, he anchored his palms on her shoulders and began to drag her upward, pulling her face close to his. His fetid, garlic-tainted breath washed over her, and her stomach roiled.

She squeezed her eyes shut and braced for whatever indignity was about to come.

An ice-cold voice intruded from behind Clara. "Take one more step, and it will be your last."

Chapter 8

Was the lady completely off her nut?

When the two women exited their cab onto the poorly lit street fronted by disreputable businesses, Stone could only stare, aghast. He watched in disbelief as they disappeared through the door of a tumbledown tenement, where numerous dangers might be lurking.

Back on Fifth Avenue, he had jogged after their cab until he could flag down one of his own. Concerned he would draw too close to the women and attract their attention, he told his driver to stop half a block past their waiting hack. They had no idea he was tracking them, a fact that did nothing to alleviate the dread that nagged at him. Two lambs to the slaughter . . .

Wasting no time, he hurried after them. Once inside the tenement, a resident told him the women had gone upstairs. He reached the third floor, heard what sounded like a fight, and kicked in a red door—just in time to see a nasty-looking fellow daring to place his filthy hands on Miss Carrington.

The sight of the scoundrel touching Clara, threatening her . . .

Fury exploded inside him. In two strides he reached her side. Grasping the man's shoulders, he threw him as hard as he could toward the wall.

The man's shoulder whacked the thin pine wall, and he snarled like an animal, taking only a moment to react to the attack. His sudden swing slammed into Stone's midsection, sending a bolt of pain up his side.

"Captain!" Clara cried behind him, her voice strained.

Stone longed to rush to her side, but he couldn't spare even a glance in her direction, or toward her maid cowering in the corner. Not when he had to deflect another strike from his attacker. He had barely risen from his sickbed before following Clara. Never before had he been so frustrated at feeling ill, feeling like less of a man.

The man slammed his fist into Stone's face, snapping his head to the side. Dizziness overwhelmed him, darts of light sparkling at the edges of his vision. If he passed out now, what would the fellow do to Clara?

By God, he wouldn't let it happen. He wouldn't lose another woman.

Not this woman. His rage began to grow, fueling an energy he hadn't felt in months. Striking out, his fist connected with the man's jaw, a satisfying strike despite how it jarred his arm and shoulder.

The man fell against the wall once more and slid to the floor. Stone pressed his advantage, lashing out with all the strength he could muster. Straddling the man's legs as the man had straddled Clara, he punched his face, over and over, raining blows on his mug until blood dribbled from a split lip and two puffed eyes.

The man cowered beneath him, his cries muting into pathetic whimpers.

"Captain, please. I'm begging you."

The pleading female voice penetrated the haze of his fury. Clara must have been tugging on his shoulders and urging him to stop for several minutes. He had no idea how long.

He stopped swinging but hovered over the man, making certain he wouldn't move. Straightening, he stepped away, only then realizing how much his hands hurt, his knuckles raw and scraped, his recently healed cut painfully tender. He rubbed them and glanced about.

Lucy stood near the door, her eyes wide with fear. She would probably have bolted long ago if Clara hadn't remained. Inside the door leading to a bedroom, a woman wrapped in a sheet stood beside a beefy, hairy man wearing nothing but trousers.

And Clara . . .

Finally, he turned to face Miss Carrington, bracing for the disgust he would see in her face. Shame filled him over his animalistic outburst, but he'd be damned if he would let her see it.

He clenched his jaw and met her gaze. Now on her feet, she looked remarkably well composed, despite the hair tumbling about her face. "Let's go." He grasped her elbow and began dragging her toward the door.

"Erin." Tearing her arm from his grasp, she ran to the second, still-closed door, and rattled the knob. It was locked. Spinning back around, she said, "The key. He must have it on him. Lucy—"

Her maid immediately reacted. Rushing to the beaten man, she knelt and searched his pockets until she came up with a key. She hurried over to Clara, and together they opened the door.

Inside the tiny kitchen were a potbellied stove, a tiny table, miscellaneous cookware—and a young girl in a stained smock who had obviously been crying.

Lucy cried out and swept her into her arms.

The girl rose on trembling legs. She was older than her cherubic face had led Stone to believe, her body that of a grown woman with a generous bosom and long legs.

Taking her hand firmly in her own, Lucy led her toward the door, Clara close behind.

"Don't you dare," came a croak near the wall.

"Shut up." Stone couldn't resist giving the man a warning kick before following the women out of the run-down flat.

Stone didn't confront her until they reached the street where the hacks waited. "If I hadn't followed you . . ." He dragged a hand through his mussed hair. His fear—an overwhelming, living thing inside him—began to transform into anger at how close she had come to disaster. "By God, woman, how foolish could you possibly be?"

Miss Carrington stared defiantly up at him, her expression remarkably placid. Without removing her gaze, she said, "Lucy, take Erin and go wait in the carriage."

"But, miss—"

"Do it, please," she said, her tone making it clear she would be obeyed. "I must speak with Captain Hawke."

Stone tore his gaze from Clara and added his own instructions. "Take the girl and go. I'll deliver Miss Carrington home in my own carriage."

Lucy looked to Clara for confirmation. Clara gave a brisk nod, so Lucy turned away, her arm tight around Erin's shoulders as she led the girl toward the hack waiting nearby. Soon the cab departed, leaving Stone facing Clara in the yellow pool of a streetlight's glow.

Her eyes studied him as if she had never seen him before—an intense expression that unsettled him. Yet *he* wasn't the one whose actions needed explaining! So easily her innocence could have been stolen from her, leaving a desolate, shattered shell, all because of her foolish generosity of spirit. The thought of what might have happened to her—of how close she had come to ruination—frustrated him beyond measure.

"I cannot believe you would be so foolish as to risk your life in such a manner. Have you taken a look around you? Do you realize what sort of neighborhood we're in?" He looked back toward the tenement, half expecting to see the man he'd beaten—or one of his disreputable cronies—coming after him. "Speaking of which, I'd feel safer anyplace else in this city."

He grasped her elbow to urge her toward the cab. She gasped and pulled her arm away.

"You're hurt?"

"A little. When I fell."

"When he attacked you, more like." He led her toward the cab, swung open the door, and helped her alight, being careful not to touch her injured arm.

He slid onto the bench beside her, aware how their shoulders and thighs pressed close in the small single-seat hack. He blinked hard to still the dizziness in his head. He had exerted himself; now he was paying the price. His nerves shook from the bloody confrontation, his scratched knuckles a fierce reminder of how completely he had lost his temper. The little bit of strength he'd summoned up for the brawl had been spent, leaving him weaker than ever.

Only then did he remember his revolver. He laid his hand on the hilt, taking reassurance from its presence. It was as well he forgot he had it, or he would have murdered the man. Yet he also knew the demons inside him had wanted to fight, dirty and physical. Wanted to defeat what threatened her, by his own hand this time.

He cocked his head and studied his companion. She sat still, prim and stoic, not meeting his gaze. She hadn't said a word since she instructed her maid and the girl to leave them. Her hair tumbled in a tangled mass down her shoulders, yanked out of place by a scoundrel not fit to lick her satin shoes. He wondered what she could possibly be thinking about her experience. About him.

Despite the exhausting yet satisfying pummeling he had given the pimp, the image of Miss Carrington flat on her back, at the man's mercy, set his blood boiling anew. As soon as the carriage began rolling down the street, he lit into her full force.

"You bloody little fool," he gritted out. "I knew

you were an odd duck, stooping to nurse me as you've been doing. Now I discover that you're raving mad! Coming into a neighborhood like this, dressed in a ball gown. You might as well wear a sandwich board reading, 'Take advantage of me.' And going into a *brothel,* of all places! I've never seen the like. If I hadn't heard you leaving the house earlier, I hesitate to think—"

"Why *did* you follow me?" she asked, her words so soft he nearly missed them.

Her question interrupted his tirade. How should he answer that? "You were going out in the dead of night, so I grew concerned."

"You were spying on me."

"Not at all. You women aren't as silent as you think, traipsing down the hall when everyone else is abed."

"So we woke you. That hardly explains why you hurried out after me. You had no idea where I was going, did you?"

"No."

"What, exactly, did you think I was up to?"

"There's no good reason for a young lady to wander the city unescorted, particularly at night. I know you Yanks have odd customs, but I'm fairly certain your culture is no different from mine in that respect. And a lady of your station particularly—"

"So you named yourself my protector, without asking."

"You're damned lucky I was there! Do you have any idea—any idea at all—the sort of trouble you were in, how close you came to being injured, or *violated* in some unspeakable way . . . ?"

She fidgeted and clasped her hands in her lap. "I'm aware of the danger. I didn't anticipate it, that's true. But I could hardly allow poor Erin to be used, not without trying to help."

"This is hardly the way to go about it. You mustn't be dashing off at all hours to the wrong parts of town."

"Of course I won't," she agreed, then added stiffly, "unless someone needs me."

He raked his fingers over his scalp, tightened them briefly, fighting the urge to pull out his hair in frustration. "I can't fathom anyone being so naive. Do you mean to tell me that regardless of the danger, you will risk yourself to help utter strangers?"

"Is that so hard for you to understand?" she asked, her tone imploring. "You should try thinking of someone other than yourself more often. It seems to have done you a world of good. I've never seen you so . . . healthy," she added. Her eyes skidded up and down his body, and he sensed an unexpected feminine interest in him.

He refused to allow her to distract him from his tirade. "I have enough difficulty making sense of my own life without indulging myself in toying with others' lives."

"I'm hardly toying with them!" Her eyes glittered in the dark.

"Yes, you are, Clara. You're dancing around the idea of helping others as if it were some grand adventure, a dalliance to assuage that big heart of yours, to make you feel as if you're repaying the blessings the Good Lord has showered upon you and yours. Or am I missing something?"

Her lips tightened, but only briefly. "You're terri-

bly cruel. Nevertheless, I appreciate you interven-
ing on my behalf," she added, effectively cutting
off his diatribe. "It was brave of you." She turned
her wide, honest eyes to meet his, and his heart
flipped over. She looked at her hands and added
slyly, "Very brave, considering you have no interest
in a young girl's plight."

"Thank you, Miss Carr—*what?*" Her sincere
thank-you had slid so smoothly into criticism, he'd
almost missed it.

"You're so wrapped up in your own misery, you
can't see the world around you," she said, leaning
close. She spoke with such intensity, she set her
hand on his knee. Did she even realize it? "Look
out these windows. There are millions of people in
this city, and almost none of them have everything
they need. Many immigrant families lack even the
basic necessities to make life bearable. Inadequate
homes without water or light, disease-infested tenements, waste everywhere . . ."

He narrowed his gaze, fighting down an inkling
of shame that threatened to rear its ugly head.
"Believe me, I've seen a bit of this world. The poor
are everywhere. *Everywhere.* And there's precious
little you can do about it," he said harshly.

"You're a fool if you think you can make a difference. You're just a girl. Besides, your money's
not even your own. Your father would rather you
confine your charitable impulses to hosting teas
and fund-raising balls, I am guessing. He couldn't
possibly approve of your gallivanting all over the
city."

She jerked back. "And don't you dare tell him!"

"Don't worry, pet. I wasn't planning to. I'm not

that much of a fool. I've been enjoying my stay in your home, and have no intention of becoming embroiled in a family squabble."

"I shouldn't be at all surprised you don't care," she huffed. "You don't even care about yourself. You were going to allow yourself to die!"

He longed to ask whether she would really care if he did die, but she pushed on, her dander up and her color high.

"You could have killed that man tonight. You would have gone to jail. Not to mention having to live with yourself when you have blood on your hands." Her tone softened. "You need to take better care of yourself, Captain. I do my best, but without your cooperation—"

"Frustrated by your lack of success with your latest charity project?" he asked, his bitterness flowing into his words. "I'm perfectly useful in that regard, am I not? You can rescue me without even leaving your home. How convenient."

For the first time since he'd known her, she appeared flustered. "That's not—I mean, in a way . . ."

He gripped her hands and stared into her eyes. "It's high time you learned something about me," he gritted out. "I am no woman's charity project. I don't need your help. I'm not some bird you've found with a broken wing, needing a patch and a kiss and all is well."

Her lower lip quivered, and he had the urge to still it with a kiss—even if he claimed he didn't need one. He'd hurt her; that was obvious. But he took no satisfaction in it.

"You *were* broken," she murmured. "You needed help. You still do."

"I never asked for your *help*," he gritted out, bitterness fueling his words. How low he had sunk! "I only sought room and board for a few nights, until I could get back on my feet."

"On your feet!" she scoffed. "You could barely stand on your own power! There's nothing wrong in accepting help if you need it."

"You know precious little about men, Clara," he said, using her Christian name for the first time. "The world is not your playground, and people are not your dress-up dolls."

Her eyes darkened in anger. She wrested her hands from his grasp. "I can't believe how angry you make me. I rarely lose my temper, but you— you're the most ungrateful, ill-mannered wretch . . ."

"So I've been trying to tell you, darling," he said dryly.

"I did the Christian thing, opening our home to you, tending to you. If you would stop moping about, refusing to take care of yourself . . . A young man like you—it's awful to see! You're not even thirty, but you behave as if your life is over. No wonder I took pity on you."

So she pitied him, just as he'd suspected. Even after tonight's awful display of violence toward another man, she saw him as less than a man himself. He had lain awake at night imagining her in his arms, in his bed, and all she felt for him was pity! Humiliation washed through him, feeding the primal urges so recently unleashed.

Damn her, he was a man, a creature with passions and desires and thoughts and feelings, someone she ought not to trust herself with. For the first time in months, he *felt* . . . Tumultuous emo-

tions rushed through him, thick and red, bringing
him back to life. Suffering the pain of his body, his
soul, he had forgotten how passion could rule a
man, could make him feel nothing else mattered
but desire and the need to possess. Now, sitting so
close beside this lovely slip of a girl who *pitied* him,
he lacked the strength to resist its call, to show her
exactly the sort of man she toyed with in her ill-
considered *pity*.

He grasped her shoulders and drew her close.
He hovered over her, their faces inches apart in
the dark cab. "This broken bird is none too safe,
Clara," he said, his tone smooth and confident with
experience born of pain and life. "You've unleashed
a predator."

Leaning down, he sealed his lips to hers.

Chapter 9

Shock buzzed through Clara as the captain's mouth expertly possessed hers. Panic mingled with delight and a trace of fear. Killian had assaulted her, threatened her virtue, even her life. She knew the captain would never harm her. Still, her fear was greater than when Killian had threatened her.

Fear she would succumb, fear she had never really known herself, fear her world was no longer the safe, comfortable place she had always taken for granted. For she enjoyed his kiss far more than a lady ever should.

And how she enjoyed it! Perhaps he had meant to teach her a lesson, but his kiss—at first punishing—gentled after the first sudden taking. The pressure eased, his lips pulling back enough to brush hers with delicate strokes. Taking pleasure in her pleasure. He made her feel so wanton! She ought not to be allowing this. She would burn in hell, or end up disgraced, or—

Her thoughts shattered into a thousand shards as his tongue outlined the sensitive corners of her lips, inviting her to tumble into the sweet ecstasy of his attentions. Like butter spread on a hot roll, his mouth slid over hers, licking and nipping and discovering outrageously responsive places she had never known existed.

Only one thought penetrated the sensual fog embracing her. *He cares for me.* Her emotions, already raw from her risky confrontation in the tenement, burst forth, obliterating her natural defenses. Tears dampened her eyes and spilled onto her cheeks.

He broke the kiss, frowning. "By God, I made you cry. What a bastard I am." He swiped at a tear with his thumb, then pulled her into his arms.

She sagged against him, sighing deeply. It felt good to allow him to cradle her, an intimacy that seemed even greater than his kiss. The scents of bay rum and gin filled her nostrils, making her feel pleasantly light-headed. "It's not you," she said, her voice thick as she struggled to hold unshed tears in check. "I mean, it is, but—"

He stroked her mussed hair from her damp cheeks. How different she must look now, compared to how he usually saw her, all neat and proper. How different everything would be between them, now that they'd opened their hearts to each other.

"But what?" he prompted, brushing away her tears with his thumbs. "Why are you crying?"

"It's everything. I'm such a baby about life. I'm a fool, just as you said. If you hadn't come to our rescue, I shudder to think what the outcome might have been."

"As do I," he murmured into her hair, his thumb continuing to skim her cheek as he pressed her head to his chest. His heartbeat thrummed in her ear, a steady, comfortable beat.

Her innate honesty made it impossible to contain her feelings. The more vulnerable she felt, the stronger the urge to share. "I only wanted to help," she explained. "This seemed something I could do—rescue Erin and relieve Lucy's heart."

"Then you succeeded. You rescued her."

"*We* rescued her," she corrected him, her fingertip tracing the sharp arc of his cheekbone, where a welt had begun to rise from one of Killian's blows. "I'm so sorry I put you in danger. But I'm not sorry you followed me. You were in such a pitiful state when you first arrived in New York, but now . . ." *Now that I know you care*, she started to say.

His entire body stiffened and he pulled back. She looked up at his sharp-featured profile and knew instantly that she had made a misstep. His eyes grew distant, his attention no longer on her. He gazed out the carriage window at the broad thoroughfare of Fifth Avenue. Their cab had joined several more deluxe conveyances taking their owners home after long evenings at balls, concerts, or the opera.

"I see no reason for this conversation to continue," he said without looking at her.

His words landed like drops of ice, chilling her exposed heart. Nevertheless, she felt compelled to try to reach him, find some way to reclaim the unexpected intimacy she had felt in his arms. "I know you feel useless right now, staying at our home, recovering. Wallowing in your misery," she added sarcastically. He still wouldn't look at her, so she continued, "You don't have to be useless. You could help me."

He laughed—an entirely humorless sound. "You must be joking. Charity parties are hardly my cup of tea." His voice sounded so bitter, it threatened to abrade her heart even further.

"Fine," she bit out, fed up with him. "If you want to sulk for the rest of your life, go right ahead. I surely won't stop you. Besides, I'm tired of trying to help you."

Finally, he looked at her. His frosty gaze chilled her to the bone. "Excellent. I'm glad you have finally heard me."

He turned away again, his posture communicating that he was through with her, in every way. After kissing her so intimately, too. How dare he! Clara wasn't about to let him off that easily. "What was that? That kiss? Why did you kiss me?"

"Because I felt like it. Now be quiet, like a good little girl."

"But—"

"It meant nothing."

Nothing? Her budding feeling she was falling in love with him burned to a cinder, along with her short-lived illusion that he actually cared for her in return. "So, you were toying with me," she said, throwing his earlier charge right back at him.

"Yes," he said coolly. "I was. I have just demonstrated how heartless bastards such as myself toy with others' lives, and it has nothing to do with charity or kindness. Never forget it, Clara. For I have never forgotten what I am."

With one stolen kiss, he had made her feel things, feel for *him*, in a way she had never felt for a man.

Shame filled her at how easily he had manipulated her emotions. "Since you have obviously recovered your health," she said, struggling to sound cool and unaffected, "you needn't prolong your visit to our home on my account. I am quite certain there is nothing more I or my family can do for you."

"Noted," he said dryly, and she felt a spurt of relief that he wouldn't fight her retraction of their hospitality. Nevertheless, the smallest portion of her heart ached to think she would see the last of this man, whose spirit was so wrought with pain he could only hurt others—and himself.

Then he added, "Though I will miss your attentive nursing. There's nothing like the touch of a woman to inspire a man." His gaze swept along her body in a familiar manner, instantly reminding her of his kiss, and earlier, that night he had held her and touched her so intimately.

Appalled at her weakness for him, she once again revised her opinion of him. How she wanted to see him gone! She never wanted to see that smirking smile again. *Please, let him pack up his things and leave the house tomorrow—no, tonight.* The moment they returned home. She would even tell the hack to wait for him, wasting no time ridding herself of his mocking presence.

Before Clara could formulate a suitably cutting statement expressing how little she would miss him, Stone sat up taller, his attention drawn to something outside the window. "We've arrived at your home." He turned back to her with a sharp look. "And it seems we're going to have company."

The hack driver pulled the small carriage to the paved walk fronting the Carringtons' elite Fifth

Avenue address. He leaped down with much more enthusiasm than he had previously shown and bowed toward the four people standing on the stoop before swinging open the door for Stone and Clara.

Her parents, flanked by a pair of uniformed policemen, rushed toward the cab as Stone stepped down. Her father shoved his way to the door and reached in to pull her onto the walk beside him. One look at his face, and Clara knew she would have a great deal of explaining to do.

Clara found it difficult to swallow in a suddenly tight throat. Her father ignored her—at first. But once he had paid off the cabdriver and the carriage had driven away, he turned to her with a chilly gaze. "Inside. Now." His eyes flicked to Captain Stone. "The both of you."

He turned and strode toward the front door, where the butler, Edgar, waited silently to close it behind them.

Clara stroked her hair from her face, knowing any effort she made to improve her appearance was fruitless. Stone gestured for her and her mother to move ahead of him.

As she walked up the path, Clara fell into step beside her mother.

"Your maid returned, Clara," her mother said, "with her cousin in tow. She told us quite a story about the night's events."

Clara's stomach tightened. Lucy had never been of a circumspect nature. She habitually embellished her stories until they were scarcely recognizable as truth. Clara feared to imagine the tale she may have shared of the night's adventures.

"How is little Erin? Lucy's cousin?" she asked, hoping to distract her mother.

"She's staying in the servants' quarters with your maid," her mother said, sounding more than a little stressed. "What am I to do with the girl? Your maid is already talking as if she's staying—according to her, we've promised to take her in permanently!"

Clara hadn't exactly made a promise, but she couldn't imagine kicking Erin out. "Her own mother sold her," she said. "Surely we can house her. She could work in the kitchen." They passed through the double doors and into the broad entrance hall. Clara saw none of her home, only her father's back before her, his shoulders sagging, his gait stiff. How she hated the thought that she had disappointed him!

"I have a full staff as it is," her mother continued. "Half of them are girls you found on the streets. Mrs. Rossi has threatened to quit, and I can't lose her."

"She's not going anywhere," Clara said. "She's been with us for as long as I can remember."

"These poor girls have no training, no experience—"

"Mother, they need us." They paused before the library doors. Her father waited inside. Clara lowered her voice, not wanting to involve her father in discussing little Erin's fate. He was in no mood to grant favors. "Erin needs us. We can't turn her out into the street."

Mrs. Carrington glanced toward Stone, standing behind them. "We will discuss it later. Right now I'm more concerned about your outrageous behavior and your involvement with these people. If what Lucy described is true—"

"Clara!" Her father's sharp tone cut her off, and Clara knew she could no longer put off the inevitable. Sucking in a breath, she followed her mother and Captain Hawke into the library. Edgar discreetly closed the heavy doors, leaving the four people standing silently in the room. Clara instinctively inched closer to Stone, her partner in crime, as both of them faced her parents. She had never seen her father so furious, not even when her adventurous sister Pauline had been caught with a boy in her room. His eyes glared hotly over cheeks, spotted with ruddy patches.

To her mortification, when her father began, he turned not on her but on Stone. "*Captain,*" he said, his voice heavy with derision, "you should be ashamed to call yourself a gentleman."

Chapter 10

Out of habit, Stone Hawke slipped into parade rest position, feet shoulder-width apart, hands behind his back, as he braced for the dressing-down he was about to receive. It wasn't long in coming. After pacing before him a moment, Mr. Carrington stopped and faced him squarely. Stone wasn't at all surprised that a railroad mogul, with the power at his fingertips that Mr. Carrington possessed, would project as much confidence as a battalion commander.

"I would have expected a soldier to be a man of honor," he began. "Instead I find you gallivanting around town with my daughter, taking her to the worst neighborhoods imaginable. Allowing her to go to a . . . a . . ." He shook his head, sending his handlebar mustache quivering. "By God, I can't even say it. And then, brawling with the proprietor, like a common street thug. All in the dead of night!"

"Yes, sir," Stone said simply. The realization that

his motives had been misinterpreted didn't surprise him at all. He was no stranger to misfortune.
Life usually dealt him a severe blow just when a
glimmer of light seemed to promise a turn in his
fortunes for the better. He nodded toward the window, where a pearly gray hue illuminated a street
awakening with early-morning delivery carts. "Actually, it's nearly dawn."

"Are you trying to be funny?" her father asked
sharply.

"If you please," Stone said, maintaining his cocky
attitude despite this newest shame fate was visiting
upon him. It didn't matter what the Carringtons
thought of him, after all. He would be out on the
street before morning. This powerful man had no
reason to take his word for anything. *He* wouldn't
take the word of a dishonored soldier such as himself. Besides, a father had every right to be distraught over his daughter's safety. And disinclined
to look kindly on a strange man being personally
involved with her.

Mr. Carrington was looking at him as if he
couldn't believe a man could be so rude in his
presence. "Don't play coy with me, son. I won't put
up with it! I'll put out word to everyone of any con-
sequence in this city, and by week's end you'll be a
pariah in New York, if not the entire Eastern
Seaboard." His cheeks had turned bright red, his
fury so palpable it vibrated in the air. "If it's the
last thing I'll do, I'll have your hide for endanger-
ing my daughter. I'll—"

"Father, stop it!" Clara cried out, drawing her
parents' gaze to her. "The captain wasn't in a brawl;
he was saving me. *Protecting* me."

Stone stared in amazement at her adamant defense of him. What did she care whether he was kicked from her home in disgrace? Especially after the way he had so brazenly begun seducing her in the carriage? He deserved no better treatment, certainly not at her father's hands.

She approached her father and laid her hand on his arm. "I would feel safe with Captain Hawke anywhere, Father. Anytime."

Stone felt as if he'd been struck by lightning. That a girl as sweet as Clara would make an effort to protect him . . .

That's why. Don't puff yourself up over it, man, Stone told himself. *She's good-hearted to everyone. Even a blackguard who takes advantage of her innocence rates a good word from her. It changes nothing.*

Clara spun on him, fire flashing in her eyes. "Captain, why won't you explain? You were worried about me." She turned to her parents and continued her explanation. "He saw me leaving the house. He hired a cab and followed Lucy and me. I was in over my head, I admit that. And if he hadn't arrived, I—"

"You *what?*" her father asked, glowering down at her.

"She couldn't anticipate what would happen," Stone jumped to defend her, earning another glare from her father and a grateful gaze from Clara.

He pointed his finger at Stone. "You stay quiet until spoken to."

"Stop talking to him like he's a child," Clara said. "He—"

"Stop defending me, Miss Carrington." Stone cut off her rant. "It's really not necessary."

"You will not interrupt my daughter, by God, or I'll—"

"All of you. Stop!" Mrs. Carrington spoke for the first time since the argument began. She grasped her husband's arm, struggling to capture his attention. "Please, Richard. There's something about Clara you don't understand."

"What are you talking about?" He gave his wife, then his daughter, a suspicious look.

"Her charity work," Mrs. Carrington continued, looking embarrassed. "I admit I haven't been as vigilant as I ought to have been. I saw no harm in giving her a loose rein. She's never before given us a moment of trouble—always thinks of others first."

"What are you blathering on about, woman? What does any of this have to do with this—this scoundrel"—he waved a hand toward Stone—"absconding with our daughter to a house of ill repute?"

Mrs. Carrington wrung her hands. "Well, Richard, you always said the girls should think of others, since the Lord has blessed us with so much bounty."

Mr. Carrington shook his head, his exasperation obvious. "Woman, you are trying my patience in the worst way."

"I've been sneaking out under your noses to help the destitute," Clara announced, her voice ringing through the room like a church bell.

For a solid minute, blessed silence reigned as all pairs of eyes focused on her.

"You *what?*" her father finally said. "You can't mean you left in the dead of night on your own."

"That's exactly what I mean," she said, lifting

her chin defiantly. "I went to rescue a little girl from bondage. And I would do it again."

Mr. Carrington stared at her incredulously for a moment, then shifted his shocked gaze to his wife. "You knew about this?"

Clara looked just as surprised by this as her father. "I pieced it together," Mrs. Carrington said. "I knew she'd gone to the Lower East Side before, but it was in daylight, and her maid accompanied her. Lucy is a very resourceful girl, if a bit . . . extreme."

"How could you allow her to run about the city like that?" her father demanded. "How could you risk her safety?"

"I never expected she would get into such danger!" Mrs. Carrington pinned her own gaze to Clara. "I understood she was volunteering at soup kitchens and escorting hobos to flophouses—that sort of thing. I never expected she would be as foolish as she was tonight."

"Only if it's foolish to save a girl's virtue, and quite possibly her life," Stone said dryly, earning a grateful glance from Clara. He gave her a brief smile, hoping it appeared encouraging. Though with the wrath of her parents about to fall on her, he wished he could do more.

Mr. Carrington turned on Stone once more. "And you saw fit to accompany her on this ill-conceived mission?"

"Father, you haven't been listening," Clara said.

"Listening to his rude remarks? I see no reason why I should pay him any heed at all. In fact, I want him gone by morning."

"Oh, come now, Richard," Mrs. Carrington said,

her abashed demeanor vanishing under a shield of motherly righteousness. "This is all so ridiculous. It seems to me that Captain Hawke did a good turn tonight in rescuing Clara. In fact, I would go so far as to say I would trust him with Clara under any circumstances."

Stone looked at her in shock. He hardly deserved that much trust. Yes, he felt protective toward Clara, more so than he ever anticipated feeling. Naturally. It was due entirely to her nature as a sweet young thing, coupled with her tendency to let her heart lead her into trouble. Any man would feel the same.

"I suppose I see your point. If it's true he rescued her," her father conceded. Still, he cast a wary look at Stone, obviously not yet ready to trust him.

Nor should he, Stone thought. If the man had any idea how Stone had pressed his daughter's body close and stolen kisses from her lush mouth . . .

"Clara, you must give up your forays into the Lower East Side," Mr. Carrington commanded. "You are forbidden to involve yourself with those people."

"Father, please don't say that. If no one helps, nothing will ever improve for them."

"Clara." His demeanor softening, he cupped his daughter's face. "Your heart is too big for your sense. I can't risk another incident like tonight's. Not with my precious girl." He patted her cheek with the air of a man who had put his foot down and expected his word to be obeyed. Clara's bow-shaped mouth turned down in a frown, her lower lip quivering.

Seeing her distress made Stone ache inside. His heart responded as if she were his own daughter—or lover. Damn the chit. She'd found a crack in his formerly stone-cold heart and slid in when he wasn't looking.

"Is curtailing her activities really necessary?" he asked her parents. "You know what her work means to her. If she promised to be safe. If someone was there to watch out for her—"

"Why, Captain Hawke, that's an excellent idea!" Mrs. Carrington swept to his side and pressed her hand on his arm. "I should have thought of it before. If a strapping young fellow such as you stands by her side, no harm will come to her."

"I suppose giving her a bodyguard is one solution," her father said, his gaze on Stone. The speculative glint in his eyes put Stone on alert. "What do you say, Stone? Will you watch out for Clara when she leaves the house on her charity errands?"

Stone hadn't intended to volunteer himself for the task. He was about to decline—until his gaze met Clara's. She looked near to panic. He realized then the prospect intrigued him. Let her feel a fraction of the discomfort he had felt in her too-familiar presence as she played nursemaid to him. Now it was his turn to drown her in overly solicitous attentions. The idea held more than a little appeal.

Not surprisingly, she didn't seem to think so, her eyes as wide as a deer's cornered by a wolf. "Father, I admit I owe him for his protection tonight, but—"

"I can think of no better way to return the favor of your hospitality," Stone interrupted, accepting his new role with a delicious thrill of anticipation. Being in the position of keeping a reluctant Clara in line, commanding her, being physically close to her for hours on end—right now, he could think of no better occupation to fill his days. In fact, he hadn't felt this enthusiastic about life in a very long time.

Chapter 11

Clara looked from her mother to her father and back again, appalled at the turn the conversation had taken. She couldn't allow this. Panic swelled within her. "It's not that I don't fully appreciate what the captain did for Lucy and me tonight. I most definitely do."

Three pairs of eyes watched her, waiting for a logical reason for her protest. "It's not that I doubt that he's capable of guarding me, but . . ." Words failed her as she struggled for a reason, any reason to keep him away from her. She had no choice but to avoid him, considering how easily she had succumbed to his attentions in the carriage. She had never felt so weak with a man, so ready to throw away all the values she had been reared with, despite knowing full well that she meant nothing to him. Truly he was a devil made flesh.

Inspiration struck, and she burst out, "You can't think it would be appropriate for me to travel about the city in the company of a bachelor, even if he is a *gentleman*." She stressed the last word just enough to draw a hint of a smirk from the captain. Oh, he knew, all right. He knew he was only playing the part, as did she.

Her mother waved her concern away with a simple solution. "Lucy shall continue to accompany you on your outings, of course. It wouldn't be proper for you to be *alone* with Captain Hawke, obviously."

"That's not the issue," Clara said, heat creeping into her cheeks. Her eyes slid to meet his, expecting that he, at least, would see reason. Instead, his face wore a triumphant smile, and she suspected he secretly reveled in her distress. Her father had it right the first time. He was a blackguard!

Quite a different thought occurred to her mother, and she clapped her hands in glee. "He even has a gun," she volunteered, apropos of nothing. "The housemaid saw it while she was cleaning. He *is* an army officer, after all."

"*Was* an officer," Clara protested, then thought of another concern. "Don't any of you remember how sick he was? Is, I mean? He's ill, and we ought not to put his health at risk."

"I wasn't too sick to protect you tonight, Miss Carrington," he said dryly, "even if I have resigned my commission."

She sent him a silent, heated warning with her eyes. "You mustn't be foolhardy. You're only recently recovered from your illness. You were weak as a kitten just days ago. I remember. I was there.

You shouldn't be putting yourself under too much stress."

He gave her a crooked, unconcerned smile. "Your hobby won't tax me excessively, Miss Carrington. Certainly no more than tonight." He looked at her father and said in a commanding voice, "An event I plan never to allow to be repeated."

His declaration earned an approving nod from her father.

"He won that brawl you dragged him into, as Lucy tells it, and came out the victor," her mother said. "That demonstrates quite well his suitability for the task."

"Mmm, yes," her father agreed. "As long as you remain safe, so that I'll no longer lose sleep worrying what you've gotten yourself into."

"But, Father, I really don't think he's the one to—"

"It's settled, Clara," he replied, his tone demanding obedience. "If you don't want his protection, then don't leave the house on any more of your ridiculous 'missions.' Understood?"

Clara nodded stiffly. "Yes, sir."

"Good. Now, it's late. Time for all of us to be abed. I won't be late for church service tomorrow. Clara, Captain." He nodded to each of them in turn. "Come, Olympia. This debacle has quite wrung me out." Tucking her mother's arm in his, he strolled from the room, no doubt proud that he had wasted no time in solving a sticky domestic problem that otherwise would disturb his smoothly running house.

As soon as the library door swung shut, Clara

spun on Stone. "I don't need you following me about. Tomorrow after church I make my Sunday visit to shut-ins and the church mission soup kitchens. Mother and Father will expect you to come with me, but I will expect you to escort me only as far as the door." She pointed in the general direction of the front hall.

"Leaving you to wander home at your leisure, without me? I don't think so." He stepped closer to her and she stiffened, bracing for whatever onslaught he might perpetrate next. Kisses, touches— she was susceptible to them all.

He took yet another step, bringing him within a foot of her. His voice dropped to an intimate murmur. "Surely being in my company can't be more frightening than what you endured this evening. What are you really afraid of, Clara?"

"Not you," she retorted, instantly regretting the telling swiftness of her response.

Lifting his hand, he ran a finger down the side of her arm, exposed in the ball gown she had worn to a party that had taken place another lifetime ago. Before tonight's events. Before the captain's mouth had possessed hers and commanded her to feel sinful, delightful things she had never imagined feeling.

"Are you so sure of that, Clara?" His teasing fingers on her flesh made her body melt from the inside out. Yearning for more, she swayed toward him, hating that she lacked the worldliness to resist him.

"Don't call me that. It isn't proper," she gasped, conscious of how her breasts pressed against her low neckline with each indrawn breath.

"*Now* you're concerned about propriety, after what happened tonight?"

"That was a mistake. I got carried away," she said so quietly she barely heard her own words. "The dark, and the danger we'd escaped from—"

"I meant the visit to the brothel, love."

She was making this worse by the moment. She had to escape his presence, before she said something even more telling. She found the strength to take a step back, breaking his contact with her. "I'm leaving at eleven. If you plan to come with me, don't be late."

Whirling away, she hurried from the room, feeling his eyes burning into her back with every step she took.

"Best hurry, miss," Lucy said in a conspiratorial voice as Clara entered the entrance hall. "Before *he* comes downstairs."

Nodding, Clara glanced over her shoulder. Neither her parents nor the captain was about. Grasping the doorknob, she yanked open the door. With Lucy following right behind her, Clara ran toward the family landau waiting for her by the curb.

Manfred looked over at them from where he lounged near the carriage's four matching horses. He didn't reach for the door as he usually did, or make a move to help them alight.

"Hurry up, Manfred. I want to leave right away," Clara said.

Manfred frowned. "I'm sorry, miss. Your father said I wasn't to take you on your errands without the captain goin' along."

Clara bristled at her father's unfortunate efficiency. "The captain isn't coming today, Manfred. Lucy and I are going on our own."

"I don't believe you are."

The deep male voice was spoken so close to Clara, she jumped. She spun to face her tormentor. "Where did you come from?" she demanded.

Stone nodded to the footman, and he swung open the door and lowered the steps. "Naughty girls, trying to give me the slip. I shouldn't be surprised. Get aboard, and let's get this jaunt over with, shall we?" He gestured for Lucy and Clara to board before him.

Clara tightened her hand on her umbrella and climbed into the carriage, ignoring his outstretched hand. Once they were on their way, she studied him as he sat across from Lucy and her.

"If you ask me, it's a blessed relief he's coming along," Lucy volunteered, voicing a most unwelcome opinion. "He's a sturdy lad, now that he's not bein' sick all over the floor anymore. He proved as much last night. I thought we were both goin' to meet our Maker!"

"Why, thank you, Lucy," Stone said, giving her maid a gentle smile that reflected nothing of his true character. "You were astonishingly brave yourself. I've rarely seen a woman so stalwart and true to her mistress, loyally accompanying her, even into the mouth of hell itself."

"What a loverly speech he has!" Lucy grinned and preened, sadly proving herself susceptible to his false charms. Well, he could win over her maid, but that was no means to herself, as she would prove to him. She expected more from a gentleman than pretty words. She expected him to have at least something resembling a heart.

"And you're looking remarkably lovely today, too, Lucy," he continued. "Despite the turmoil of last night."

Lucy giggled and pressed a hand to her chest. "Oh, goodness me! Such a silver tongue. I must say, you're looking right handsome yourself. A far sight better than when I first saw you, all weak and sweaty like a sick colt."

Unfortunately, Lucy's assessment was accurate. Captain Hawke had never looked better, despite having so little rest the night before. His color was healthy, his pronounced features looking not so much sharp as sculpted, his face the perfect model for a classically trained artist. His dark brown hair had been smoothed back with a touch of bay rum tonic, his face was clean shaven, and his tan suit was clean and pressed.

"Thank you, Lucy. That's kind of you to say," he said.

"I ain't lyin', that's for sure. You're very easy on the eyes, Captain. Very easy." She gave him a flirtatious smile.

A shaft of jealousy cut into Clara. She had never been jealous of Lucy, but seeing her flirt with Captain Hawke touched tender places in her heart that he alone had awakened.

Irritated, she interrupted their mutual admiration, giving Stone a cold glare. "Since you insist on coming with us today, I expect you to help."

He rolled his shoulder in an insolent shrug. "I am helping. I'm keeping you out of trouble."

"I'm quite sure you can make yourself truly useful, Captain, if you try. And that means doing more than sweet-talking my maid."

Lucy began to blush, her freckled face turning bright red in a matter of seconds. "It don't mean nothin', miss. Truly."

Stone arched his eyebrow. "You're making Lucy feel bad," he said bluntly.

Instantly, Clara regretted her words. She hadn't meant to hurt her maid's feelings. She glared at Stone. He had caused this conflict, the devil! He prodded her in her most vulnerable places, without even trying.

"I'm sorry, Lucy," she muttered.

"T'weren't nothin', miss."

Stone grinned at Clara. "That's a good girl. Behave yourself from now on."

"Why, you—" Clara began.

Stone cut her off. "After all, you needn't feel so possessive toward me. I promise you, milady. I'm more than willing to fulfill your every desire," he said, his voice thick with suggestion. His familiar gaze made it clear he hadn't forgotten their intimacy of the night before.

Lucy's eyes grew round as she stared at each of them in turn.

Clara clenched her fist to keep herself from slapping the knowing smirk off his face. How dare he talk to her in such an audacious manner!

Last night's intimacy returned in a flash, deflating her anger. He dared because she had allowed him to hold and caress her, of course. *It was only one kiss,* Clara tried to rationalize to herself. *Thank goodness he doesn't remember how he caressed me during his illness. That would truly give him something to crow about.*

Chapter 12

Stone followed closely behind Clara and Lucy, watching as the ladies lifted their skirts to avoid a steaming pile of rags and debris. Their pressed, well-tailored clothing stood in marked contrast to the stained, damp garments hanging from clotheslines strung between the narrow tenements.

His eyes traced Clara's back. Her dove gray tailored suit was among the least fussy garments he'd seen on her—or any woman of her class. A thoughtful choice, considering the neighborhood. Clara was always thinking of others.

Meanwhile, *he* was thinking of *her*. His eyes played over her hips, her woolen skirt swaying enticingly with each step she took. Her matching dinner-plate hat rested atop a psyche knot, and she clutched a black brolly in her gray-gloved hands. Ever the proper miss, she had no idea of the sensuous thoughts that spun through his head when he looked at her.

Certainly, studying her as she worked entertained him more than the work itself.

He had never known a lady with so much energy. He had already accompanied her to a rat-infested tenement to bring food to a mother with tuberculosis and her three children who had no means of support. Then they had delivered food and medicine to a poorhouse where most of the residents knew her by name. Still they weren't finished.

Clara led the way toward a run-down single-story building on the corner. A small wooden sign was posted beside a cracked pine door. Crudely painted lettering spelled out FIRST EPISCOPALIAN MISSION and THE LORD WELCOMES YOU. Clara pushed the door open as if she belonged there. Perhaps she did.

They entered a stuffy room filled with the scents of cooking vegetables and cigarette smoke. Long wooden tables and simple pine chairs filled most of the space. A half-dozen hobos in tattered coats and shirts sat at the tables, waiting for the food to be ready.

A portly white-haired man wearing a clerical collar pushed through a swinging door, bearing a heavy pot, which he placed on a table beside a hodgepodge of tin mugs and chipped china bowls. Looking up, he spotted Clara, then smiled and hurried over to meet them.

"Miss Carrington, Lucy, good morning. I see you brought a friend. We can always use more helping hands." The minister smiled at him and extended his thick hand reddened from hard work. "I am Reverend Jasper Jones, with the East Side Episcopalian Church."

Stone clasped his hand in a firm shake. "Captain Stone Hawke. I'm willing to help, as long as Miss Carrington is volunteering." He glanced at Clara pointedly, and she nodded appreciatively.

"That's marvelous!" Jones said, clapping him on the shoulder. "It isn't easy finding people to volunteer. Miss Carrington is one of the few of her set willing to donate her time on this side of town." He glanced toward the door as two more men entered. "Well, we'd best get to it. The natives are getting restless, and we'll be needing more soup than I've prepared, I can see that already. It's a hungry day."

Once the soup was hot and being served, rarely did a chair remain empty for more than a few minutes. Stone stood awkwardly by the wall, feeling out of place while Clara dashed about the rundown building, knowing where to be and what to do at every moment. She seemed oblivious to the vast difference in her lofty station from that of the destitute out-of-work men and homeless families who streamed to the mission for handouts. She only paused when the preacher gave his sermon, which he kept blessedly short. The clank of spoons on cracked china and tin bowls didn't cease even while he spoke.

Over the next three hours, Stone helped when requested, but he lacked the innate awareness of others' needs that Clara possessed, anticipating needs before they grew critical. She assigned him a few simple tasks—slicing vegetables, ladling soup into bowls, helping inebriated fellows to chairs. Even so, she had to direct him, making him feel next to useless. Still, when tired men and hungry children accepted the soup from him with a smile, he didn't feel entirely bad.

As the afternoon drew to a close, Clara crossed the room to Stone's side. She swept a hand over her forehead, pushing a damp tendril of hair from her face. His previous lady friends had told him how stifling their corsets could be, and he'd witnessed the deep indentations their whalebone stays made in their tender flesh. Despite wearing such a garment, Clara showed no sign of slowing down.

While he stood there feeling uncomfortably out of place, she spotted a family in need that Stone hadn't even noticed: a woman near the corner of the room, holding a little girl's hand. The child appeared scared, her eyes big as she gazed at the woman, and the woman—only about seventeen herself—looked as if she had been crying. The little girl's thick black hair hung down her back in a tangled mass, and her too-thin frame was garbed in a worn smock that looked two sizes too big.

Hurrying over to them, Clara knelt and spoke to the older girl. He watched as she turned her attention to the little girl, cleaning her face with her own lace handkerchief. Soon both girls were smiling at her.

Stone marveled at Clara's ability to touch the hearts of total strangers. Until now, he had believed Clara's commitment to charity work was as shallow as that of most debutantes, who engaged in a few acts of "basket charity" as a moral obligation. He had imagined her work was a lark that enabled her temporarily to escape her otherwise constrained life. True, she had gone out of her way to rescue her maid's cousin. Still, he hadn't really believed she was committed to relieving the suffering of total strangers. He hadn't believed—hadn't wanted to see—that Miss Carrington was different. Special and unique. A true angel.

He enjoyed watching her work. Even better, he enjoyed being in her company. Her inborn strength and sterling character were unlike any he had encountered in a lady before. Her grace and kindness shone like a beacon in the dreary lives of those she helped. In contrast, his own soul hung like a black stain in this place of hope, a wasteland of dead dreams.

Good Lord, he thought, catching himself. *You're getting bloody maudlin over this girl.* As he watched her work, he realized she had a purpose that sustained her. As for himself, he was useless here. Worthless. He had nothing to give to these people, no false words of hope to ease a troubled brow before they went once more into the harsh light of the world outside.

Then again, his darker side questioned what good she was really doing. True, Clara's concern and a hot bowl of soup may ease their suffering for a few hours. But these people's lives were no better than before.

Clara was speaking to a boy of about five, who was sitting silently against the wall, when her bow-shaped mouth turned down and sadness filled her eyes. Concerned for her, Stone crossed the room to her side.

She lifted the boy in her arms and rose to her feet. "This is Dobry Delinski. As near as I can gather, his father left him here so he could look for work. His older brother is only nine, yet he's the only breadwinner the family has."

"He has a job?"

"At a textile factory on Twenty-seventh. He loads spools onto a weaving machine for twelve hours each day, except the Lord's Day. Today, he's home sleeping."

The little boy said something in a language Stone couldn't identify.

"Polish," she informed him. He marveled that she knew enough of the language to understand the child. Certainly she hadn't been taught Polish along with her schoolroom French and Latin.

"His mother died of the white plague—tuberculosis—just last month. Now his father struggles to tend to him," she murmured, "while trying to find work."

"What sort of work?"

"The docks, I believe. He's been taking odd jobs, trying to put food in his sons' bellies, and his own." Her calm gaze lifted to his. "This is only one family. There are dozens more just like them, with even more children, and parents out of work. Or dead."

Despite himself, Stone felt compassion for the struggling family. "Life is hard for most of us," he felt obliged to point out.

She narrowed her eyes at him. "And some people's problems are of their own making."

"Miss Carrington?" The Reverend Jones stood fifteen feet away, gesturing to her. "Dozens more people came in over the past hour, and the soup is almost gone."

Clara nodded, then handed the boy over to him, forcing Stone to reach out and take him. "Take care of him," she directed. "Make him feel he's not alone, that someone cares." She began to walk away.

"Clara, I can't—"

She shot him a stern look over her shoulder. "I would like to believe, Captain Hawke, that you aren't completely heartless. Prove me right."

He watched her hurry toward the soup table, filled with confidence and purpose. Then he turned his attention to the burden in his arms.

A pair of large brown eyes met his. The little boy said something unintelligible and pointed toward Clara.

Stone said ruefully, "It seems you're stuck with me."

The boy frowned, probably more of a reaction to his expression and tone of voice than to his words. Stone forced a smile to his face and bounced the boy in his arms. "There, there, mate. Don't fret. She'll be back soon. She'll know what to do."

A tentative smile replaced the boy's frown, and Stone marveled that he could have such an effect on him with just a few words of encouragement. Perhaps Clara was right, and encouraging people would make a difference.

He put the boy down, feeling ridiculous, like he was playing a part. He had nothing to offer the child. To his surprise, the boy grasped his hand. He looked down to find the little boy craning his neck, his dark, soulful eyes gazing up at him worshipfully.

"Don't look at me like that," he groused, glancing frantically around for Clara to take away this burden she had foisted upon him.

The boy tugged his hand, drawing his attention again. He lifted his arms in the air and said something.

"What is it? What do you want from me? I have nothing—"

"Don't be daft! He wants ye to pick him up," Lucy said from beside him.

Embarrassed, Stone gave in. He crouched down before the child. The boy wasted no time wrapping his thin arms around Stone's neck.

Stone lifted him and turned to Lucy. "I'm not used to children," he explained, feeling incredibly thickheaded.

"It only takes a little love," Lucy said, giving him an encouraging smile.

"Something our captain has in short supply."

Stone stiffened at the insult. He turned and stared down at Clara. She met his glare unflinchingly. "If you'll put the boy down, you can fulfill your duty and escort me home. Lucy and I"—she nodded toward her maid—"our work is done here, for now."

Stone's jaw tightened. He didn't miss that he had been left out of the equation. Not that he should have been included. He had done a good job of warming the wall with his back for most of the afternoon.

Still, he didn't appreciate Miss Clara's pointed comments about his lack of feeling. So he wasn't a bleeding heart for every downtrodden soul in the city. Few people were as giving of themselves as

Clara, after all, and he was no exception. That didn't mean he was completely dead inside.

With a start, he realized he cared what she thought of him.

Central Provinces, India

An arm . . . It was a human arm.

Wisps of smoke curled from the white sleeve. A man's shirt. Its owner could be anywhere in the smoking rubble. Could be any of his men, except those on evening watch. Stone tried to recall the duty roster and failed. He had no idea of his men's whereabouts. At this time of evening, while most of the men might be enjoying a drink or the cantonment club, others would have already retired to the privacy of their bunks to play cards or read letters from home.

Or die.

Residents of the cantonment were beginning to gather near the devastation, their response building into a thunderstorm of shock and anger. As confusion transformed to understanding, questions became shouts and curses. Soon, the women, hampered from running by their stays and petticoats, caught up with the men, adding their cries and screams to the confusion.

Men formed a line to bring water to the still-burning timbers. Others found a handful of wounded and dragged them to safety. One man's foot was mangled; another had sustained a head wound. For another, the lower half of his face had been blown away. He would die a few days later.

Over the next hours, the reality of their loss became clear. Fourteen men died in the explosion—one lieutenant, three subalterns, nine privates, and one Indian servant. Except for Witherspoon, all of the murdered soldiers had been under Captain Hawke's command.

One woman had also died: Miss Penelope Flynn, his fiancée.

The regiment commander had responded to the unheralded attack that very night. The men had been called to arms and immediately rode out to hunt down and punish the offending tribal group. Several other regiments had joined them.

Stone recalled little of the skirmishes that followed. Soon after the explosion, he fell into a numbing fog. He did as he was told, passed instructions to his men, used his rifle against poorly armed natives, killed in his turn. He experienced no joy, and knew he had lost his will to soldier. Even the desire for revenge couldn't seduce him. The explosion had killed more than a dozen innocent people. And it had killed the man he thought he was.

At age twenty-eight, he knew he had already begun to die.

New York City

"Your methods are clumsy and inefficient."

Stone's tossed-off comment threatened to ruin a perfectly lovely afternoon. After returning from another foray into the Lower East Side, her mother had insisted that Clara rest. She had finally agreed to take tea on the lawn, to rest and restore her energy. To her surprise, Stone had joined her.

At first delighted despite herself, she was beginning to wish he hadn't taken the wrought-iron chair across the tiny linen-covered table. She was in no mood to defend herself and her work against his worldly pessimism.

She shot him a stern look over her porcelain teacup. "How can helping people ever be termed clumsy? Following one's desire to help can only reap blessings. That would be obvious to anyone who *had* a heart."

He sipped his own tea, then set it down firmly on its gold-rimmed saucer. "Criticism of me aside, your efforts are hit-or-miss, scattershot all over the city, each day a different goal. Yet, despite your considerable efforts, you are having no discernable effect on these people's lives."

No effect? All her hours of work, and he dared to say that to her? Sometimes Stone made her so angry, she wanted to scream. While he held himself aloof from the poor she worked to help, he never avoided an opportunity to needle and tease her.

This morning, he had trailed along while she and Lucy brought hot soup and bread to the Zepetnek family, an invalid mother and her six children who had no means of support after the father had died in a factory accident.

"You're being needlessly judgmental, Captain," she said, gently stirring her tea and trying to appear as if his criticisms didn't bother her. "I am certain those I help do not feel that my efforts are useless."

"Of course not." He shrugged amiably.

She continued with asperity, "I help those who I am told are in desperate need. I can only do so much, but I like to think my efforts alleviate true suffering."

"And that's admirable, I'm sure," he said with a sardonic twist to his lips. "Mrs. Zepetnek will eat well for a few days. But what about next month, and the month after that, and the month after that?"

Clara's conviction that she was right became a shade tarnished. "I'll visit again," she said defensively.

"Neglecting all the other souls you've helped before?"

"You seem determined to make me feel bad."

His smile gentled. "That's not it at all. I'm merely pointing out the basic flaws in your campaign."

"Campaign! This isn't a war."

He leaned forward, his eyes intent on hers. "Isn't it? Every day you take to the streets, determined to fight hunger or want, or disease, or whatever problem Lucy or the other servants have brought to your attention. Your energies are being divided exponentially." Sitting back, he shrugged. "At this rate, you'll run out of energy in a matter of months and, consequently, be able to help no one."

She hated his detached attitude, his lack of concern for the individuals she helped. But she had to admit he had a point. "I suppose you have experience helping the poor?" she said coolly.

"I *have* planned strategic battles. One begins by

considering his resources, determining his strengths and weaknesses and those of his opponent, mapping out a workable campaign . . ."

Despite being somewhat impressed by this new side to the captain, Clara couldn't readily equate his war experience with her charity work. "What does any of that have to do with bringing soup to shut-ins?"

"You should choose your field of battle, and focus your energies and resources toward that battle. Choose one, any one. But stop spreading yourself so thin, or you'll simply grow more and more frustrated." He muttered softly, "And I can't abide the thought of you losing your enthusiasm for helping others."

As he sipped his tea, Clara bit her lip, considering his words. So many problems in the city screamed for attention. She had to admit that her efforts, though admirable, had almost no effect on the overall situation of the poor and downtrodden.

"It seems as if you've given this some thought," she gently suggested.

Setting his cup down, he frowned and cocked his head, his eyes not quite meeting hers. "It merely seems obvious. However, if you feel my ideas have merit, I might be able to think of ways to improve your effectiveness."

"I appreciate your offer. I see no reason not to explore your ideas. Not that I'm ready to commit to anything, of course," she added, determined not to allow him to think she prized his opinion too highly.

He nodded, the corner of his mouth lifting. "Of course."

Their eyes met over their teacups. At his perusal, Clara began to feel warm all over. He had the power to make her forget her proper upbringing, to think about things quite apart from her charity work. *I could lose myself in those eyes,* she thought, quite off the subject.

"Miss Carrington, you're not ready! We'll miss the play if we don't leave immediately."

The intrusion caused Clara to jerk, and tea sloshed from her cup onto her afternoon tea dress. "Oh, no."

Stone jumped to his feet to confront Gerald Burnby. "Blast it, you idiot. You've ruined her dress."

"I didn't intend—say." Burnby gave Stone a suspicious stare. "What are you doing out here, anyway? I thought you were ill."

"Not too ill to know how to approach a lady," Stone retorted.

Clara rose and dabbed at the tan stain with her napkin, but it showed up clearly on her white chiffon skirt. "Mr. Burnby. I didn't see you approaching. I didn't realize it was so late." She would have to change to evening attire before going out, and that could take more than an hour.

Stone whipped his pocket watch from his vest and checked the time. "Hmm. I don't believe you have time to catch the theater show." A flicker of a smile danced across his lips, and he pocketed his watch. "Sorry, Burnby. You're out of luck."

Mr. Burnby frowned. "I can still escort her to a late dinner, even if we miss the play. I'm quite willing to change my plans. That is, if you agree, Miss Carrington. Unless you would rather not, of course. I only hope to please you."

"How accommodating of you," Stone said dryly. "No wonder her father thinks so highly of you, seeing as you lack a proper spine."

Mr. Burnby took a step back, as if Stone might infect him with a dreadful disease. "And you, sir, lack manners."

"I don't coddle Miss Carrington, because she doesn't need it. If you saw *her,* instead of her father's money—"

Stone was dancing far too close to the truth for Clara's comfort. "Both of you. Stop it!" She spun on Stone. "Your enthusiasm is misplaced. Father may have wanted you to protect me in the city, but I hardly need protection from Mr. Burnby."

"Is that a fact?" Tugging her arm, he turned her away from her gentleman caller and whispered urgently, "I'm willing to bet this sodding idiot will attempt to press his suit in a matter of weeks, if not days. If you're not careful, you could end up engaged before you know what hit you. Trust me, I have experience in these matters."

"Stop it." Clara tried to tug her arm away discreetly, but he refused to release her. "Stop treating me like—"

"Like what?"

She stared straight into his eyes. "Like I belong to you. For I certainly do not."

He let go of her arm, his face turning as dark as storm clouds. "God forbid you ever do," he said, a brittle laugh erupting from him. "You'd turn *me* into a sodding idiot, doling out my hard-earned savings to everyone on the street, kissing dirty babies' faces. Never measuring up to the paragon

that is Clara Carrington. I'm an unfeeling monster, if you haven't figured that out yet."

"I think I have," she said, proud that her voice
sounded even, despite the hurt and anger brewing
inside her. He had finally stated what he really
thought of her, and it wasn't kind. He thought her
a saint! How insulting. She lifted her chin and attempted to look down her nose at him, despite his
height. "I have figured it out. Finally."

He shot a scathing look toward Mr. Burnby. "Try
to enjoy yourself, Miss Carrington. I'm sure Burnby
here has no problem kissing babies, though I
doubt I can say the same when it comes to women."

"That's completely uncalled for," Clara said, giving him the harshest stare she was capable of. "My
relationship with Mr. Burnby is none of your affair."

His lips thinned into a tight line, and his eyes
darkened. "I wouldn't dream of interfering in
your perfectly ordered fairy-tale life. God forbid
anyone set you straight about human nature."
Jamming his straw hat on his head, he turned heel
and began striding away across the lawn.

"What a rude fellow," Mr. Burnby said as they
watched Stone's departure. "He's hardly a proper
escort for you. I don't understand why he's linger-
ing about. Taking advantage of your family's hospitality, I suppose."

Clara was in no mood to explain how Stone had
been designated her protector. She had a hard
enough time trying to contain her anger at his rude
treatment of her guest. Sometimes he was such a
brittle, cold man. And angry. And passionate.

And not at all cold, she amended, despite his disdain for her. She had felt his passion, hot and intense. Had longed for it to consume her. She felt none of that passion for the man beside her, but she did feel safe. "It doesn't matter, Mr. Burnby. *He* doesn't matter. Not tonight."

She gave him a smile, hoping to make herself forget the captain, at least for a while. She ought to be glad Mr. Burnby didn't upset her. Perhaps feeling safe was just as important as passion. Perhaps.

"I'm so glad to hear that, Miss Carrington." With a victorious smile, Mr. Burnby tucked her arm in his and escorted her back to the house.

Clara, Stone, and Lucy exited the mission. This had been their fourth visit in two weeks, and the situation for the poor was worse than ever, Stone reflected. They just kept coming, with no end in sight. As he'd advised Clara, she needed to become more effective if she ever hoped to make a dent in the needs of New York's populace.

He fell into step beside Clara and noted with annoyance that she increased her pace to make it difficult for him. As usual, Lucy hurried on ahead, not interested in becoming embroiled in their arguments. He couldn't blame her. Clara and he were increasingly rubbing each other the wrong way. She bristled at his oversight and inability to leap in and help wherever needed; he detested that she thought him a coldhearted monster.

Yet, watching her work with others, bringing hope into their lives, however ephemeral, was vastly more satisfying than attempting to do the same. He could offer them no comfort, not when he felt none in his own life.

Clara continued to attempt to ignore her protector.

"Afraid to walk beside an unfeeling monster?" he asked, goading her.

She showed more interest in her parasol than in answering him. Popping it open, she twirled the expensive confection, its pastel green ruffles dancing in the late-afternoon breeze. "Despite how well your name suits you, *Stone,* I cannot believe your heart is as stone cold as you would like others to believe. A little more effort would go a long way, but apparently you're too wrapped up in your battle campaigns to see that."

He slowed his pace, and she followed suit, to his satisfaction. Both of them seemed to seek out these confrontations despite their better sense. "You don't know me that well, Clara. It would probably surprise you to learn that I noticed something today, about human nature. About you."

That caught her interest. She paused and looked up at him, her eyes wide with interest. "And what might that be?"

He began slowly, feeling awkward putting into words his private feelings. "I was watching you today, helping people you don't even know. Seeing you with the people—with the children—I don't believe I've ever seen anyone enjoy herself more . . . outside of the bedroom." He added the last under his breath, to remind her in no uncertain terms what sort of man was protecting her.

Clara gave him a stern look but didn't respond

to his suggestive remark. "Helping others brings joy to my life." Despite her obvious fatigue, she glowed with pride.

"That much is clear," he said dryly. True, he questioned the value of her efforts in solving the problems of this teeming city. Yet he couldn't help admiring this slip of a girl for her determination and sense of purpose. How he missed that feeling, that sense of knowing where in the world you belonged. He had once enjoyed a sterling military record, been a man on his way up the ranks who believed himself perfectly capable of overseeing the men in his company. How little he had really considered what it meant to hold their very lives in his hands, until it was too late.

"I believe helping others is beginning to bring out the best in you as well," Clara said, drawing him from his dark reverie. "I didn't hear a single caustic remark from you the entire time we were at the mission. A rare experience indeed."

"That's a naive assumption," he said, instantly on his guard. He had confessed his observation of what her work did for her, but that in no way meant he was similarly affected. It was picturesque to imagine Clara's optimism, the joy she found in life even in the world's saddest corners, rubbing off on him, shining through the cloud that had surrounded him for so long.

But he knew that while he might greatly benefit by being in her company, she benefited not at all being in his. His sarcasm and realism could only taint her goodness. He was the worst influence possible on her life, a demon poisoning an angel with his black outlook.

He grasped her upper arms, his hands tightening enough to remind her how lacking in sentiment he really was. "It obviously hasn't occurred to you that there is no 'best' in me to bring out. It's your fantasy that there's anything good in me. Worse, you're trying to force me to change. I am not that malleable."

He dropped his hands, then turned again toward the carriage, where Lucy had already boarded.

Before he reached it, Clara's light touch on his arm brought him up short.

"Captain," she said, coming around to face him. He found himself gazing down into troubled eyes, her brow creased in concern. "You're right," she burst out, her ready acceptance of his criticism shocking him. "No one has ever questioned my motives before, but I believe your criticism may have a kernel of truth."

At her admission, the corners of his mouth began to lift in a smile. Until she continued speaking. "For I want you to change into a happy man. I want you to feel like living again. And, as John Donne said, 'No man is an island.' I firmly believe that happiness cannot be achieved if one is lonely. And caring means being a part of the human race. You can't isolate yourself from caring, from giving and receiving love. Not if you really want to live."

Her pleading gaze seemed to him an invitation, a promise of great rewards, if he dared take the risk. He took a half-step closer to her, so close she had to crane her neck to meet his gaze. Lifting his finger, he traced the curve of her jaw, then skidded his touch along the vulnerable arch of her neck to the lacy, proper collar of her gentlewoman's dress.

She trembled under his touch but didn't move back. No, she was far too proud for that, he reflected. Too determined to prove her mettle to reveal any weakness.

"Miss Carrington," he murmured, challenging her with his gaze. "Do you care? Do you really care? For me?"

"I . . ." She stared at him, her pretty lips frozen in a delicate gasp, her eyes wider than he had ever seen them. How unlike Penny she was, without the studied flirtatiousness, without the deliberate touches and words. Miss Clara Carrington was unguarded territory, waiting to be explored. A tiny flame of hope ignited in his chest as he gazed into her upturned face. Perhaps, in some unforeseen way, she *was* his ticket to happiness.

His heart thumped hard in his chest, then again, then a third time, every beat a measured moment in time as he awaited her response to his invitation. One more heartbeat. She swayed toward him, the briefest fraction of movement. Then she lowered her eyes and took a step away from him.

His heart crashed to his feet, hope snuffed in an instant. Her rejection of his overture told him all he needed to know. He replaced his derby and tugged the brim down. "I suggest you cease commenting on my personal life, Miss Carrington," he said, infusing his voice with the chill that had overtaken his heart. "And I shall stay out of yours."

Chapter 13

Clara maintained her composure admirably, she thought, during the short carriage ride back home that Sunday afternoon.

Captain Hawke had no clue that hot tears, spurred by a tight pain in her chest, were begging to be released. For the first time, the captain had frightened her, shaken her faith in her motives.

When she finally found herself alone in her room, she allowed the tears to flow. What was this power the captain had over her? Why did his cutting remarks affect her so?

"Do you really care? For me?" A few simple words, and she had lost faith in her own sense of honesty. She sagged against the pillows in her canopy bed and thought about everything she had done and said since he had appeared on her front porch.

Had her desire to tend to him, to help him out of his dark melancholy, come from selfish motives? Perhaps not at first. But ever since the night he had cradled her, had touched her in an intimate way only lovers shared, she had been drawn to him as more than a "charity case," as he liked to call it. She had been drawn to him as a man.

The truth settled in her heart, and she began to accept it. She was falling in love with him. She sighed and dragged an arm over her face. What should she do about it?

"Clara?" Her mother's voice sounded at her door. "Are you well?"

"Yes, come in," she rushed to assure her, then pulled herself to a sitting position. "I was just resting."

Her mother pushed open the door. "Look who's here!"

"Hello, sweet pea!" A flurry of white cloth and golden hair burst into the room. Her younger sister, the baby of the family, rushed to her side and threw her arms around her.

"Meryl! You're home." Clara's chest filled with happiness. If anyone could distract her from thoughts of the captain, it was her spunky little sister.

Meryl released her with a bright laugh. "That's obvious, silly goose."

"Is the term over? I didn't realize it was so late in the year." Ever since Captain Hawke had arrived, she had been floating in a dream, day to day, thinking of little else but his welfare. She hadn't realized until this afternoon, until he had confronted her, how much of her heart she had given to him.

"The term ended yesterday," Meryl explained. "Two more years and I'll be the first woman in our family to graduate something other than a finishing school."

"That's wonderful." Clara gave her a hug, ignoring her sister's opinion of her own education. A dutiful if average student, Clara hadn't always enjoyed her lessons in French and etiquette. People meant much more to her than book learning.

Despite their differences, Clara had always felt closest to Meryl. The youngest of the Carringtons' five daughters, Meryl was nearest Clara's own age. Clara hadn't confided in anyone her growing feelings for the captain, but she had never been very good at keeping secrets from the perceptive Meryl. "I've missed you more than you know."

Meryl pulled back and gave her an assessing gaze, her sharply intelligent blue eyes showing more worldliness than might be assumed from her girlish, pixielike face. "Something is different. *You're* different. What is it, Clara?"

"Don't be silly." Clara patted her hair, checking to see if her practical bun was still in place after her crying jag. She patted her cheeks, too, to make certain they weren't still wet.

Meryl nodded. "You've been crying."

Clara sighed and dropped her hands. "You're far too observant."

"That's what my professors say, too. Except they call me 'precociously curious.' " She grimaced. "I take great satisfaction in keeping them on their toes."

She grasped Clara's hand and pulled her to sit by her on the bed. "Now, then. Tell me your problems, so we can fix them."

"It's not that simple, sweetie."

"Of course it is. Someone has hurt your feelings, and they should pay. Or, someone close to you is hurting, and we'll fix it. Or . . ." She narrowed her gaze and examined her sister. "Or, some cad broke your heart, which would be the most interesting problem to solve. You weren't in love at Christmastime, so—"

"I'm not . . ." Clara began, then stopped. Perhaps she was. She had to stop lying to herself. "I'm not *sure,*" she finished.

"It *is* a man! That's wonderful. I mean, I wasn't sure you'd ever find a fellow who was good enough for you."

"What do you mean?" Clara asked warily, not sure she wanted to hear the answer.

"You know. Your standards are so high when it comes to people. Wishing everyone were selfless and giving. I figured it would be hard for you to find a husband. You know, a fellow who met your expectations of what a man should be—honorable, giving, caring, all those mushy, lofty things. I figured you'd fall for some preacher at some point, and together you'd work to save the world from sorrow by helping the needy. Is that what he is, a preacher?"

At Meryl's assumptions, Clara's stomach tightened and her chest thickened with a tangle of painful emotions. Perhaps Clara *had* envisioned herself with such a paragon. She didn't know. She hadn't spent much time thinking of men at all, until now. She had danced with them at parties and balls, allowed a few to court her, but never felt more than friendship for any of them. She had never intended to give her heart to the wrong man, to a man incapable of loving himself. How proud did that make her, to think herself above the vagaries of the human heart?

For she had never once imagined herself falling in love with an injured soul like Captain Hawke.

What did that say about her? That she shouldn't feel these things for the captain? Or that she was foolish to put such boundaries on her love for a man? Regardless, loving the captain was a fool's game. She knew that with a certainty that scared her.

"Do you really care? For me?" Perhaps he believed he returned her feelings, but until he began to live again—truly embrace life—he could never truly love. Not her. Not anyone. If she allowed their relationship to advance, if she became even more emotionally bound to him, he could quite easily grow tired of her once his spirit healed. If it ever healed. For a broken bird could not possibly fly.

He was right. She had been longing to change him, just enough to make him a man she could love and live with. Even she, with her limited experience with men, knew how foolish such a hope could be. She had known enough ladies who entered into a lifetime commitment with a fellow who indulged in drink or women, or was in other ways unsuitable. Women longed to believe their tender mercies could save a man from himself. Yet they usually wound up lonely, their hearts aching every day as their love wasn't returned.

She refused to be one of them. The captain himself had warned her she couldn't force him to change.

Therefore, she had to do her utmost to stop thinking about him.

"You're wrong, Meryl," she said, speaking firmly to brook no argument. "There is no man." She silently added, *Not if I can help it.*

"Thank you again, Miss Carrington. I enjoyed myself immensely."

Mr. Burnby lifted Clara's hand in his and bowed over it. "I would dearly love to call on you in Newport. Your father mentioned his family was moving there for the summer this coming week. He extended me a great honor, suggesting I travel with him for his weekend visits. So we'll be seeing much more of each other."

"Yes, we go to Newport every summer," Clara said, her eyes caught by a shadow moving beyond her beau's shoulder, near the alcove holding the inset doors of the grand Louis XV salon. Someone was watching them, she was certain of it.

"I hope that pleases you," Mr. Burnby said, tightening his grip on her hand.

Clara hardly heard him. The tall silhouette had disappeared into the alcove. "Yes, it's fine."

"Excellent! May I count on being your escort to the Goelets' ball, then?"

"Mm-hmm." Lifting her skirts, she began edging around her guest toward the man in the shadows.

"Miss Carrington. Clara."

His use of her Christian name drew her full attention. No man except her father and the captain ever called her Clara.

"If I may." He took both of her gloved hands in his and drew her close. "Clara," he murmured. "I can't begin to tell you how much being in your company has come to mean to me."

"That—that's nice," she said, flummoxed by the intensity of his gaze.

He continued in earnest, "Every moment I spend in your company is an honor. No, better. A blessing. It should be apparent that I'm . . . I'm starting to grow quite attached to you."

"Oh." When had this happened? They'd gone to a concert in the park, to the opera, to a few balls. While his company provided a nice distraction, she hadn't begun to feel seriously about him. "Um, thank you," she said, not wanting to encourage him nor discourage him. Not until she determined her own feelings in the matter.

Mr. Burnby looked less than ecstatic over her response. "These things take time, or so my father tells me. Perhaps . . ." He glanced around, then leaned close. The scent of peppermint from his breath washed over Clara's face. "If you'll allow me . . ." He touched his lips briefly to her cheek. Straightening, he smiled victoriously, then settled his derby on his cropped, oiled hair. "See, Clara? There is nothing to be afraid of. Not with me."

"I wasn't—" she began to protest, but Gerald had already turned toward the door, confident in his victory over her maidenly modesty.

"Don't worry, I shall let myself out. I'm almost a member of the family, after all." He smiled at her once more, before closing the front door behind him.

Clara sighed. She knew she wasn't the best companion. Try as she might, she felt as if she were acting a part when she was with any of her half-dozen suitors. Burnby in particular had grown quite attentive, demanding more and more of her time.

Yet, regardless of where they were or what they were doing, her thoughts insisted on returning home, to Captain Hawke—wondering what he was doing, worrying about his health, thinking of him.

The hovering shadow had vanished, but she sensed he remained nearby. She had seen him; she was certain of it. Annoyance filled her. Though her father had mandated the captain accompany her on her charity outings, that in no way gave him the right to spy on her when she was being courted by gentlemen suitors.

She pushed open one of the fifteen-foot-high gilt doors leading into the grand salon. "Captain?"

The door slammed shut behind her. She whirled and found herself facing him. Despite her better judgment, her heart began to race. He looked dashing and dangerous as he leaned nonchalantly against the door, his arms crossed, his expression dark and forbidding.

"What are you doing, skulking about the house?" she demanded, determined not to let him affect her.

"Out again with Burn-me?" he asked. "Let's see. That makes for . . . how often? Three times in one week? My, my. It's getting quite serious, isn't it?"

"Possibly," she shot back. Did it bother him, thinking she might be falling for another man? The thought thrilled her, but she attempted to shove down her delight.

He took a step toward her, imitating her suitor with a falsetto voice. "I'm growing quite attached to you. Let me kiss you, Clara, darling. Marry me and give me your millions."

"You're being quite rude."

"Oh, Clara, darling," he said, continuing the mocking falsetto. "Your mummy and daddy want you to marry me. Stop making me work for it. Give in already."

"Stop it!" Clara tightened her fist, longing to smack that smug look from his face. "It's not like that."

He returned to his normal deep voice. "Isn't it? He seemed darned impatient to me."

"He's not impatient. It's not like that," she repeated, beginning to doubt the veracity of her words.

The captain chuckled, the rich timbre of his laugh lacking any true humor. "If you had given him the slightest bit of encouragement, he would have proposed."

"That's silly. We're only friends."

"Trust me, little girl, friendship is the last thing on his mind. He wants you to marry him and set him up for life in your father's company. You can't possibly be so naive that you don't realize that."

"Of course I realize it," she snapped, knowing it would be foolish to deny the obvious. "I'm not blind."

He closed the distance between them and gazed into her eyes. "But do you ever ask yourself, what does he have to offer *you*?"

Clara edged backward, until her hips pressed against a marble-topped occasional table. Unable to retreat further, she went on the offensive. "I happen to like the fellow. He makes for very pleasant company. He *enjoys* things, unlike some men. He enjoys being with me."

Stone's mouth twisted into a harsh line. "Does he, now? I should think any man would enjoy being with an heiress."

"Not you, apparently," she said dryly.

"What makes you so certain?" His hands locked on the edge of the table on either side of her hips, imprisoning her.

Too close. He was far, far too close for either propriety or comfort. Not that she expected comfort from him. Being in his presence set her every nerve on edge. Her gaze lingered on his mouth as it slowly softened and relaxed, gently parting, his fuller lower lip slightly moist.

"What about after the wedding?" he said, his voice tight and dangerous. "Do ladies like you ever think of that? Do you ever think past your corsets and crinolines?"

Clara stared into his face, so compelling despite the danger she sensed in his tense muscles, the hard planes of his face. "What are you talking about?" she demanded.

"Giving yourself to a man. If you offered Burnme the ultimate prize. If you offered to take him to your bed. Trust me, little girl. He would not have refused. Not if he had a breath in his body."

"That's—that's wicked," she said, struggling to find the strength to deny his words while they rang in her head and her heart. The ultimate prize. Did he truly consider *her* the ultimate prize, and not her family's millions? "I would never do such a thing, never."

"Never?"

"Not as long as I live and breathe. Not for a moment. Not . . . not . . ."

Rational thought fled as pleasure assailed her, caused by the audacious brush of his lips on her neck. "You shouldn't be doing that," she finally managed to gasp.

"I'm quite aware of that." He caressed her cheek as if it were made of the finest porcelain, his voice filled with wonder. "What is it about you that draws me? I hated seeing Burn-me touch you. I feel I am the only one who should be touching you."

"You mean—" Her words were cut off, drowned in a sea of passion as his mouth claimed hers. Grasping her waist, he pressed against her, pinning her between the table and his own hard, unforgiving physique. Reaching behind her, he shoved aside an expensive urn that threatened to tumble to the floor.

She moaned and arched into the kiss, half of her mind seeking escape from him, the other half relishing the feel of his hard chest flattening her breasts. He buried his hand in her hair, shoving his fingers deep into her chignon, sending hairpins across the table and the Aubusson carpet.

He drew his legs closer, trapping her thighs between his own. A hardness pressed into her belly, and Clara vaguely understood this as insistent and undeniable evidence of his need.

His tongue teased the corners of her mouth, drawing a groan from deep within her. Clara admitted to herself how much she had enjoyed his kiss the first time, how much she wanted it now. She reached for him, exploring his chest with her palms, sliding her hands over his lapels, then under his jacket and along his woolen vest. She slid her fingers around his neck, marveling at the softness of the skin beneath his hair.

"Does Burn-me make you feel like this?" he whispered.

"No," Clara murmured, unable to lie, especially not now, in this most intimate of circumstances.

"Good." He slanted his mouth over hers, opening both their mouths wider, plundering all the softest places as his tongue dueled with hers.

"Oh, my goodness. Clara!" Meryl's voice penetrated the fog of desire in Clara's mind.

Chapter 14

Instantly, the captain broke the kiss. Clara fumbled away from him, then faced her little sister. She felt her cheeks heating to a bright pink. "Meryl," she said breathlessly. "Um, hello?"

"Hello to you, too. And Captain Hawke." Her unflinching gaze assessed him. "I understood you were suffering from malaria, but you certainly don't look ill now. I take it you're cured?"

"I'm feeling remarkably well, thank you, Miss Meryl." Unlike his behavior toward Clara, Captain Hawke always treated her little sister with gentlemanly deference—even now, having been caught in an intimate embrace. Clara envied his composure.

Meryl crossed to Clara and took her arm. "If you'll excuse us, Captain, I need Clara for something."

"What?" Clara asked.

"Just . . . something." Shooting the captain a curious look, Meryl propelled her sister through the salon doors and up the stairs to Clara's bedroom.

Once there, she locked the door and spun on her sister. "Tell all."

"What?"

"Captain Hawke! You didn't let on a peep that you fancied him. I've hardly seen you two in the same room since I came home. Now, tell me everything about your lover, before I tell Mother and Father."

Clara stared at her, aghast. "You wouldn't! And he's not my lover."

Meryl arched a blond eyebrow. "Is that a fact? Then what were his hands doing roaming all over you?"

Clara felt a fresh blush coming over her again. "Don't say that."

"You were doing it. Why not talk about it?"

"We weren't doing anything. Much," she added, recognizing how ridiculous that claim was. Sagging onto the bed, she asked her sister, "Am I terribly bad?"

Meryl rolled her eyes. "Oh, good grief, Clara. Stop being so darned good all the time. As long as you don't let the spooning go too far, you'll be fine. That is, if you truly like the fellow."

Clara's eyes widened in shock. "Of course I do! I wouldn't let him—that is, I wouldn't want to—I mean, if I didn't, I wouldn't . . ."

Meryl propped her hands on her hips. "Then what are you going to do about it?"

She stared warily at her sister, almost afraid to hear her elaborate. "What do you mean?"

"Do you want the fellow? I mean, do you want to marry him? If you marry him, you can kiss him to your heart's content and stop feeling so guilty about it. Trust me," she said with an air of authority. "I know what I'm talking about. My sorority sisters and I discuss boys all the time."

Marry him . . . Clara hadn't allowed herself to think of such an outcome. Now, faced with Meryl's pointed question, she found herself imagining it. Her entire being began to fill with pleasure at the possibilities . . . only to be followed almost immediately by discouragement. "I shouldn't marry him if he doesn't love me. I couldn't stand that. Yet I'm not sure he's capable of loving anyone. He's rather . . . broken inside."

Meryl sat on the bed beside her and pulled Clara's hand into her lap. "Then we'll just have to mend him, won't we?"

Clara met her smile, hope filling her. For the first time, it occurred to her that she was meant to rescue Captain Stone. Meant to heal him. Meant to love him. He had been delivered to her doorstep for a reason. She finally understood that reason, and accepted it wholeheartedly.

Her parents may have hoped that she would marry Gerald Burnby, but they would understand. No one would be able to deny that her destiny lay with Captain Stone Hawke.

It didn't take Stone long to pack. He owned very little.

He yanked open the door of the armoire and grabbed his satchel. Throwing it on the bed, he began stuffing his few articles of clothing into it. Last in was his toiletry kit, given to him by the British Army.

He grimaced. The army—when he used to be a man of character.

He swiped a hand over his mouth in a futile effort to banish the tingling sensation of Clara's lips responding to his. Perhaps his illness had driven him mad. That might explain why he found it so difficult to resist her charms, why he burned to possess her sweetness, body and soul.

This time, he couldn't convince himself that kissing her meant anything other than his desire for her. He wasn't trying to teach her a lesson, wasn't trying to show her how hard and cruel he could be, how undeserving of her pity. He wasn't thinking at all, only feeling.

On the contrary, he wanted her to want him. Wanted to make her feel pleasure, wanted her to think well of him. *Wanted her love.*

"Damn fool," he cursed under his breath. A dishonored soldier had no right to the heart of an angel like Clara. No right to kiss her or make her gasp with pleasure. The thought he would never see her again made him ill deep in his gut, compounded by a growing nausea that felt all too familiar.

Not now. Please, not now. He shook his head, determined to keep his thoughts clear. His gaze fell on the bottle of quinine by the bed. He hesitated only a moment before grasping it and stuffing it into his duffle. She would want him to have it in case the sickness returned, which the doctor explained was likely.

He tied his bag closed and grasped the handles,

then slipped silenty from the room, and from the mansion on Fifth Avenue.

"A sudden exit from our lives," Mrs. Carrington observed, glancing over the note that had been left for her in the guest room Captain Hawke had occupied. She sat in the blue parlor, in her favorite chair by a stone-carved fireplace that had been imported from a French chateau.

Clara sat across from her, trying to appear less miserable than she felt at the captain's sudden disappearance.

"He has a neat hand and a way with words," her mother continued. "He thanked us quite graciously for taking him in—in his writing, at least. I don't recall his words reflecting the same level of grace. A bit of a dragon, he was."

Clara may have once agreed. She knew him so much better now, knew how vulnerable he was inside, how badly he needed her. How could she hope to mend him if she had no idea where he had gone? Overnight he had vanished, leaving only these two notes behind.

"I suppose his departure now is for the best." Mrs. Carrington folded her note and placed it on a nearby occasional table. "We'll be leaving for our Newport cottage in three days, and he wouldn't fit in well with the community there."

"He doesn't fit in anywhere," Clara murmured as she studied the neatly penned words in a second note addressed only to her. How she had longed to change that! Despite her best intentions, that opportunity had passed. She had truly failed him.

She read his parting words again, her throat tightening with secret, unshed tears.

Dear Miss Carrington,
    I cannot put into words what your care and concern for my welfare have meant to me. Now that I am past the worst of my illness, I find I am ready to move on. As we discussed previously, I have enclosed some thoughts on how you might conduct your charity efforts with greater efficiency. Feel free to adopt or ignore them as you see fit.
                                    Sincerely,
                                    Stone Hawke, Esq.

Clara bit her lip, trying hard to read between the lines, to gather some clue to where he'd gone. She found none.

He had never discussed his plans with her. Where was he going to sleep tonight? What did he intend to do next? He had no job, had never mentioned any family or friends, other than her sister and husband back in India.

She tried to imagine what it must feel like for a career military man to lose his commission. Though he never discussed it with her, she imagined he must feel completely at loose ends.

She stared out the window at the broad sweep of Fifth Avenue, bustling with morning traffic. The city was so immense, home to one and a half million souls and more immigrants each day. He could be anywhere—assuming he even intended to stay here in New York. Instead, he could take the first ship back home—to India? Or England? Where was home for him? Would she ever learn what had become of him?

She folded the note he'd written her and slipped it into the pocket of her day dress. He'd given her no less than five pages filled with suggestions about her charity work. But his personal note to her had been ridiculously short.

Her mother might think his words were filled with grace. But the scoundrel hadn't had the grace to grant her a proper good-bye. He hadn't thought of her feelings at all. He had simply chosen to vanish from her life.

Irritation swelled in her chest, dispelling some of her sadness. He had appeared one night in her life, drawn her in with his melancholy smile, his sensuous kisses, and simply left her. His kisses . . . Was that why he had fled? How foolish of him to think that necessitated his departure. He hadn't ruined her, for goodness' sake. And she'd been a willing participant. More than willing.

He couldn't have gone far. She would be leaving for Newport with her family in three days. She had that long to find him, to make certain he was well situated. To say a proper farewell.

Or a new hello.

Clara entered the front hall, narrowly avoiding a pair of servants manhandling one of her mother's steamer trunks. On the broad marble stairway, two more men were carefully maneuvering another trunk to the front hall, to add it to the growing pile of luggage going with the ladies of the house to Newport.

That afternoon, they would be leaving Manhattan for their summer cottage, and not returning until fall. Clara had just come from visiting flophouses in the Bowery, desperate to find Captain Hawke. Hour upon hour during the past two days, she had looked for him, climbing rickety stairs, knocking on faded plank doors in the most disreputable neighborhoods. She had been determined to visit every flophouse and hotel in the Lower East Side, the Bowery, and the Five Points—all the neighborhoods her parents hadn't wanted her to enter without the captain guarding her.

And she had failed. No one fitting his description had been seen. He may not even be in the city anymore. Her chances were diminishing rapidly, along with her options. In the past day, she had come to realize that it was partly her fault that he had fled. She had scared him off with her bold willingness to enjoy his advances. Now he could be alone on the streets without a penny to his name, possibly ill with fever.

Desperate, she turned to one of the men. "Have you seen my father?"

"Yes, miss. Heading to his study."

"Thank you, Wills." Clara hurried down the hall to her father's sanctuary, the darkly paneled male domain where he retreated from his wife and daughters and thought about his railroads, smoked cigars, and imbibed more whiskey than Mother would have approved of.

Clara didn't knock. There was no time. She burst into the room.

Her father glanced up from his desk. "Clara. I was just thinking about you. I'm trying to decide on an appropriate philanthropic gift to the city, to leave my mark. Carnegie has his hall, and Vanderbilt has the opera house. I don't want to copy them. What do you think?"

Clara couldn't focus on his question, only on how rapidly time was ticking away. Once she departed Newport with her family, the chance that she would ever see the captain again were next to nothing. "Father, I would like to remain here in Manhattan for the summer. With you."

He arched a gray brow and stared at her. "I can't imagine why. All the parties and teas and whatnot that you young girls love so much will be in Newport. There is nothing for you to do here."

"Yes, there is. My charity work—"

He folded his paper and stood up. "Ah, I see. You feel you will be abandoning those you enjoy helping. Clara, dear, it's time for you to start thinking of yourself. You're young! You need to enjoy life."

"But I would enjoy staying here in the city during the week."

"How about if I donate to that mission of yours? Funds to tide them over while you're gone, so that you needn't fret." Opening a drawer, he pulled out a large draft book and began filling out a check. "That should do it."

He came around the desk and showed the check to her. "What do you think of that? I'll have Benson mail it out today."

"Thank you, Father. It's very generous." Her father seemed to think the matter resolved. Desperate, Clara realized she had to tell him the truth. "I want to find Captain Hawke. I'm worried about him."

Mr. Carrington pursed his lips and gave her a dubious look. "I know how personally you take your projects, Clara, but it was time for him to get on with his life. I paid him for his service in aiding you, and he seemed in good enough health. He could hardly be expected to remain with us indefinitely. Besides, with you going to Newport, you won't need his protection. And," he added pointedly, "I expect once you're married, your indulgences in these areas will be replaced by more domestic concerns."

"But, Father, if he's not well situated . . ." *I will never forgive myself for driving him away. . . .*

Slinging his arm around her shoulder, he steered her toward the door. "Your Mr. Burnby will be coming to Newport on weekends with me," he said with a wink. "That should please you. Why don't you go check on your maid? Make sure she's packing your favorite bonnet or frippery or whatnot."

He ushered her out the door. Before he closed it on her, Clara stopped it with her hand. "But, if the captain should need help . . . The doctor said his illness would return. You *would* be willing to help him again, wouldn't you? We could hardly turn him away."

A trace of annoyance flitted across his face. "Of course. Go along, now. Help your mother pack." He closed the door solidly behind her.

Clara pulled in a deep breath and squeezed her eyes shut. Her last hope had vanished. Only two hours remained before she would be forced to leave town. And leave Stone behind.

Two hours . . . At least she had that. She had to keep trying. She wouldn't forgive herself if she stopped looking now.

Clara paused before a nondescript door pointed out to her by a man outside the tavern across the street. It looked familiar. Had she already tried this flophouse? She wondered if she should waste a precious handful of minutes talking to the proprietor. Maybe she should move on to the next street.

She knew she was probably retracing her steps in her frantic search for Captain Hawke. All the streets and buildings had begun to look alike. "I think I came here before." Lifting her gloved hand, she tapped on the rough wooden door.

Meryl sidestepped a pile of garbage against the wall and came to join her sister. "I can't believe you spent the last two days doing this," she said, shaking out her skirts. "I already feel like I need a bath. We've probably picked up fleas just walking up here."

"Shhh." Clara nodded toward the door, which cracked open. The occupant gave them a careful look, then swung the door wider, displaying a stained undershirt and scraggly gray beard. A soggy cigar hung from the corner of the man's mouth.

Clara forced herself to smile brightly, hoping her positive demeanor would encourage the fellow to share any information he might have. "Excuse me. Has a young gentleman come here? British, slender yet well built, wearing a worn army uniform.

Except it had no insignia on it. And his eyes—he has these penetrating dark eyes that make him seem a thousand years old."

The flophouse manager stared at her in silence, his eyes traversing her well-dressed figure. His too-familiar gaze made Clara's skin crawl.

He chewed the end of his cigar, then thrust it back into his mouth. "What's it to me?" he asked around it.

"I'm desperate to find him," Clara started to explain.

"Ain't seen no one like that." The man stepped back and closed the door.

Clara sighed and turned to Meryl. "See? No one has seen him. He's probably left the city by now."

Feeling awful for lying, Clara had told her mother only that she had shut-ins to visit one last time before they left town. Her mother had insisted Meryl accompany her—but not before both of them had finished breakfast and directed their maids in packing for the summer stay in Newport.

Finally, she had received leave to go, after reassuring her mother that Lucy could oversee the rest of the packing and make certain her belongings were delivered to the station along with the rest of the family's.

The family carriage waited behind them on the street. Manfred kept giving Clara pointed looks, extracting his pocket watch from his vest and perusing it, wordlessly making it clear that time was running out. Already the noon hour had come and gone. The train to Wickford, across the sound from Newport, would leave Pennsylvania Station at two-thirty.

Her feet aching, Clara turned to lead the way down the stairs to the street.

"You're not giving up *that* easily," Meryl said. "The man hardly listened to you."

"He said he hasn't seen him." Clara shrugged.

"No wonder you've had no success. Let me show you how this is done." Raising her fist, Meryl rapped hard on the door. After a moment, the man opened it again, not hiding his annoyance at this second intrusion.

Drawing open her reticule, Meryl extracted a smooth dollar bill and waved it at the man. "Listen carefully. A British fellow, dark-haired, tall. Have you seen him? And don't lie."

Using only his tongue, the man shifted his cigar to the other side of his mouth. Moving surprisingly fast, he snatched the bill from Meryl's hand. "Yeah, I seen him. Across the street at the tavern. He was lookin' for a place to stay."

"And?"

"And what?" he replied, his eye on Meryl's draw-string satin reticule, lavishly decorated with ribbons and a beaded fringe. Clara herself always carried a practical bag tucked inside her pocket in these neighborhoods, so as not to tempt the desperate or weak-willed into thievery—something she wouldn't put past this particular man.

Meryl pulled out another dollar and waved it in the air. "If you have information, you may have this. If not, you can't. And if you're lying, our carriage driver will make you pay."

Clara stared at her baby sister, aghast. Where had this confident, worldly creature come from?

The man snatched the bill from her hand. "I ain't

got no room here, so I sent him to Mrs. Drawer's flophouse on Tenth, behind the tannery."

"Why, thank you, sir. You've been most helpful." With a perky smile, Meryl tucked her reticule away and spun about, striding toward the waiting carriage. Still amazed by her quick success, Clara hurried close behind, hope blooming in her chest. He was so close. Tenth Street was only a few blocks away.

At the carriage, Manfred stood, pointedly tapping the face of his pocket watch. "We have to get to the station, miss. Your father hates to be late."

"But we're so close." Clara stared from Manfred to Meryl, panic threatening to overtake her.

"Relax, sweet pea," Meryl said to her. "Father owns the line. And Mother isn't about to leave the city without us."

Manfred shook his head. "She gave me strict instructions to deliver you home on time, Miss Meryl. We'll barely make the train if we leave now."

"We can't leave now," Clara said firmly, making it clear she would brook no argument and earning an approving smile from Meryl. "We have one more stop to make."

Chapter 15

A warm shaft of light crossed Stone's closed eyelids. He blinked, opened them, and found himself looking at the world speeding by. A steady rhythm gently rocked his bed from side to side, and he realized he was on a train.

What the . . . ? He blinked and studied his surroundings. He'd been tucked into a lower berth, in the most luxurious railcar he had ever seen. Sconces of polished brass hung from walls paneled in polished black walnut, and framed mirrors hung between the curtained windows. Rich embroidery covered the seat cushions. Deep, royal blue carpeting covered the floor and led his eyes to a pair of stylish leather boots. He looked higher, up a slender blue skirt, past a neatly tucked blouse with wide leg-o'-mutton sleeves, and into a pair of concerned blue eyes.

"Are you feeling better?" said a voice he had

consigned to his memories. "You look a good deal better."

"Clara," he growled. He sat up and discovered he wore no shirt. He was naked from the waist up. A quick check assured him he wore his underdrawers, at least.

How had he gotten here—wherever here was? He concentrated, trying to think. He remembered collapsing in the flophouse the second night there, having barely made it back from looking for work before passing out from a fresh bout of fever. After that came the nightmares—fire and flames, devastation and death, the unholy screams of the wounded filling the evening air.

Then darkness. The last thing he recalled was being pushed and prodded and spoken to as if he were a child—by the very same woman who now puttered about his train compartment as if she belonged here.

She bustled here and there, arranging his medicine and a spoon, retrieving a towel from the floor and draping it over the towel bar near the sink, making herself at home despite the fact he was nearly undressed. God, how presumptuous she was!

"What in the hell am I doing here?" he ground out through a scratchy throat.

"You don't remember? Meryl and I found you in a filthy, flea-ridden flophouse, out of your mind with delirium. I rescued you from that awful place and brought you here."

"I'm so sorry my choice of accommodation didn't meet with your approval, Miss Carrington," he drawled. "But what the bloody hell are we doing here? This is a train."

She smiled gently at him. "Very observant. That proves you're no longer out of your mind with ague."

He glowered at her. "I'm not in a humorous mood, woman. You took me against my will."

"Don't be silly. You needed help." Leaning over, she began fluffing the pillow behind his head.

The patronizing gesture snapped his last bit of patience. He grasped her hands free of the pillow and yanked her to face him. "Damn it, Clara. I left to get away from *you*."

That succeeded in making her smile fade. "Your plan didn't work, did it? You're lucky I convinced my father to take you back in. I had to tear him away from his grand plans for a gift to the city to do it, too. And that's no small feat."

He could not care less about her father's grand plans. "Where in the hell are we going?"

"Stop swearing. I'm taking you with me to Newport. We'll be in Wickford shortly, and from there we'll take a steamer to town. My family has a cottage by the sea, and you'll get plenty of rest."

He shoved her hands away. "Don't be daft. Go back to your parties and suitors and get out of my life."

"That's a little difficult when we're on a train heading to the same destination." Leaving his bedside, she filled a glass at the sink, then brought it to him. "Besides, what plans did you really have? To lie in that awful place until the fever took you again, this time robbing you of life?"

He emptied the glass and passed it back. "I have plans. Options. Opportunities," he prevaricated, doubting she would believe his lie.

"Such as?"

"It's none of your business."

She gave him an indulgent smile. "Mother agreed you should travel with us to the shore. The sea air will do wonders for your health; I'm certain of it."

"Certain, are you? And what am I to wear?" He glanced about. His suit wasn't visible.

"Your satchel is in the armoire. We can buy you more clothing in Newport. Worth has a boutique there."

Worth. By God. He could never afford a Worth suit, or even a Worth tie tack. "You make me feel like a kept man," he said, his words tinged with a bitterness he could not hide. What use was he to anyone anymore? Why not resign himself to being Clara's plaything? Let her move him about and dress him up like one of her china dolls.

Her expression grew troubled. "I'm not sure what that means, but whatever it is, I don't mean any insult." She leaned over and pressed her palm to his forehead to check his temperature, like a good little nurse. His malarial fever had abated, but her gesture sparked a different sort of bodily heat within him.

"Being kept means you want to provide for me, so that I'll always be at your beck and call." He slid his arm about her waist and jerked her toward him.

Her lithe body fell forward, her breasts nearly landing against his face. At the last moment, she caught herself on her extended arms.

"Is that what you want, Clara, to make me yours?"

Her face was right above his. He found himself

recalling so clearly how delicious she tasted. His body responded with fierce need, his blood pounding hotly in his veins, anger and desire warring within him.

He felt so trapped then, so consummately weak. He could not escape her, despite his efforts. She had taken him against his will, captured him and bound him, and still his body thrummed with longing for her.

He had to end this relationship, make her understand that he didn't need her. Because he didn't. He refused to need her. Frustrated beyond measure, he flipped her onto her back and locked her wrists against the bed on either side of her head. On the narrow bunk, she lay almost beneath him, her svelte curves deliciously tempting.

"Captain . . ." She struggled against his hold, but only for a moment. Then she relaxed into him, her blue eyes large, waiting, watching to see what he might do.

"You make me so furious," he gritted out. He shook her wrists briefly. "Furious."

"Captain . . ."

"Damn it, woman. Call me Stone." He moved his mouth to just above hers.

Her eyelids fluttered and lowered. She sighed deeply, and he felt her life's breath reaching out, surrounding him, drawing him the last inch to her. She exhaled, and his name rode on her breath like a prayer. "Stone."

Whether she closed the final distance or he did, he couldn't say. In the next breath he was kissing her, hot and deep, her entire body molding beneath his like she was meant to be there. His naked skin slid against her curves, and his body burst to life. Suddenly, he felt more alive than he ever had.

Her hands dug into his bare back, her fingertips tracing the muscles in wide, sweeping arcs. *She wants me,* he thought, pleased beyond bearing. Despite feeling unmanned by her attentions, her trembling told him the truth—she hadn't wanted to let him go.

When their lips parted, each of them gasping for air, she cried softly, "I thought I would never see you again. You left without even saying goodbye." She kissed his cheek, then his lips.

"You know why I left when I did."

Her hands on his shoulders, she stared into his eyes. "I don't."

"Yes. You do." His thumbs slid along her silken lower lip. "You know what you feel. You should not have sought me out—again."

The heat of her determination filled her eyes. "Of course I should have. We seem to be making a habit of you slipping away, so that I have to search for you. But I would do it again."

His hold on her wrists relaxed, and she lifted her hand to caress his face. Her fingers traced his cheek, his forehead, his sensitized lips. "You were all alone. You needed me. Now that you're getting well again, I hope we shall start fresh, and be honest with each other."

Was he really going to be well again, as she said? Would he ever be? The ghosts of his past were not so quick to forgive. "Clara, love, you expect too much of me. Of who I am."

"Who you *can* be. I know you care for me," she

murmured. "You cannot pretend that you don't." Her thumb teased his lip, and his groin tightened with such fierce need, he thought he might burst.

"This is an incredibly dangerous game you're playing," he warned her. His words had no effect on her. Her wide eyes gazed into his, opening herself to him in a way he had never seen a woman do. She did not keep herself aloof as other young ladies did, especially those of her station. Silently, with her eyes alone, she welcomed him in.

"Stone," she murmured, continuing to stroke his chin, his cheekbones. "I want you to touch me, like you touched me before."

He rested his forehead on hers. "You mean when I kissed you."

"I mean when you were ill the first time." Grasping his hand between her own, she turned it palm up. Stone waited in anticipation, wondering what she intended to do.

"You pulled me into your arms, and then you—did this." To his shock, she did the unthinkable, and laid his hand on her breast.

He gazed down at her in awe. He thought he was well past finding wonder in life, but this slip of a girl, so innocent and untried, had managed it. He molded his fingers to her full curve, his thumb sliding along the lace of her bodice. "I have no recollection. . . ." His eyes met hers. "How could I forget this?"

She pulled in a trembling breath, her chest rising and falling under his touch. "You were hallucinating. You thought I was a girl named Penny."

Penny. He stiffened and yanked his hand away. So easily he had forgotten who he was. So quickly he had shoved memory of his fiancée from his mind.

Clara knew nothing about his true character, despite the fire that burned between them. If anything, his willingness to explore physical delights with her virginal body should prove to her his lack of moral fiber. Probably, in her schoolgirl's experience, she fancied him some kind of war hero and painted their liaisons in a nonsensically romantic light.

Anger pumped into his veins. He could never be what she so clearly believed, wanted, deserved. He hadn't been what Penny wanted. He had tried to leave her, lied to her, pushed her away—until his lack of love ultimately killed her.

Now Clara thought she could change him. Fury filled him, leaving one clear thought on his mind— to teach her a lesson she would never forget.

He cupped her breast, caressing the globe above her corset through her sheer bodice. "Do you like this?" he asked, his jaw tight.

Her eyes closed; she didn't react to the change in his demeanor. "Yes," she panted through parted lips. "Stone, you make me feel as if I've entered paradise."

"Paradise? No, Clara. This is paradise." Reaching down, he expertly flipped up her skirt and petticoats, exposing her hose-clad legs. He slid his palm along the creamy length of her inner thighs. She trembled beneath him, her chest shuddering with her gasps, but she did not protest.

Sliding his hand farther upward, he encountered her bloomers. His fingers dipped into the opening provided for personal matters. Still she didn't protest.

Then he touched her. Curls softer than he had ever felt greeted his questing fingers. Her feminine lips were silky soft, damp with desire, welcoming him. He shuddered, clamping down on his own passion as he sought to violate her sense of security in his presence.

"What do you think of this, Clara?" he asked, tracing the inner folds of her femininity.

She responded with a moan, her hands still wrapped about his shoulders. Not enough—not yet. He pressed his fingers inside her moist heat, deep, then deeper still, allowing his thumb to make small circles at the apex of her pleasure.

Her fists tightened on his shoulders. "Oh, my goodness," she burst out, uttering the strongest exclamation her angelic nature would allow.

If she spent time with him, she'd learn quite a few more colorful phrases, he thought ruefully. But he was doing this so she would no longer want to spend time with him—so she would understand the dangerous game she played.

His rhythm intensified, his fingers moving in and out, his thumb pressing and retreating in a steady beat. She bucked on the bed, gyrating her hips downward, seeking completion from the pleasure he gave her. Her head tossed back, she cried his name like a lover.

Lover. The little fool.

Frustration churned inside him, dampening the passion he felt, extinguishing his inclination to finish what he had started. He rasped into her ear,

"I could so easily take your virtue, Clara. A single layer of cloth, a thrust of my hips, and I would be filling you. You would be a fallen woman, *my* plaything. Think about that the next time you try to help me, and count yourself lucky."

Before Clara could take another breath, could even think about the cruel words he had uttered, he had pulled away.

In a heartbeat, he had withdrawn his hand and sat up, not even looking at her.

Her body ached with a need so fierce, it consumed her. Need screamed through her, obliterating reason and thought. For a long moment, she didn't care what he had said. If he would only return to her side, caress her again, stroke her *there*.

Somewhere in the distance, a guttural horn shrieked. He pulled the sheet about his shoulders, stealing his slim, muscular body from her view, and rose to his feet. He looked through the curtain on the compartment window. Without looking back at her, he said, "We're arriving at the station. Straighten your clothing and your hair. You look like I've had my way with you."

His mocking statement cooled her passion. Her mind began to clear, and the blunt words he had uttered came crashing back. *"You would be a fallen woman. My plaything."* Hurt stabbed at her, and her eyes filled with moisture.

Trembling, she sat up and stared at him. He was so strong yet also so weak, this man she thought she knew, the man she thought cared for her in return.

"Do you hate me that much, to threaten me so?" she finally said to his strong, impervious back.

"That should be obvious." His words fell on her like ice water. Yet he wouldn't look at her.

Clara's hurt began to subside, along with her frustrated passion. She began to think clearly, to see him through unfogged eyes. To understand.

Despite what he had told her, despite how he had intimately teased her, Clara could not put him so easily from her heart.

She pulled herself to her feet. Her legs nearly gave out from under her. "Then why didn't you?" she asked boldly.

His shoulders stiffened. "Didn't what?" he asked with feigned casualness.

"Take me." Just saying the words made her tremble with need.

He didn't answer, and she knew she was right to have faith in him. She took a step toward him, raised her hand to touch his shoulder.

"Get out so that I may dress. I don't want to appear stark naked to my generous and socially prominent benefactors." His words were filled with sarcasm.

The hurt, the silent pain, radiated off him in waves. And why shouldn't he ache? She had inadvertently damaged his pride with her generosity.

Understanding this, she had tried to show that she was acting out of more than charity. She had physically opened herself to him, needing him to see the truth, see that she cared deeply for him. Perhaps, in some ways, she needed him as much as he needed her. She had never felt so stimulated, so alive, as when he came into her life, challenging all her notions of what a gentleman truly could be.

At some point, possibly during that military explosion he had endured, his spirit had taken a direct hit. Oh, he might fool others with his cold demeanor, his cutting comments. Might even believe he could fool her. He may try to hurt her—may actually succeed, as he had today. But Clara knew the truth.

Again she approached him, determined to let him know she saw right through him.

The horn sounded again, and she felt the train slowing. They had run out of time. "Very well, Stone. Perhaps later—"

"I said, get out."

Resigning herself to waiting, she slipped from the compartment—right into the path of her curious mother.

Chapter 16

"Clara!"

Clara stiffened and released the handle to Stone's compartment door, then slowly turned to face her mother. Mrs. Carrington's neatly tailored traveling suit and hat stood in marked contrast to Clara's mussed state.

"Mother, hello. I was checking on the captain. He's doing much better. The fever has broken."

Her mother narrowed her gaze. "That's good news. He may have a relapse, however. Isn't that typical of malaria?"

Clara began to nod; then her mother said suddenly, "Why is your dress wrinkled? And what happened to your hair?" She lifted a hank of hair that had come loose from her coiffure.

Clara touched her hair self-consciously. She hated lying, so she settled for a half-truth. "The captain— He reached out in his delirium, and it came loose."

"Did he, now? I thought you said his fever had broken?"

"It did," Clara said, feeling flustered. This is why she rarely lied. She was terrible at it. "After. His fever broke after."

"Hmm. Well, straighten yourself. Style your hair and put on your hat and gloves. We'll be at Wickford in less than five minutes. You know other members of the Four Hundred will be at the landing to board the same steamer to Newport. I won't have us entering Newport looking less than our best."

"Yes, Mother."

"Now, where has your sister got to?"

Mrs. Carrington continued down the passageway with a confident stride, her thoughts turned to Meryl.

Clara sighed at her close call. Thank goodness her mother had no idea what had really happened in Stone's compartment.

"Now that we're away from the city, you can stop thinking of others and start thinking about yourself and your future." Mrs. Carrington glanced at Clara while overseeing the unpacking of her daughters' trunks. "There are no missions here to distract you, only the cream of society. And plenty of social events with plenty of eligible men."

Clara set her jewelry case on the dressing table. Her bedroom in her family's Newport home wasn't much different from the one in New York. Unlike New York, however, there were no soup kitchens or tenement dwellers—only the top strata of society with which to fill one's days.

"I know, Mother. I'll hardly have a moment to myself." While charity work energized Clara, the whirl of social events during a Newport summer would weary even the most energetic soul. She picked up the schedule her mother's secretary had prepared, and flopped into an overstuffed wingback chair to read it over. Though she had arrived only the day before, perusing tomorrow's agenda filled her with a sense of exhaustion.

After a large breakfast *à l'anglaise* at eight, the girls would change into their riding habits. Following the morning ride, they would change into day dresses and join their mother for a jaunt to the Casino in the family phaeton. Its low sides were the best for displaying their expensive Parisian fashions.

At the Casino, they would visit the Worth boutique, watch tennis, and gossip. To close out the morning, they would be expected to spend an hour at Bailey's Beach, dunking themselves in the water and pretending they were swimming.

Mother particularly looked forward to luncheon on the Astors' yacht, anchored in the harbor, more so she could compare her jewels with those owned by other matrons than for the food, even if it would be served by a French chef on fine white linen. Debutantes weren't allowed to wear their jewels until evening.

The afternoon was booked with a drive to the polo field to watch a match. Then at three, despite being tired from the endless socializing, she and Meryl would put on their afternoon dresses, climb into the carriage, and promenade from home to home, leaving cards at friends' mansions along Bellevue Avenue and the Cliffs.

Clara thought about her mother's specific instructions for the promenade. "When we pass an acquaintance in another carriage, only nod—no more, no less. If we pass them a second time, you may smile."

"What about a third time?" Clara had asked.

"Then you must look away, so as not to appear too forward."

Clara hoped she wouldn't forget and embarrass her family.

Even after the promenade, the day was far from over. From five to eight, the family would take tea on the terrace. Afterward, Clara might have an hour to herself while she dressed for dinner and the evening's events.

Every night's entertainment was unique—tonight they were attending a ten-course dinner hosted by the Astors, followed by a specially arranged play by performers from Broadway, then a housewarming dance, and a second supper at midnight.

The next day, it would all start again. And nowhere was time allowed for her to spend with Captain Hawke.

Her mother pulled a lavender chiffon dress from the steamer trunk and passed it to Lucy. "Have her wear this to the polo match this afternoon, and the mauve and gold to dinner. Don't forget the matching hat and gloves."

"Yes, mum." Lucy curtsied, no easy task while balancing three voluminous dresses over her outstretched arms.

Mrs. Carrington began flipping through the

dresses hanging in a second steamer trunk. Clara's wardrobe included no less than ninety changes of clothing, so that she would not commit the faux pas of wearing the same dress twice. Besides dresses and gowns—all of which came with matching parasols, hats, and gloves—clothing in her five trunks included riding habits, a bathing costume, and bicycle bloomers, so that she could take part in all the summer activities of the enclave.

"Two engagements have been announced already, and it's barely July!" her mother exclaimed.

Clara only half listened to her mother's gossip. She was much less interested in discussing engagements than in the answer to a particular burning question. For she hadn't laid eyes on Stone since the train pulled into the station. On the platform, he had met her gaze only briefly before entering a carriage shared by the servants.

Her mother might grow suspicious if she showed too much interest in the captain. Then again, she knew Clara was concerned for his welfare. Gathering her resolve, Clara posed the question. "Where is Captain Hawke? I haven't seen him since the carriage brought us from the station."

"Oh, yes." Her mother didn't meet her gaze when she replied. "I know you're concerned for that Englishman, which is why I allowed you to bring him along. But that's no reason for you to neglect your purpose in being here, which certainly isn't to wait on an army captain."

Clara nodded, not in agreement, but to end the discussion. Still, it satisfied her mother, for now. Clara was far less satisfied, still not knowing what had happened to him.

"By the way," her mother continued, as if it were an afterthought. "I've arranged for him to stay on the beach, in one of the caretakers' bungalows. The sea air will do his health good."

Clara frowned, a sinking feeling in the pit of her stomach. Did her mother suspect she harbored feelings for him? "You didn't give him a room here in the house?"

"I felt it wouldn't be appropriate. Newport Society is extremely closed, Clara. People would talk."

She does suspect. Clara hadn't told a soul the depth of her feelings, not even Meryl, and she trusted her sister not to spill a single word about catching them in an embrace that day in the parlor.

She had no illusions about her ability to hide her feelings—or lack thereof. Her mother could probably read her affection for Stone in her eyes.

Anxious to keep her secret, she averted her gaze and tried hard to sound nonchalant. "Goodness, Mother, we have twenty-four bedrooms here at Elmhurst. Surely we can spare him one."

"Hosting him in the city is different from hosting him here, Clara. In Newport, everyone's business is known. It wouldn't be proper for us to host someone who isn't *in.*"

By "in," she meant accepted into the highest echelons of society; in other words, suitable marriage material for the daughters of the elite. Clara didn't need to be told why the penniless, connectionless captain didn't suit. "I understand that, Mother, but we can't simply leave him alone in a cabin. He needs to be tended to. Cared for."

"Yes, dear. By someone other than my well-bred

daughter. I've hired him a nurse. Once he is well, he will be ready to resume his life—whatever that might entail."

Clara sat back in the chair, frustrated yet unable to come up with any reason things shouldn't be as her mother had arranged. If her mother had done as much for any other charity case of hers, Clara would not have minded. But how could she possibly explain her need to be near Stone, when that need grew out of her most personal, feminine heart?

Her mother gave her a sympathetic gaze. She set down a hat she was holding and crossed to her chair, then laid a hand on her shoulder. "Dear, I don't mean to diminish the good you've done in donating your efforts to help this fellow. But it's past time for you to turn your energies elsewhere, to enjoy yourself with friends of your own class."

"Friends like Mr. Gerald Burn-me—I mean Burnby," she quickly corrected.

"Yes, exactly." She ignored the petulant tone in Clara's voice. "He's a solid catch, dear. Several of the ladies have set their caps for him, but I can tell that he has eyes only for you."

Clara laid her head back on the chair and pressed her eyes shut. Marrying Mr. Burnby would make for an easy life. He was of her class, her family approved of him, and he worked in the family business. Besides that, he was good-natured and kind.

Nevertheless, she felt no passion for the fellow. She could not imagine Mr. Burnby igniting the fires within her that Stone could with a single glance. If

Burnby touched her as Stone had . . . She shuddered and bit down a smile, the image both ridiculous and horrifying.

She knew the captain would be a difficult man to live with—sometimes irritable, always challenging her. Yet she found the idea irresistible. Despite their conflicts—or because of them?—he brought fire to her life. He was unlike any man she had ever known.

Her mother's declaration cut into Clara's reverie. "Some of the most eligible men are being snatched up. I hope by the end of the summer to hear good news regarding you and Mr. Burnby."

Clara snapped open her eyes. "I'm in no hurry."

"If you won't marry Mr. Burnby, then you must get busy with the other bachelors. Getty's son is visiting from Pittsburgh. Rumor has it his heart was recently broken. I know how you love to mend broken birds. Why not him?"

"Mother, I'm not ready."

Mrs. Carrington ignored her protest. "And while we have plenty of connections to the peerage because of your sisters, one more can only be an asset for our family. You might cast your eyes toward Lord Sotheby. They say he's here from England for the sole purpose of finding a wife."

"Marvelous," Clara said, her dry tone reminding her of the captain's. His mannerisms were rubbing off on her, something her mother would no doubt hate to see.

Oh, Stone . . . What are you doing now? Has your fever returned, leaving you shivering alone in your bed? Do you miss me as much as I miss you?

Once more scanning the day's schedule, she

sighed. When would she find time to see him again? And did he even want to see her, after their encounter on the train?

Nothing was settled between them, and she knew he ached still, whether or not he was racked with malaria.

So much healing left to do. And instead of helping him, she would be wasting hour upon hour watching polo matches and dancing quadrilles.

Trying to appear as if she were taking an innocent stroll on the beach, should anyone see her, Clara exited the Cliff Walk onto a rocky path leading to the shore. At the far edge of the pebble-strewn beach, a half-dozen clapboard bungalows sat perpendicular to the coast. Here, away from the center of town, the caretaker and his staff lived year-round.

Clara had learned from Lucy that Captain Hawke had been put up in the cottage closest to the sea. Its whitewashed walls were bright against the azure sweep beyond. Ocean breezes buffeted her navy blue serge skirt against her legs and snatched at her blue-and-white-striped parasol, making it difficult to navigate the uneven, rocky slope.

As she reached the bottom of the path, a fresh gust tugged at her straw hat. She pressed it to her head, thankful that a silk bow held it in place. She lifted her skirt but couldn't keep from dragging the hem in the hillocks of sand sculpted by water and wind.

The closer she drew to his cottage, the faster her heart beat. Thoughts of his ironic smile, his penetrating gaze, his incendiary kisses flashed through her mind. Had he missed her? How would he react to seeing her again?

A month had passed since her family arrived in Newport. In that time she had seen Captain Hawke exactly once. And he had been asleep, resting after a bout of fever. The dour, mean-faced nurse attending him had insisted Clara leave and return another time if she wished to speak with her patient.

Clara prayed the nurse wouldn't interfere this time. She stopped before the clapboard door, its red paint weathered, its knob rusting. She tentatively tapped on it with her gloved hand, uncertain who would answer.

After a painfully tense wait, the door swung inward, its hinges squealing in protest. For a long moment, she stared at Stone, drinking in the sight of him. He wore only a shirt with his trousers—no vest, no jacket. His cuffs hung undone over his wrists, and his collar lay open. She had the hunch he had pulled on his clothes to answer the door.

He hooked his thumbs through his suspenders and shrugged them on. As he moved, her eyes played along his arms, flexing under his shirt's cotton fabric. She well remembered the look of his naked physique, lean yet powerful, like a thoroughbred racehorse. She recalled the warmth of his skin under her palms, the smoothness of his neck, the roughness of his beard stubble. She knew the softness of his thick brown hair wrapping around her fingers. Now his hair looked windblown, and she longed to brush back an untamed lock falling over his forehead.

His lips twisted in a mocking smile, as if he had

been reading her thoughts. How would he treat her? With more of his cutting comments, his insistence that he was beneath her?

She wasn't about to let his thorny attitude defeat her. Steeling her resolve, she took a step forward, silently demanding entrance.

He gave in, retreating into the room. "Here to finish what we started on the train? By all means, come in."

She ignored his jibe. Snapping her parasol closed, she stepped inside and looked around. The little cabin had only two rooms: the main room, where they now stood, and a kitchen in an alcove past a spindle-legged pine table. Her eyes fell on the narrow, unmade cot where he slept. So hard and unforgiving! How could he be comfortable here?

He must have read the distress in her eyes. "Don't fret. I'm used to rustic conditions. This is not unlike my bungalow in Nagpur." He shoved the door shut behind her.

"I'm sorry," she said, her eyes following him. She couldn't get her fill of looking at him.

His eyes flashed in annoyance. "Aren't you supposed to be somewhere? Dancing or playing cribbage or whatnot?"

"Swimming," she tossed over her shoulder on the way to the table, where she deposited her parasol.

"Ah, swimming." He watched as she reached up and unpinned her hat, then laid it and her gloves on the table. "I rarely enjoy a sight more than the humorous image of ladies bobbing in the waters offshore, their huge hats flopping, wearing so much clothing one expects them to sink."

Clara bit her lip as she fought a smile. His description was very like her own impression. "Not exactly my favorite activity."

She pulled out one of two rickety straight-backed chairs from the tiny pine table. Turning it around, she sat down facing him. "I think it's a waste of time to parade down to the beach just to bob about in the water for a few minutes before the men arrive and we have to leave. It's silly when there are better things to do."

He smiled wryly. "Like visit me?"

"It's difficult enough to find time to visit you while attending what Mother calls 'essential events.' And there are dozens and dozens of those. Last week I attended one at the Breakers," she commented, trying to ease into her request.

"That new palace they built in place of the one that burned?"

She looked at him in surprise.

"The caretaker mentioned it to me."

"That's right," she said, infusing her voice with enthusiasm. Everyone had been curious about the new mansion. Even the captain couldn't be entirely immune. "Everyone agrees the new one is the grandest home in town, even bigger than Marble House."

"How nice for the Vanderbilts," he said dryly but without malice.

Clara clasped her hands. "Yes, well, that ball was the first in their new home. A coming-out party for their daughter Gertrude."

He arched an eyebrow. "How nice for Gertrude."

"I think the house was the greater draw."

He studied her closely for a moment, then asked softly, "Clara, why are you here?"

She swallowed, then faced him squarely. "It's quite simple, really. There's another ball at the Breakers tonight—"

"How nice for *you*."

". . . and I'd like you to be my escort." There, she had said it.

He pulled himself upright and uncrossed his arms, his face showing genuine surprise. "Me? Seems to me there are much more suitable beaux in the neighborhood."

"I want you."

He arched a brow, and she realized how suggestive her words sounded.

"To escort me to the Vanderbilts' ball," she clarified. "It would do you a world of good."

He extracted a cigarette from his jacket pocket and tapped it against the mantel above the rustic stone hearth. "And it would cause you a world of trouble."

"No, it won't. There will be close to three hundred guests—cousins, friends from out of town. No one will think it odd if you're there. Besides, you need to get out. Meet people."

"Impress your parents?" Striking a match on the stones, he lit his cigarette and inhaled deeply.

She chose to ignore that remark. "Does your nurse approve of your smoking?"

"My nurse." He chuckled. "My prison warden, more like. She finally left. Deemed me well enough to manage myself. Of course, my lack of tact and appreciation for her efforts probably played a role in her declaration."

Clara narrowed her eyes at him. "Did you cause her trouble?"

"No more than I caused you."

All she could think about was the way he had embraced her, fondled her, driven her mad with passion. "You didn't!"

He shook his head in annoyance. "Don't be daft. Trust me, I no more wanted to manhandle Nurse Detwurst than I would Mrs. Astor."

"You are an extremely rude man," she declared, despite privately agreeing with his assessment of society's reigning monarch.

"So I've been trying to tell you. And that is why, my dear, I cannot escort you to your ball."

"Yes, you can." Clara rose and approached him. Drawing close, she laid her hands on his arms, felt his muscles tense under her palms. She gazed into his eyes. "Please take me. I don't care if you're rude to Mrs. Astor herself. You're handsome and well spoken, and you can be gallant when you want to be. Besides, I rather like you."

He chuckled and shook his head. "Persistent little chit, aren't you?"

"So I've been trying to tell you." She grinned. She had never attempted to use her feminine wiles on any man. And she couldn't now. What she could do was express to him in the most heartfelt terms how much she longed for him. "Please, Stone. I am so sick of the men my mother keeps shoving my way. Please come with me, and give me at least one night to remember fondly from this long, dull summer."

"As dull as all that?" he murmured.

"Dreadfully dull, without you there to annoy me." She slid her hands up his chest, then locked them behind his neck, feeling she belonged there, in his arms. "Please."

"Well . . ."

Rising on her toes, she arched her back and pressed her lips to the soft spot beneath his earlobe. He pulled in a soft breath as she whispered once more into his ear, "Please."

Heat wound through him, delicious and dangerous. They were alone; she was speaking seductively to him. He imagined pulling her onto his cot, finishing what they had started right then and there. "Clara," he murmured, his voice shaky from the tantalizing feel of her lips traversing the sensitive spot under his ear.

"Mmm," she purred.

His desire grew so intense, he had to force his hands flat against his thighs to keep from pulling her hard against him. "Clara, you have to go now. This isn't a good idea."

She pulled back and looked in his face. "But you haven't agreed—"

"And I'm not going to. Not now. Time to go." He swept her hat, gloves, and parasol off the table and pressed them into her arms, then maneuvered her toward the cottage door. She must have felt the pulse of desire, too. Instead of tensing with resistance, she felt as soft as warm butter, leaning invitingly into him, allowing him to move her where he willed.

Out on the front step, he released her. "Go home."

Her forehead creased. "You are still a rude man." She popped open her parasol. He ducked to avoid being hit in the face with it. Spinning on her heel, she began marching back across the sand toward the trail leading to Newport's loftier realms.

Central Provinces, India

"Where is he? Where is Roddy?" The young woman stepped over the debris left by the explosion, her eyes darting over the wreckage, her hands desperately clawing at the charred timber that used to be the regimental barracks of the Ninth Jodhpur Dragoons. "Roddy!" she screamed.

Her wild eyes caught on Stone, and he froze as cold as his name. Trying to make her way to him, she stumbled on a steaming board, damp from the fire brigade's buckets. He caught her arm and righted her.

Almost as quickly, she snatched it back. "You. Captain Hawke. You're Roddy's commanding officer. Where is he? Where's Roddy?"

He could barely bring himself to look in her face. Didn't she realize she was looking at a ghost? "I don't know, miss," he said, his voice flat. "I don't know what happened. That rebel tribal group—"

She shook his arm. "My baby brother's missing. Don't you know that? Don't you know anything?" Her shrill voice abraded his nerves. "He's missing! He's missing, I tell you. He went in there, and now he's missing!"

He forced his brain to work, his mouth to respond, all the while thinking about Penelope and Witherspoon, who had been standing on the bar-rack veranda, and were now nowhere to be seen. "There was an explosion. Dynamite, I imagine."

Her eyes were huge, her face contorting as hysteria overtook her. "How? Tell me how? How could you let this happen?"

He stepped away from her, but she pressed toward him, refusing to let him escape. "It's your job to watch out for Roddy. Do you even know which one he is?"

"I . . . I'm not sure." God, he was a miserable excuse for an officer. He didn't know which man in the regiment she was talking about. He hadn't paid attention. Now her brother might be dead.

The woman's panic transformed into rage. She gritted her teeth, and her hands clawed. Any minute he expected to feel her fingernails sinking into his flesh.

"You *bounder*," she spit out, her voice snapping with pain. "If he's in there—if he died—why weren't you with him, protecting him? Protecting all of them? Why?"

Why? . . .

Newport

Stone jerked awake, his eyes wide open as if he hadn't slept at all. God, how he hated the nightmares. Memories that haunted him like living things, reaching out from the past to hold him down, remind him who he was, demand that he not forget.

He sat up and pressed his hands to his face. How long would this continue? How long would he let these memories conquer him? He had to start making choices in his life, find reason where none existed. If he didn't, he would go mad.

Warily he eyed the long box that had been delivered to his cottage from Worth's boutique. It rested on his narrow bunk. Inside lay formal regalia for the well-turned-out gentleman.

Don't do it. Don't dare to dance with the angels. His gaze lifted to the window, and the twilight settling around the mansion on the crest above.

He might as well be in purgatory. He had been expelled from the glittering heaven where his own angel resided. He had understood—more than understood—when his benefactress had sent him to stay here instead of so near her lovely daughter. How could he fault a protective mother, when he had treated her daughter so brashly?

And his ploy hadn't come close to working. His taste of her lushness had only served to fill his days with dreams of her, fantasies of bringing her to crashing completion, dreams of lying naked beside her in the sweet glow of fulfillment.

His chest tightened with a fierce, burning longing. *She wants me beside her, tonight, at least.*

Perhaps she merely wanted to flaunt him in her mother's face, as a rebellious child might. Perhaps she meant to use him to turn Burn-me's affections from her, or to make him jealous. No, that didn't sound like her. More likely, she wanted to prove to her satisfaction that she had "saved" him.

Whatever her motive, he couldn't help longing to take her up on her invitation. Every night he watched the gilt carriages congregate on the broad sweep of Bellevue Avenue, harness bells jingling, hooves clopping, ladies as colorful in their gowns and feathers as tropical birds.

Every day he wondered what Clara was doing. Who she was seeing. Who she might be kissing. The pain in his heart when he thought of her with other men was his just reward. He had no one else to blame for becoming involved with her.

To keep himself occupied during his lonely hours, he ran on the beach, farther each day, building up his strength. And he wrote letters. Correspondence filled his small writing desk, letters to potential employers, mining companies, oil concerns, engineering firms—anyone who might be interested in hiring an educated military man with colonial experience, a man willing to take a position in some far-flung outpost. Anywhere except India.

He would never again set foot in that damned country. India—a place of such promise when he first arrived—had witnessed the death of his dreams, the destruction of his innocence.

Now innocence reached out to him again, in the form of Clara Carrington.

She believed he could be saved yet, that there was something inside him worth saving.

Sitting on the bed, he lifted the tuxedo jacket from the box and held it up. Perhaps tonight, just for a while, he could pretend she was right.

A dozen pairs of eyes turned to follow Clara as her captain escorted her into the great hall at the Breakers, a four-story Italian-style mansion inspired by the sixteenth-century palaces of Genoa. Liveried footmen stood at attention between the Corinthian columns lining the hall.

With the house's—and their daughter's—coming-out party behind them, the Vanderbilts had decided to host a more frivolous event. The theme this night was yachting. Huge sails hung from the high gilt ceiling, painted like the sky, and marine signal flags decorated the buffet table and orchestra stand. Many of the men wore faux "admiral" uniforms. Even the ladies had sailor themes in their clothing.

Clara tightened her hand on his arm as they entered the ballroom. He looked down at her, and she saw worry in his eyes, the fear that he was overstepping his bounds. "You are the most handsome man here," she assured him, and meant it.

A ghost of a smile appeared on his lips, and his eyes warmed as they met hers. *Thank you,* he silently mouthed.

The marine theme had been carried inside the ballroom. An entire sailboat had been brought in, and dancers circled around it. A plank leading up to it allowed the guests to sit on deck. The jovial guests greeted each other with calls of "Ahoy, matey."

"Cute," Stone said dryly. "It always amazes me how the wealthy spend their time—and money."

Looking at the party from his eyes, Clara could only agree. It was rather silly. Jaded aristocrats always sought new ways to amuse themselves, and costume balls were a favorite. Because this was their first—and perhaps only—ball together, Clara had decided they would wear the traditional ball gown and tuxedo rather than a costume.

"At least you're a real captain and not a pretend

one," she said, nodding at acquaintances who pointed discretely at the captain and whispered to each other. The socialites always took note of new faces intruding on their "set." "Even if you were with the army and not the navy."

"I *was* a captain. Not anymore." For once, he didn't sound bitter about it.

"Clara!"

Meryl had been waiting for her near the entrance. She hurried over, wearing a captain's jacket with a braided cap—a daring costume for a debutante. "Good evening, Captain Hawke."

"Miss Meryl," he said with a nod. "You look lovely tonight. Rather intimidating, actually."

"You wouldn't expect me to wear less than a captain's uniform, would you? Not if I'm going to run Father's company someday."

Stone chuckled. "I would expect no less, Miss Meryl."

"Daring, Meryl," Clara said, not at all surprised her sister had chosen such a costume. Other ladies had come as mermaids and sailors, but not captains.

"Not as daring as what you're up to." Her eyes flicked up and down Stone. "If you'll excuse us for a moment, I need to talk to my sister."

Meryl pulled Clara aside and lowered her voice. "I knew you were waiting at home for a suitor to bring you, but never expected it to be him. My, he cleans up nicely, doesn't he? I heard Sandra Underhall speculating that he was a European prince, of all things."

Clara had arranged for top hat and tails to be delivered to Stone's cabin. To her delight, the tuxedo fit him as if it had been tailored just for him. The swan-tail coat emphasized his height and lack of excess flesh. With his hard physique, he needed no girdle to keep his stomach in check, as she suspected Mr. Burnby did.

Yet his natty attire was only one aspect of his appeal. His dramatic features and dark coloring made most of the young eligibles appear washed out and tepid by comparison. Ladies nearby were admiring his severe, aristocratic features, which, given his aloof expression, made him seem of a better breed than everyone there.

Clara had never felt more proud to be on a gentleman's arm, to show off her "catch" as so many young ladies did, though she expected her fantasy to be short-lived once his identity was tossed about by the gossiping herd. Not that she cared. She was doing this for Stone and no one else. Not even herself.

"Does Mother know?" Meryl asked, emphasizing the conflict to come.

Clara tried to sound unconcerned as she saw her mother look their way, then begin separating herself from a knot of gossiping matrons. "She will soon. She's coming this way."

Chapter 17

"Captain Hawke," Mrs. Carrington said. "I didn't expect to see you tonight. Nurse Detwurst told me you no longer require her services. You *are* looking remarkably well."

Clara tensed despite her mother's pleasantries. She would never make a scene in public, after all.

"Thank you, Mrs. Carrington. I can't tell you what your generosity has meant to me. I'm in the process of finding a position, so that I will no longer be a burden on you and yours." He gestured to Clara.

"You are?" Clara asked, her pleasure that he was embracing his future mingling with sadness that he might walk out of her life.

"Clara, if I may?" Her mother gestured with her fan. Clara released Stone's arm. Bracing herself, she followed behind her mother to a small alcove on a side corridor leading from the ballroom.

"What is going on here?" her mother asked as

soon as they were alone. "Why is he here, and why are you hanging on his arm? He is hardly a member of the set."

"I felt he needed company," she said, her chin high. "People who suffer from melancholy should never be left alone for long. They need the company of other people."

"Melancholy, is it?" her mother asked archly. "I thought it was malaria."

"The malaria caused the melancholy. Or, the melancholy made him susceptible to the malaria; I'm not sure."

"Nurse Detwurst never said a thing about melancholy, and she's a professional."

"She doesn't know him as well as I do."

Her mother gave her a studious look and tapped her folded fan on her gloved fingers. "How well *do* you know him?" she asked, her tone deceptively casual.

Clara shifted her feet, deciding to stick to the truth, even though it failed miserably to capture their complex relationship. "I like to think he's a friend. And I'm not ashamed of that."

"Nothing more?"

"Mother, please. I thought an evening out would be good for his disposition, which can often be quite sour."

Her criticism of the captain seemed to please her mother. "What about Mr. Burnby? I've seen him standing alone. He looks rather put out."

"Don't worry, Mother. I'll still dance with him. He can spare me for this one ball. There's one almost every night of the week."

"Very well. This will take some explaining." She

gave a heavy sigh. "I swear to the good Lord, Clara, your good heart causes me more trouble than Meryl's high jinks ever did."

"Thank you, Mother. You're the best." Leaning up on her toes, Clara kissed her mother's cheek. Whirling, she hurried back to the ball, and her captain.

Over the next hour, Stone lost himself in a wealth of feelings he had forgotten he could experience.

As Clara's escort, he allowed his old self to return, giving her a glimpse of the officer he had once been, a man accustomed to escorting ladies about the cantonment. A product of the British military, he could play the gentleman as well as any man, and he decided to demonstrate that to Clara. He wouldn't allow her to regret placing her faith in him.

He gazed at her by his side, as regal as a princess, wearing a tapestry gown shot with metallic gold and trimmed with sapphires that matched her eyes. While her skirt was full, the bodice appeared minuscule. Her waist was tiny, and her low-cut bodice revealed a generous expanse of cleavage. As much as he longed to hold her, to caress those curves as he had before, he found her most attractive feature to be her face. His first impression had been of an angel, but now he recognized the steel and desire in her eyes. A fascinating combination, one that promised every good thing he had once thought forever lost to him. How could he resist giving this amazing creature, even more beautiful inside than out, anything her heart desired?

He had never been much of a dancer, but he relished the excuse to hold her in his arms. When they weren't dancing, he discovered he enjoyed playing the role of attentive beau, finally taking his turn to see to her needs instead of letting her tend to his. When she was thirsty, he brought her punch. When she was weary, he found her a chair to sit in. He waited while she danced with other men, biding his time, counting the minutes until they were alone again. When she returned to his side, her angel's face lit up, and he knew she had eyes only for him.

And, for the first time in ages, he felt happy.

Halfway through the ball, Clara pulled herself from Stone's side to visit the ladies' reception room, decorated in suitably feminine eighteenth-century rococo pastels. On her way back to the ballroom, she passed an alcove off the central courtyard, where a pair of familiar voices were engaged in an intense discussion.

Her mother. And Mrs. Astor. Talking about Captain Hawke.

Clara's footsteps faltered. She paused and leaned her shoulder against the wall nearby, hoping her eavesdropping didn't appear too obvious to the ladies passing along the corridor to the dressing room.

Mrs. Astor was chastising her mother. "Olympia, I'm surprised at you. I've never known you to *confuse* society in this way."

Her mother gave a small laugh. "I'm afraid I don't understand."

Clara smiled ruefully. Unlike herself, her mother was an accomplished liar.

"You're sponsoring an ineligible," Mrs. Astor said. "As I understand it, this captain of yours has no title, no wealth, nothing to offer our daughters, yet you allow him access to them. He is in no way suited to court our debutantes, not even your Miss Clara, who seems quite enamored of him, I've noticed."

"I explained about that. He's a hobby of hers, one of many good works she engages in. It's not at all of a personal nature."

Mrs. Astor sounded unconvinced. "We have built here in Newport a society of the elite. What good is allowing only the best people in, if those very same people bring in outsiders?"

"He is only visiting, Caroline. He'll be returning home soon, to Britain or . . . wherever." Her mother then took advantage of the opportunity to remind Mrs. Astor of her "upstart" family's social success. "With my Pauline married to the Duke of Bathurst, and Hannah the countess of Sheffield, I can afford to be less demanding of Clara's choice of a husband."

At her words, joy bloomed in Clara's chest. Her mother knew her feelings for her captain! She would allow her to marry him, if he should ask her. Until now, she hadn't realized that was her dream. To have him profess his love, his desire to live his life with her by his side . . . She closed her eyes, filled with the fantasy, knowing in her heart she had dreamed of such an outcome long before now, even if she hadn't admitted it to herself.

Her mother's next words dashed her hopes.

"Trust me, Caroline. She won't be marrying the fellow. I would never allow it to go that far. Clara is as good as engaged to Gerald Burnby, a protégé of my husband's."

Clara squeezed her eyes shut, fighting against the pain filling her heart. How foolish of her to imagine they might wed. Even if he asked her—which he hadn't—she had never imagined going against her parents' wishes for her. She found it hard to imagine doing so now. *Unless . . .*

Deep in thought, she returned to the ballroom. Like a magnet, her gaze was drawn to Stone, who remained by the potted palms where she had left him, waiting for her and her alone. A pair of ladies approached him, probably angling for dances, but he shook his head and they soon departed. He looked toward where she had disappeared. When he spotted her watching him, his expression softened and he strode over to her.

His eyes darkened as he looked at her face. "Are you quite all right?" He gave her elbow a furtive squeeze.

"I'm not sure," she said honestly, trying to sort through her feelings.

"Come with me. It's far too stuffy in here." Tightening his hand on hers, he led her through the ballroom doors. They began strolling sedately down a hallway. After rounding a corner and finding no one else about, Stone broke into a jog, spiriting her away with him as if he couldn't be alone with her fast enough.

She struggled to keep up with him, lifting her skirts high with one hand, her other hand locked in his. A giddy heat stole through her, and laughter burst from her.

He chuckled in response. "You ought not to make so much noise. People will wonder what you're doing away from the ball, with a man that causes you to giggle." He winked at her.

They passed through a door to the outside and found themselves on a stone loggia, its archways framing the sea. As she caught her breath, Clara studied the stars, pondering what the future held in store for her. What role would this man by her side play? Once he left her life, would she ever see him again?

"You're far too serious for such a beautiful evening," he said, for the first time more cheerful than she. "Look about you. Isn't the moonlight lovely on the waves?"

"So now you're a poet," she commented, afraid to look at him for fear he would see the naked yearning in her eyes.

"All of us melancholy blokes are." His hand encircled her waist.

She sucked in a breath at the dance of electricity that swept through her at his touch. Needing desperately to gather her thoughts, she spun away—and came up short.

"My skirt. It's caught." The decorations on her tapestry skirt had snagged on a rough stone, and it stretched suspended from her body like a ship's sail.

"By God, woman, your ankles are showing," he gasped in mock horror.

"Stop teasing and help me free." She tugged on

the fabric and heard the sound of fine threads
snapping.

He knelt before her. "Let go so I can see what to
do. You're just making it worse."

She released the fabric, and he attacked the
problem with the determination of a man refusing
to let female fashion defeat him. The sound of
rending fabric soon accompanied his efforts.

"Blast," he said mildly, holding up the torn sec-
tion. "That didn't go quite as I expected. Ah, well.
What's done is done."

Tossing the fabric aside, he moved close to her
and slid his arms around her waist, this time giving
her no opportunity to escape. "I would much rather
be doing this anyway." Lowering his head, he began
pressing tender nibbling kisses along her neck,
each touch of his lips sending darts of pleasure all
the way to her toes.

Clara closed her eyes and pulled in a ragged
breath, giving up on her feeble attempts to put off
the inevitable. This was what she wanted, from the
moment she imagined inviting him to the ball.
This was exactly what she hungered for.

Her eyes slid past his shoulder to the glistening
Atlantic. Soon she would have to return to the
ball, or risk being the brunt of gossip. "It's easy for
you to dismiss the damage to my gown. But everyone will wonder how I tore it."

"That's simple to explain," he said, his hands caressing her back through her tight, low-cut bodice.
He touched his nose to hers. "You're a very naughty
girl."

Naughty. . . . She had always been lauded for
her virtue, had never done anything naughty in her

life—until now. Stone's description of her made her feel naughty, yes. But also delicious and daring. And she wanted that feeling. She wanted it so badly, it frightened her. "No one but you would call me naughty."

"No one but me is allowed to touch you here." He kissed the sensitive notch at the base of her neck. "And here." His whispered words lingered on her bare shoulder before his mouth skimmed her. "And here." His lips lowered further, to the swell of her breasts, his tongue darting into the dark hollow between them. Scandalous. He was simply scandalous.

Clara sagged back against the stone wall, allowing him to support her. "God, you taste like heaven," he said softly, his tongue swirling along her skin, continuing to do amazing—and, yes, naughty—things to her body.

The sheer impossibility of what he made her feel, of what they were doing together, tugged at her pleasure, dimming it. "Mother wants me to marry Gerald Burnby," she announced into the still night air.

The delicious torture of Stone's tongue ended. He paused a moment, his breath hot on her breasts. Then he raised his head and looked at her.

"The hell. If anyone is marrying you, it's going to be me."

Chapter 18

Clara cupped Stone's face in her palms, joy filling her. He had asked her, and she knew her answer already. She knew that despite what her parents might say, she would marry this man.

Happiness consumed her, a sweet, joyous promise of a lifetime of love. Throwing her arms about his neck, she gave him a fierce hug. "Yes, I accept."

Stone swore under his breath, muttering a colorful phrase she didn't recognize. He slid his hands up her back, then gently pulled her far enough away that he could look in her eyes.

"Clara, darling. I wasn't planning on proposing."

"But you did." She caressed his face, a face she would never tire of looking at. "You did. Didn't you? Or are you taking it back?" Doubt began to dim her joy. She couldn't imagine holding him to his words if he hadn't meant them with his whole heart. "If you didn't intend to say it, I understand."

He shook his head, his eyes filled with amazement. "You're so damned understanding. I want you in my life, with me, as my wife, more than I can say. But I'm not yet a man you should be marrying. I shouldn't be marrying anybody. I'm just now feeling like I used to, like I can take on the world. But I cannot say it will last." He pulled her hands against his chest. "Being here, near you, has been like living another life, it's so far removed from who I really am. But it can't last. Eventually I'll have to wake up from this dream and face myself again."

"I'll wait for you."

"I have no right to ask that of you."

"You don't have to ask. I'm offering."

"You're far too good for me, Clara. And I don't mean your dowry or your station in life." He placed his hand on her chest. "I mean your heart."

"You have my heart, Stone. I'm in love with you." The words came so easily, she wondered that she had never said them before. To him, to herself. To the whole world. "I adore you."

Her pronouncement failed to bring a smile to his face. "I was afraid of that."

"Don't be afraid of my feelings for you. Please. Just let me love you." Sliding her arms around his neck, she drew him close and pressed her mouth to his, without hesitation, wanting desperately to show him he was worthy of love.

"Clara," he gasped, returning her kiss, "if I could possibly make you happy—"

"You will." She would brook no uncertainty, no question that they would end up together, married and in love. Whatever it took to prove that her love was true, she would do it. *Oh, yes, she would do it. If only she had the opportunity* . . .

He kissed her long and deep, sending her into a sensuous haze that dimmed time and place. After a while, he pulled away and put distance between them. He yanked on his tuxedo coat and smoothed his trousers.

"Much more of that and I'll forget where we are," he said, echoing her own feelings. "We have to go back in now. Your mother is probably frantic with concern."

Her mother . . . A sick feeling grew in the pit of Clara's stomach. How would she ever convince her mother that Stone was the proper husband for her?

I will. I will convince the world. As long as he is by my side, we can accomplish anything.

Stone grasped her hand and pulled her close again. He tucked a loose strand of hair back into her upswept coiffure, beneath the jeweled comb that held most of her hair in place. "There. Better. If no one looks too closely, your reputation will be secure."

"Except for the tear in my gown."

"With so many yards of fabric, no one will notice."

"And if they do?"

He grinned wickedly. "Tell them a clumsy fellow stepped on it during a dance. A man by the name of Gerald Burnby."

Good Lord, how she loved him, irascible fellow that he was. Rising on her toes, she kissed his cheek. "Thank you for watching out for me, Stone. You're a true gentleman."

A shadow crossed his eyes, causing Clara's heart to skip a beat. So many mysteries about this man she loved. So many unanswered questions. Perhaps he was right—until he trusted her love enough to open himself fully to her, they should not commit to marriage.

Hanging tightly to his arm, she pondered what secrets he might be keeping as they walked back to the ball.

Gerald Burnby met them just outside the glass ballroom doors. Stone had the feeling the dandy had been looking out for them, spying on Clara to see what they might be up to.

The man's soft features were creased with annoyance. He glared at Stone while addressing only Clara. "Miss Carrington. I wondered where you'd got to. I was about to alert the authorities." Though he smiled at his quip, Stone had the hunch he wasn't joking.

"You needn't have worried," Clara responded, her eyes sparking. "I was feeling a little light-headed. Captain Hawke was kind enough to escort me for a walk on the loggia, the one that fronts the sea."

"You should have asked me." Burnby maneuvered himself between her and Stone, then lowered his voice. Still, Stone heard every insulting word. "You're such an innocent, Miss Clara. I would hate to see your reputation suffer due to your . . . questionable associations."

Remaining composed, Clara cast him a cold look, then swept past him without a word. Warmth filled Stone at her silent support of him.

Burnby hurried and caught up with her again. Not willing to let the dandy at her alone, Stone joined them just in time to hear Burnby saying, "There's something you don't know."

"Why don't you share, then?" Clara said hotly.

"Yes, Burnby. Share," Stone said. "I'm sure we would all like to hear whatever you have to say."

Gerald's eyes shot daggers at him. "I'm not so sure of that," he said dryly. "Captain Hawke, you were with the . . . what were they called . . . the Jodhpur Dragoons? Such quaint names the Brits give their fighting regiments."

"The Ninth Jodhpur Dragoons, yes," Stone said slowly. He was uncomfortable discussing his military career with anyone, especially this ponce. "It seems you're remarkably acquainted with my personal history."

Burnby shrugged nonchalantly. "Oh, I wouldn't know a lancer from a Bengal, except that I met a woman here tonight who has lived in India. I thought she might know of you. It turns out she does. A lovely lady. She's here visiting her aunt, the wife of a Pierpont."

"This woman knows you, Captain?" Clara looked from one man to the other. "What's her name?"

Burnby ignored her question. His gaze remained fixed on Stone's face, as if looking for any sign of weakness. "She's right over here." He gestured broadly toward a corner of the room where a dozen guests congregated. Stone and Clara had no choice but to follow him.

Burnby stopped behind a tall brunette in a red gown. He tapped her on the shoulder. Even before she turned around, Stone knew who it was. His stomach clenched into a painful knot. *Not here . . . Please, not here. Not in front of Clara . . .*

Too late. The woman turned. Her good humor vanished, replaced by eyes glinting with hatred. "Captain Hawke. He told me you were here. I prayed he was wrong."

Miss Jenkins. Sister of Roddy Jenkins, the late Roddy Jenkins. His stomach churned and the hairs on the back of his neck tingled. He wouldn't feel worse if he were walking to his own execution.

Clara's hand tightened on his arm. "Stone?" she whispered, her soft voice a reminder of all the good things he had tried to grasp, once more impossibly out of reach. His brief flirtation with happiness already seemed like a distant dream.

Sensing his consternation, Clara gripped his arm tighter. While he appreciated her support, she would soon realize she should have nothing to do with him.

The young Englishwoman still hadn't removed her eyes from Stone. "It is him," she told Burnby, who had moved to stand beside her. "Just as you said."

"So, you two know each other after all," Burnby said with false jocularity. "What a marvelous coincidence."

"Not at all marvelous," she said bluntly. Stone's stomach twisted at the accusatory gleam in her eyes. "I left India to escape the terrible memories. Now I find myself back there, as I stare at your devil's face."

"Don't call him that," Clara said hotly, and despite himself, Stone reveled in her defense of him.

Miss Jenkins ignored her. "Captain Hawke. I had prayed never to set eyes on you again. Prayed you had slunk into a hole and never returned to the light of day—as snakes are apt to do."

"Please, stop insulting him," Clara insisted.

Miss Jenkins finally tore her eyes from Stone and looked at her, one narrow brow arched. "My brother Roddy—may he rest in peace—served under the captain. He *trusted* him. Put his life in his hands. This man . . . this *excuse* for a gentleman—failed to protect him. He *killed* him."

Clara glanced from Miss Jenkins to Stone and back again. "But—don't officers send men to their deaths all the time? Isn't that the job they perform?"

"Roddy wasn't on duty," the woman said, her tone communicating that Clara was a fool for even bothering to defend him. "He was in his barracks, probably asleep. Nothing more risky than that."

The time for pretending with Clara had ended. His own vanity—his own weakness to need and be needed by a lovely woman like Clara—was about to cause her awful pain, and it was all his fault. "She is right, Clara," Stone said, his voice low but firm. "That's all you need to know."

Clara placed herself in front of Stone, her face tight with determination. "Why won't you defend yourself? I *know* you. You wouldn't shirk your duties, or put your men at risk—not without good reason."

"Clara always sees the good in people," Burnby said. "Even when there is none to see."

"There is plenty of good in the captain. I know him. I—"

"Miss Carrington." Stone cut her off, worried that if she said any more, her reputation would indeed be endangered, as Burnby had warned. "I shall take my leave, then." He stepped back from the gathering, which had grown to a dozen guests as the confrontation progressed.

"Captain, wait." Miss Jenkins stepped right in front of him. She stared up into his face for a long moment. Then, without a word, she lifted her gloved hand and slapped him across the face. The slap wasn't hard, and made little noise in the din of the ballroom. But it drew the notice of everyone within fifteen feet of the confrontation, and soon the room was buzzing with talk of it.

Like the soldier he once had been, Stone spun smartly on his heel and strode swiftly from the room, eyes and voices following his exit.

Clara had glimpsed heaven, then watched it slip away, helpless to hold tight to its promise.

Everyone nearby watched Stone take his ignominious leave. Mrs. Astor herself, the matriarch of New York society, stood a mere twenty feet away, witnessing the entire scene. Those around her took their cue from her. When Miss Jenkins turned toward them, they accepted her with softly murmured words of condolence.

Miss Jenkins's high-flown connections guaranteed they would take her word over the captain's. Worse, he hadn't even offered any words of defense against her slanderous charges. Why?

Despite his admission of guilt, she could not accept that he was completely at fault. Not without learning the entire story of what had transpired. Not without talking to him and making him finally open up about all those secrets he held so close to his chest. Secrets that threatened to destroy him once and for all.

She had no idea what part Penelope played into Miss Jenkins's story. The two threads of his past had to be related. What had happened to him?

"Good riddance," Gerald said, his voice painfully loud in the void left by Stone's departure.

How dare he pour salt in Stone's wound! Clara cast him a stern glare over her shoulder, then began to hurry after Stone—only to be stopped by her mother.

"Clara."

Mrs. Carrington spoke her name with uncharacteristic harshness. She gripped her daughter's elbow, preventing her from taking any more steps toward Stone. She looked close to panic, her demeanor tense.

"Don't you dare move a muscle," she whispered harshly, her lips barely moving. "Now, follow me. Keep your head high and your eyes forward. We're going home. Where is your sister?"

Olympia Carrington's clipped words quivered against the rollicking tune played by the orchestra across the ballroom. Dancers swirled by in the intricate steps of a favorite dance, the mazurka. Despite the appearance of normality, heads turned to them as they strode past; voices murmured; smiles turned to frowns of disdain.

With a single pointed look, her mother summoned Meryl from a group of gossiping ladies. She led her two daughters to their hostess, Mrs. Alva Vanderbilt, and said quick but polite good-byes. Mrs. Vanderbilt nodded politely at her mother and sister, then turned such a frosty glare on Clara, it chilled her even through her heavy ball gown.

"I'm sorry, Mother," Clara said.

"Hush! Not here." Head high, Mrs. Carrington led her through the crowd to the entrance.

The moment their front door had closed them off from the world at large, her mother broke into a tirade.

"Never have I been so humiliated in my life! Your father and I know you've been concerned with this fellow more than is proper, but we know your caring heart. Taking him to the ball was worse than foolhardy. I never thought you would be so inconsiderate of my feelings—and your sister's. I was always so proud of you for never giving me a moment of trouble. That's why you've been allowed to help the poor. We gave you a great deal of freedom, and this is how you repay us?"

"I never meant to hurt you or Father. Or Meryl. If only you knew him as I do, you would never think—"

"That he lacked character and good breeding?" She slammed her fan down on a hall table. "That is the truth of the matter."

Clara shook her head, desperate to make her mother understand. "I wish you could see the man I see. See his heart. If you did, you would grow to love him, as I do."

Her mother's eyes widened in shock. "*Love* him? Oh, my Lord. This is so much worse than I ever thought. I had no idea he had seduced such feelings out of you."

Seduced her . . . The word, even though her mother hadn't intended such a meaning, brought a blush to her cheeks. "He hasn't—he hasn't fooled me, Mother. I know him better than anyone. He's hurting . . ."

"He has wormed his way into your good graces and used you to attempt to ingratiate himself with our set."

"No." Again she shook her head, knowing no matter what she said, she would never convince her mother to look kindly on him again. "I begged him to come. It was all my idea. I wanted everyone to see the man I see, to see his heart."

"You don't know the first thing about love. You're just a child! From now on, you shall have nothing to do with this . . . this *captain*, do you hear me?"

Clara had always obeyed her parents. Now, she found it impossible to assent, even to nod her head a fraction of an inch. Her heart felt torn from her chest. Moisture flooded her eyes. Unable to comply yet unable to express rebellion, she turned and hurried up the stairs to the safety of her bedroom.

"Oh, miss, that was brutal," Lucy said, the moment Clara entered her room. "I can't say as I'm surprised, hearin' all the gossip that's been goin' around."

"You shouldn't believe everything you hear," Clara said sharply. Even her maid believed Captain Stone had no honor! And she had always liked the man.

"He said so hisself," Lucy said defensively. "If what I heard is true—"

"That doesn't matter. I'm certain there's more to it." Clara pulled off her shawl and tossed it on the bed.

"Miss, if I may say so . . ." Lucy hesitated, becoming uncharacteristically solemn. "Some men ain't worth it. They's all handsome and charmin' and all, and wantin' to spark with you. But they ain't the sort to be makin' a home with."

"Even you, Lucy?" Despair filled Clara. No one was willing to stand up for Captain Stone Hawke except her. Not even *he* would stand up for himself. *He has no one. Except me.*

Determination filled her. She would find him and prove to him he was worthy of her love. Prove it to all of them, Lucy and her mother included.

"You're wrong, Lucy. All of you are wrong. And I intend to show it." Snatching up her shawl, she re-settled it on her shoulders and turned to leave the room.

"You won't find him, not at that bungalow on the beach," Lucy said in a soft voice.

Clara spun around. "Tell me."

Lucy glanced about hesitantly, clearly torn between her loyalty to Clara and her belief that her mother was right.

"Tell me." Clara had never spoken to her so firmly before.

"We were havin' our Saturday evenin' get-together, down to the Forty Steps. You know the place. We dance 'n' all. The hands from the houses up and down the avenue. Guthrie has his accordion, and McDermott plays his pipes, and we dance—"

"Tell me about Stone."

"Yes'm. He came up the Cliff Walk, right through our crowd. I almost didn't see him. He weren't talkin' to nobody. Then he went down the steps."

Constructed of wood some years before, the Forty Steps led straight down the cliff face, right above the crashing sea. It was a wonderful place to feel the power of the ocean. Flat rocks and a small cave nearby beckoned adventurous explorers— during the day. In the evening, going down the rickety wooden steps was foolish at best, pure madness at worst. What could he have been thinking? What crazy thoughts were spinning through his mind? "So, Lucy, you saw him go down. Then what? Where did he go after that?"

"Well, y'see, miss, it's like this." Lucy twisted her pale hands, looking more nervous than Clara had ever seen her. She lifted her wide, pale blue eyes to Clara. "I never saw him climb back up."

The bicycle's large, thin wheels squeaked against the dirt path. The broad seat beneath Clara vibrated harshly, and she fought to keep her balance while steering along a path made for walking.

Fifty feet below the path's left edge, the Atlantic churned against the rocky cliff face. Clara kept the bicycle to the far right of the path, knowing a small turn in the wrong direction could send her careening down the cliff. Still, the bicycle had been

Clara's best solution to reach the Forty Steps—and Captain Stone Hawke—quickly.

He needs me. He needs me, he needs me, he needs me. The words thrummed in her head, in rhythm with every push of the pedals.

A nearly full moon illuminated the dirt path. The Cliff Walk, a favorite strolling path by day, made for a dangerous and bumpy path upon which to ride a bicycle, at any time of day. By night, it was downright idiotic.

Worse, after Lucy's story, Clara hadn't taken the time to change into her bicycling skirt. Perhaps she was being foolish, like the night she went to the Lower East Side in a ball gown. That gown hadn't survived that night's adventure, and neither would this one. Already torn from the loggia where she had lingered with Stone (how long ago that already seemed!), her gown was bunched in her lap, freeing her stocking-clad legs to churn the pedals.

At least she'd had the foresight to bring along a lantern. It rested in the basket on the front of the bike. If he was at the base of the stairs, she may need it to find him.

He'll chastise me for this, she thought, taking an odd comfort in the thought. His honesty, at first shocking, had brought her alive in ways she had never foreseen. That's what he did for her. In turn, she hoped to free him from his pain. Hearing him say he would marry her, she thought she had succeeded. Now she knew that had been nothing but a fantasy. He could never be free to love her with the shadow of the past pursuing him.

It never occurred to her to lose faith in him. Soon she would see him again, tell him she still believed in him, tell him to stop fleeing the demons that pursued him.

Tell him I love him. And more. Show him I love him. Show him I belong with him. She had realized, after the confrontation with her mother, what it really meant to leave one's parents in order to cleave to a husband. For he *would* be her husband. There was no other path to take. They belonged together, for better or worse, no matter what had happened in his past, or what had happened in her future. If he could only leave his past behind, leave Penelope behind—

Her front tire hit a rut, throwing her off balance. The bicycle veered dangerously close to the cliff edge, made even more dangerous by shrubs that hid the actual drop-off. Panicking, she yanked the wheel to the right, losing hold of the yards of heavy cloth squeezed between her legs. The skirt of her gown snagged in the spokes of her back wheel, yanking her to an abrupt stop. She tumbled to the ground in a tangle of cloth and metal.

Pulling herself up on her arms, she rolled onto her bottom and sat up. Only a few scratches— nothing serious, she quickly assessed. She tried to stand but found her skirt trapping her. She yanked furiously at the heavy cloth. It gave with a satisfying rip.

Standing, she retrieved the lantern that had tumbled from the bicycle's basket. The head of the Forty Steps was only thirty feet ahead, so she left the bicycle behind.

At the top of the stairs, she paused to light the lantern, then held it up. It was almost better to go by moonlight. The lantern cast a circle of yellow, blotting out the world beyond, making it impossible to see the ocean crashing against the rocks below, or anything beyond five steps ahead. Gripping the rickety handrail with one hand, she lifted the lantern with the other and nearly tripped on her torn skirt.

A jolt of terror caught in her throat. She had come extremely close to tumbling down the steep incline. Juggling the lantern, she flipped the excess fabric over her arm and got a better grip on the handrail.

Toward the bottom, the steps were slick with seawater. She could slip off at any moment. And she didn't even know that he was down here. She was four times the fool.

Still, she had to check. It was her fault he'd been humiliated at the ball. She had wanted him to escort her to prove to her family—prove to everyone—that he fit in with their crowd. It had been working beautifully—until Miss Jenkins called him out.

With a relieved sigh, she reached the bottom step—and saw no sign of him. Her heart pounded hard in her chest. "Stone!" she called into the sea-misted air, hardly hearing her own voice above the ocean's roar.

Only a few yards below her feet, the sea gathered and swelled, then shattered against the cliffs, sending cascades of water down the rocks. Fingers of spray teased her bare face and arms. Lifting her lantern, she glanced around and saw no sign of Stone. He may have left hours ago. Perhaps Lucy hadn't seen him leave. He may be back at his bungalow after all. Or he could have left town.

Yet she had come too far not to be certain. If he was here, he would have to be in the tiny cave notched into the cliff face. Unless . . .

She squeezed her eyes shut, refusing to visualize how easily the churning waters below could have swallowed him whole. Several times during his recuperation, she had suspected he harbored such a melancholy of spirit that he pondered taking his own life. She refused to believe he would do such a thing, not now that he cared for her, perhaps even loved her. *Please, let him realize he has a reason to live.*

Trying not to think of such possibilities, she picked out a path along the slab of rock leading to the cave. Bracing one hand on the arched opening, she peered inside and saw nothing but inky darkness.

Clara lifted the lantern, illuminating the small enclosure. The closeness of the air inside drew around her like a cloak, and she shivered. Golden light shone off damp walls made smooth by centuries of tidal storms.

Then she saw him. Her heart jammed in her throat. He sat with knees up, back propped against the cave wall. His tuxedo jacket hung unbuttoned, his collar unclasped.

Her gaze played over Stone, looking as unlike his name as she had ever seen him. His pain hung on him like a shroud. His emotions, usually protected under a heavy layer of bravado, lay raw on the surface. His agony was so obvious in his eyes, in the set of his jaw, in his deeply furrowed brow, it tore at her heart.

He lifted his eyes to meet hers. "Clara," he said,

her name barely audible against the background of the ocean behind her.

She stepped farther into the cave and set the lantern on the ground, near a pile of rocks by the opposite wall. She extended her hand, anxious to comfort him, but he gave her such a hard stare, it stopped her cold. That's when she saw that he was holding something.

A gun.

"Oh, no," she whispered. Would he—if she hadn't found him, would he truly have done it? Did he still intend to use it, despite her arrival? Nothing mattered so much right then as getting that devil's implement away from him.

"Don't you have somewhere else to be?" he asked caustically.

"Haven't you learned yet you can't frighten me off with your acidic tongue?" Paying no mind to her gown, she knelt on the sandy floor in front of him.

He dropped his head back on the cave wall. "Very well, tell me how you found me *this* time," he said dryly.

"I'm looking forward to the day I won't have to chase after you. Why did you come here, and with *that?*" she pointed at the gun in his hand.

He spun the revolver's cylinder, filling the cave with a clicking echo. "It seemed as good a place as any."

"As good a place for what?" Her eyes nervously migrated to the revolver, then back to the empty, aching sadness in his eyes.

He toyed with the gun, his long fingers caressing the barrel, toying with the cylinder, his thumb clicking the hammer—on, off. On, off. On.

Desperation filled her. She longed to snatch the deadly revolver out of his hand but feared there might be a struggle, that it might go off. She trusted him not to hurt her, not intentionally, but he wasn't thinking clearly. In his reckless frame of mind, he honestly believed he had nothing to lose.

His sharp gaze nailed hers. "I thought you had more sense than to climb about on slick rocks in a damned ball gown."

"I felt I shouldn't take the time to change."

"Your parents will be looking for you."

She shrugged her bare shoulders. "They think I'm in bed. Asleep."

His eyes darkened into twin pools of anger and desperation, and she knew she had to get the gun clear of him, at all costs.

Inspiration struck her. Instead of rising to her feet, she scooted closer and presented her back to him. "Would you undo my dress for me, and my corset? The whalebone stays are digging into me." Over her shoulder, she carefully watched his reaction.

Her words accomplished what she intended. The hard edge in his eyes softened with heat, skidding across her back and sparking her own senses. For the first time since she entered, he truly noticed her.

As he stared at her, his hand loosened enough on his revolver for her to pluck it from his palm. She scrambled to her feet. "We really won't be needing this anymore."

"Don't you dare," he said as she headed for the cave opening—and the ocean beyond. "That's my service revolver."

She cast him a glance over her shoulder. "Ah, so you do care about things. About life. As that is the case, I'll merely remove the bullets." Like many women of her set, she had experience with sport shooting. Popping out the cylinder, she emptied the bullets into her palm. And was dismayed to discover he had filled each of the six chambers.

She tucked the now empty gun behind the rocks near the lantern. This time she did step to the cave opening, and threw the bullets as hard and far as she could. They sank into the ocean below, safely out of harm's way.

"Very cheeky," Stone said behind her. "You didn't think I would use that on myself, did you?"

She turned to face him. "Wouldn't you?"

He sighed, the sound drawn from deep in his soul. "I'm too much of a coward."

She studied him silently for a moment, then gently asked, "Do you have any idea how much it would hurt me if you had?"

He gave a humorless laugh. "I'm good at hurting women. No reason to change that now. Hurting women, killing friends . . . What else could you possibly want in a suitor?"

"I'm glad to hear you call yourself my suitor."

"Enjoy it while it lasts," he shot back. "Get out of here, Clara. Out of this place, and out of my life. I never want to see you again."

Her earlier thought was wrong. His acidic tongue *could* hurt her, very much. Nevertheless, she bit back a retort that rose to her lips. She was about to tell him once again how much she longed to be with him, when he added a final, cold statement.

"I wish I had never met you."

Chapter 19

Clara's eyes filled with tears, and Stone knew he had hurt her. "I don't believe you. I will never believe you don't care for me."

God, couldn't she simply leave him be? What was she trying to do, kill him with slow torture? He couldn't take much more of this—seeing her there before him, unable to touch her, unworthy to have her. "Get out of here, Clara. Think of yourself for once. Go back to your fancy parties and gilt ballrooms and uncomplicated Burn-mes."

She shook her head, sending her golden curls dancing against her naked shoulders. She looked as ethereal as a wood nymph, as untouchable as an angel. "No. No, I won't leave you. I'm no good at leaving people in distress. You should know that about me by now. In fact, I won't leave until you tell me what Miss Jenkins was talking about. You've been harboring this secret of yours for so long, it's eating you up inside, worse than your malarial fever. You need to speak of it. To me. *Now.*"

He eyed her with surprise. She certainly had a commanding way about her. Despite her angelic appearance, she had a spine of iron, he well knew. And he wasn't going to get away without spilling his guts to her, without bleeding all over the cave floor. He could see that now.

Once he exposed his weak underbelly, showed her who he really was, he would have no trouble seeing the last of her. His heart clenched in a painful spasm. Never to see her again, never lay eyes on her and be transported to heaven . . .

Don't tell her. Let her think better of you than you deserve. "Clara, get out of here."

"Tell me," she insisted, her expression determined. "Stop running away, Stone. I've been pursuing you all over this city. And you fled India, too, didn't you?"

His jaw clenched. "Damn it, Clara, I told you I was a coward."

She shook her head. "You're not a coward. There's a part of you that loves living, or—or you would have used that thing." She nodded toward the rock behind which she had placed the gun.

"You don't know me, Clara. If you did . . ." His voice cracked despite himself.

"That's because you won't share your secret with me." Curling her legs under her, she sat beside him and cupped his cheek in her palm. "Tell me."

For a long heartbeat, he gazed at her, knowing then how far he had fallen, fallen so deep into his need for her. He could deny her nothing, not even the baring of his soul. Sucking in a breath, he confessed his deepest sin. "I ignored a warning that rebels might pose a threat. Her brother died as a result, along with a dozen others. To put it bluntly, I sent my fiancée and my best friend to their deaths."

Central Provinces, India

"Sir, the reports are fairly reliable."

Captain Hawke glanced up. He sat at his desk in the small pine-walled office, dealing with the raft of paperwork assigned to him. "Fairly reliable? Is that the best you can do?"

The man squirmed under his senior officer's perusal, his discomfort not at all surprising to Stone. He was thought a good officer, but he lacked the open, friendly demeanor to be a truly popular one.

"Well, sir," the subaltern tried again. "It's from a man whom I often converse with in the market-place. He told me the tribe in question is unhappy with the Army's position on recruiting members to the Indian Corps. They have a rather high mortality rate, apparently."

"That's too bad. But what does it have to do with us?"

Having snagged Stone's interest, the subaltern warmed to his tale. "This man, Riva is his name. He told me that his brother saw a hut with boxes stamped with the words *British Army*. They could be guns. Or explosives."

Stone sighed and shuffled through the reports he had to complete. "Good God, man, you know the Indians scavenge our boxes. They're probably being used to store cotton or opium."

The subaltern looked doubtful. "He didn't seem to think so."

"Riva?"

"His brother."

"Is this all you have? We can send a man 'round to inspect the boxes."

"Yes, sir. But as I believe I mentioned before, the marketplace is buzzing with talk of a—a strike against us."

Stone leaned back in his chair. "How long have you been in India, son?"

The subaltern—Stone never caught his name—cleared his throat uneasily. "Four months, sir."

"And this makes you an expert on tribal relations?"

"No, sir, but I thought it might mean something."

"If you had served here longer, you would know that the infernal marketplaces are always buzzing with rumors. Unless you have something more specific?" He pointedly raised his eyebrows and glanced toward the door. He was determined to get through the pile on his desk before afternoon parade.

The subaltern opened his mouth, then abruptly closed it and shook his head. "No, sir."

"Then I suggest you get back to your duties."

The young soldier nodded and left. In less than a minute, Stone had forgotten the warning, brushed off the rumble of unease at the base of his nerves. It meant nothing. And he had forgotten about the mysterious boxes, which—he realized later—had contained dynamite stolen several weeks earlier from a supply train down south.

The moments after the subaltern left were among the precious few he spent secure in the knowledge that he was where in the world he was meant to be. That he knew how to do his job. That his men were right to trust him.

The very next evening, his world turned inside out.

In the smoking ruin of the barracks, bodies lay twisted among charred timber that continued to bake like a campfire left untended. Tendrils of smoke painted the air above the cantonment with a rancid charcoal smell. He shuddered to think of the source of the stench underlying the wood smoke.

But an even more potent image haunted his days and his nights.

As he stared in shock at the destruction, a crowd began to gather. Soon members of the cantonment banded together into a bucket brigade to put out the fire, while others searched for survivors and tended the wounded.

And Stone was frozen in impotence, his attention stolen by a pair of crumpled bodies thrown several yards by the blast. His friend Witherspoon—half his face had been blown away, but he recognized his curly hair. Blood covered the front of his usually neat uniform.

Right beside him, her face remarkably peaceful-looking in death, lay Penelope. His fiancée, the woman he had been avoiding. If he had been a man, if he had gone to meet her at the club, neither of them would now be a corpse baking in the Indian sun.

If he had told Penelope he couldn't marry her . . .

If he hadn't sent Witherspoon to take care of his own damn business . . .

If he had listened to the subaltern's warnings . . .

But he hadn't, and he didn't. Even now the horror froze him as stone cold as his name. He wasn't a man of action, a man able to think on his feet. He was the worst excuse for a British officer. The worst excuse for a man.

Newport

"And that is why Miss Jenkins took me to task," he finished, feeling utterly exhausted from his foray into the past.

He waited for Clara to pull back, to find an excuse to leave him. He wouldn't blame her in the least. It wasn't in her nature to be rude, but there was no doubt she would now leave him. If she had held him in any kind of esteem before, she would no longer.

After a long pause, she did nothing of the sort. Instead, she leaned closer and wrapped her arms around him. "Oh, Stone, so many memories. So many wrong choices. But you can't let it keep you from being who you were meant to be."

"And who might that be?" he croaked, his voice thick with tears.

"My husband. You said it yourself."

Her husband . . . She still wanted him! He lifted his hand and traced the curve of her cheek. "Clara," he murmured, "you make me believe it might be possible, even though I know it can't be."

"Don't say that, Stone." Grasping his hand, she pressed it between hers. "Did you love her?"

"As much as this cold heart is capable of love," he said, his lips twisting into a rueful smile.

"You are so wrong about yourself. You're not cold. Quite the opposite." Leaning close, she slid her fingers over his chest, a surprisingly sensuous gesture that sent his heart pumping. "I believe you feel more deeply than most. That is why you continue to ache over things that you can't change."

He tightened his hand on hers, longing to keep her close. "Sweet Clara. I am constantly astounded that you believe in me. Especially now."

"Of course I do. Because I love you." She kissed his forehead.

He gazed at her in amazement. "How can you, Clara? How can you?"

"No one expects you to be perfect. Least of all me."

"Not perfect, no. But at least a man of honor."

"You never meant to hurt anyone. Please, listen to me." She directed his eyes to meet hers. "You must accept that you cannot control everything or everyone around you. You have already suffered enough for the past. Let it go, Stone." Her voice dropped to a tempting whisper. "Let it go."

He leaned forward and pulled her into a tight embrace, finding comfort in her arms, in her complete acceptance of him. "I wish I could believe you," he murmured. "It amazes me how you're able to see the good in things. In people. In me." Looking in her face, he traced her lower lip with his thumb. "You almost give me hope."

"Only almost?" She smiled, and in that simple moment, he knew the truth.

The past was releasing its hold on him, letting go, freeing him to feel. To love. Gazing at this angel before him, his heart brimmed with hope. The sweet sensation of happiness began to fill him, dispelling the shadows that had dragged him down for so long.

Only one thing remained. To tell her one last truth about what lay in his heart. "About Penelope," he said suddenly. "I never loved Penelope. Not like this. Not like I love you."

She anchored her arms around his neck and touched her lips to his. Pleasure filled him at her gentle yet sensuous touch, at her total acceptance of him. He closed his eyes and let her in, welcoming the kiss, using the embrace to demonstrate just how much he loved her.

She pulled away from the kiss just long enough to flash him a triumphant smile and say, "I know." Then she pressed her mouth once again to his.

Their kiss began to grow more heated, his desire to demonstrate his feelings overwhelming any sense of propriety. Nothing mattered but her, here in his arms. He anchored his arms around her, desperate to keep her there, yet knowing she would willingly stay.

Her hands cradled his cheeks, then slid upward along his scalp, her fingers weaving into his hair. Pulling up to her knees, she pressed unashamedly against him. The fullness of her breasts, thrust forward by her corset, smashed against his chest. Her hands slid under his jacket and shoved it from his shoulders, a move that nearly undid him.

"Oh, Clara." He broke the kiss and lowered his mouth to her exposed collarbone, licking and nipping at her creamy shoulder. He reveled in her clean, sweet scent, in her sheer beauty. He wanted more, had to taste her, all of her. He slid his lips higher, to relish the scented skin at the curve of her neck.

"Stone," she urged breathlessly, "I want you to kiss me. Everywhere."

"Yes." Rational thought failed him. Sliding his palms down her satin-clad back, he cupped her bottom.

She swayed against him, and he realized he was supporting her weight. The knowledge of her passion acted like an aphrodisiac on his senses, sending desire pulsing through him. He gave her bottom a squeeze, a prelude to even bolder caresses. She pulled in a sharp breath at his rough intimacy.

The sound startled him from the haze of passion that had engulfed him. Though she continued to fall against him, he pulled back and grasped her shoulders, pushing her away until he could look in her eyes. Her face—God, her gorgeous face!—bore an expression of utter rapture. Rapture he had caused.

He knew then he could have her if he wished. Right here, right now. And how he wished it! But not if what he suspected was true.

"Clara, look at me."

She did, pulling in a deep breath and sinking back on her heels. "If you mean to tell me we shouldn't, I don't care. I'm not a foolish girl, Stone. I have thought about this. More than I should. And I still want you. I want you so badly, it's a physical ache in my chest. And . . . other places." She blushed slightly but didn't look away.

"Darling," he said, stroking loose tresses from her cheeks. "My sweet darling. You give of yourself so much. But doing this for me . . . it's asking far too much."

She stiffened and pulled away from him, confusion tracing her features. Then she frowned. "You don't really believe I would do this out of charity. Please tell me that isn't what you think."

"Damn it, Clara, how can I doubt it? I have never met a more giving, caring soul. Sacrificing your virtue in a misguided attempt to heal my broken spirit—"

She cut him off and leaped to her feet in a fury. "You think I can't love you, is that it? You think I don't love you enough to . . ."

He had never seen her so angry. "I merely thought—"

"You aren't supposed to think so much, Stone. You're supposed to *feel*. With me." Dropping to her knees again, she caught his gaze with her own. "What do you feel when you're with me? What do you desire?"

His throat clogged with emotion, and he barely managed to speak the word. "You."

Her lower lip trembled. "Then stop putting me on a pedestal. All I want is for you to treat me like a woman. But if you refuse to . . ." She began to rise to her feet again, but he stopped her with a hand on her shoulder. He pressed her back down, then angled her so that her back was turned toward him. The brush of his fingers along her sensitive nape sent delicious chills of pleasure and anticipation down her spine. "What . . . ?"

"You wanted help with your corset, remember?"

That had seemed so long ago. In just a few hours, they had come so far together. She squeezed her eyes shut, poised on the brink of realizing her most secret dreams. She gave herself up to his experienced touch as he began freeing her from her restraints. Starting at the top of her bodice, between her shoulder blades, he slipped each black-pearl button from its loop, not stopping until he reached the waistline seam just above her bottom.

He touched me there, she thought, the memory one of a dozen thoughts spinning through her mind. One of a dozen new sensations his kisses and caresses awakened in her.

Not once did she doubt she was doing the right thing. She had always followed her heart, even to the worst neighborhoods in the city. This time, her heart led her into Stone's masculine arms.

While he seemed to have no difficulty undoing the buttons, he also seemed to be taking his time. Each passing second, each brush of his fingers along her spine, stoked the rising passion within her. His tongue tickled her exposed skin, dancing down her spine, tantalizing forbidden regions of her body, building greater and greater anticipation within her.

Her bodice now sagging, she lowered it into her lap. He leaned forward and kissed the sensitive spot at the base of her neck, sending fresh tingles through her. His warm breath stirred loose tendrils of her hair, and she shivered with delight.

She felt the tug and release of her corset laces as he began working them loose from each eyelet. The stays pulled away from her chemise-covered flesh, releasing her aching breasts. She pulled in a deep breath of relief, felt prickles of delicious sensation darting from her distended nipples.

His palms slid around her sides, under her chemise, massaging her where the stays had imprinted her flesh. "Wearing that damn thing so long. I'll fix it."

"Yes," she whispered. "You will."

"Confident of that, are you?"

"More than you know."

His hands slid upward and cupped the undersides of her breasts. Lifting them from underneath, he gently massaged her, soothing her skin with a rhythmic touch. She closed her eyes and melted into him, sinking back against his chest.

His caresses turned more ardent. Sliding his hands upward, he began rotating her nipples against his palms, sending a burst of sensation through her entire body. She gasped at the sheer pleasure of it.

"Face me."

His command tingled through her. Even though he had been caressing her, she glanced down at her exposed breasts, then crossed her arms over them before she turned.

When she was facing him, she looked into his eyes, and her momentary fear dissolved. He looked as a starving man might while gazing at a feast of culinary delights. Her arms relaxed, her hands dropping into her lap. "You like what you see."

Lifting a finger, he teased her nipple. "I love what I see."

She bit her lip as a fresh dart of pleasure shot through her, straight to her womanhood. The flickering lantern light lent an unreal feeling to their intimate encounter. He drew her near and caressed her breasts, her shoulders, the smooth planes of her back, as if it was his right, and hers, to enjoy such intimacy. As he gazed into her eyes, she believed nothing could separate them. She had nothing to hide. Not anymore. She was his, and he was hers.

He shrugged off his shirt and undershirt. Then, together, silently sharing caresses and kisses all the while, they removed her heavy ball gown, leaving her in petticoats and underdrawers. He spread the gown and his jacket on the sandy cave floor. As he lowered her with him to the cloth-covered ground, she thought vaguely how glad she was to have worn this particular gown tonight. The heavy fabric made for a surprisingly comfortable bed for lovers.

Stone kissed her forehead and face, then lowered his mouth to her left breast. His lips surrounded her nipple in wet heat, nipping and tugging, drawing from her a shuddering gasp of pleasure. She dug her fingers into his hair, anchoring herself tightly to him as he worked magic on her body.

His fingertips stroked along her stomach, and in a remarkably short time, he had untied her petticoats, leaving them spread beneath her like a fluffy cloud. She floated in a sea of pleasure, which began to build to unquenched desire the longer his explorations continued.

The sensitive spot between her thighs began to dampen her cotton underdrawers, and she found it difficult to lie still while he touched her. "Stone," she said, running her palms along his corded torso. How perfect he was! Lean and hard and strong. Intense desire built within her to submit to him, to possess him, though she didn't completely understand what that might mean.

But Stone knew. In answer to her moans, he briefly stroked his fingers *there*, between her thighs.

"Stone, yes," she murmured, encouraging him. "Show me more."

"I will, darling." He hooked his thumbs in the waist of her bloomers and urged them below her hips, then pulled them completely off. She was as naked as the day she'd been born. Naked, and so hot, despite the cool night air wafting off the ocean crashing below.

Somewhere, somehow, he had shed the last of his own clothing. The golden lantern light revealed him stretched beside her in all his glory, from his bare feet to his jutting hipbones, to the broad sweep of his chest. A body so unlike hers, yet so gorgeous it made her chest hurt. For a long moment, she found it impossible to breathe. That sleek torso she had long admired led to strong thighs of bunched muscle. At their juncture, his manhood jutted from a wealth of dark curls. Without thinking, she stretched out her hand to touch that male prominence.

Reading her intent, he grasped her palm and placed it on him, allowing her to explore the length of him. "Warm," she murmured. "Smooth and warm."

"And extremely hard," he supplied, his lips quirking.

She lifted her gaze to his. "Because of me?"

"Because of you. By God, woman, if you don't stop . . ." He pulled in a ragged breath and lifted her hand away. Dropping a kiss on her nose, he pulled her fast against him, bringing their bodies as close as possible. His hand slid down to caress her thighs in feathery arcs that came ever closer to the juncture of her thighs but, teasingly, avoided direct contact. She squirmed under him, desperate for more. "Touch me as I touched you. Touch me there, please."

His eyes opened, sparking with humor and pleasure at her forwardness. Then he settled his palm on her moist womanhood. She jerked, her hips arching toward him.

But that was only the beginning. He began to stroke her, moving his palm against her, building the pleasure into regions of unbearable sensation. Clara arched her head back, lost in sensation. Such amazing feelings had been nothing but a feminine promise at the edge of her awareness, until now. Until Stone.

He slid his fingers into her slick sheath while his thumb circled around the moist nub of her pleasure. She squeezed her eyes and cried out, need engulfing her as the tantalizing pleasure mounted. "Please, Stone. Please."

He urged her thighs wider apart, and she submitted easily, already so loose-limbed, he could have molded her into any shape he wished. Sliding atop her, he braced himself on his elbows, his manhood prodding where his fingers had explored. "This will hurt."

Hurt? She couldn't imagine pain, now—

A bolt of lightning shot through her as he pushed inside, and she cried out with the sudden, searing pain of his entry. Still, she found herself thinking beyond that, to the wonder of their joining. *So, this is why I'm made the way I am. Why he's made the way he is,* she thought in amazement. It all made perfect sense.

She opened her eyes to find him gazing down at her with uncharacteristic concern. "Are you in very much pain?" he asked softly, his thumbs tracing her jaw.

She shook her head, for already the pain had subsided to a dull echo. "Is this all there is?" she asked with a trace of doubt. She bucked under him, aware that he filled her, aware that she wanted him there, but still she was missing . . . something.

He smiled. "Not quite." He began to pull out of her, and she panicked, locking her legs around his hips.

"Shhh," he soothed. "Easy. I'm not going anywhere. Not this time." And he came back to her again. And again.

Over and over, he stroked inside her, leaving, returning, each time taking her higher into realms of longing on the edges of ecstasy.

His fingertips danced in her curls as he moved inside her, drawing from her waves of desire so intense, she feared she would die from it. Pulling back with a cry, he crashed hard against her womanhood, and it happened.

The stars fell to earth; the sun rose; her body melted into heaven as fire consumed her. She rode the intense, shocking wave of pleasure, gripping him around the shoulders as if to let go meant to fall to her death. For she feared that was exactly what might happen, since he'd borne her to heaven.

He stiffened in her arms, his primal cry echoing around the narrow cave walls, blending into the thrum of the sea below.

He rode her through his own pleasure, and hers. Eventually, he relaxed in her arms, his head nestling against her shoulder. After a while, she felt dampness on her skin. Concerned, she lifted his face to hers and found his eyes moist. "Darling?"

He shook his head and smiled tremulously. "God, it's nothing."

"It's something," she countered, determined not to let her taciturn lover hide his feelings from her.

He gave in with a sigh. "I have never felt so . . . *right* before, love. Right, and happy."

Then he smiled, his expression so joyous, it made her heart pound in delight. She slipped her fingers into his hair. "It feels good, doesn't it?"

"Oh, yes," he murmured. His lips danced over hers. "Oh, yes."

She pulled back and gave him a teasing smile. "I believe I know why I love you."

"Because of my sunny disposition?"

She laughed. "Because I can trust you to say what you mean. Everyone is so careful in my social set. No one wants to say or do the wrong thing for fear of being taken to task. That's why I never lost faith in you, even when Miss Jenkins treated you so cruelly. I know better than to believe everything people say."

He gazed at her as if she were the most precious thing on earth. "I'm astounded by you, Clara. I've never met a woman so willing to see good where there is scant evidence of it."

She teased his sharp cheekbone with her fingertip. "You're far too hard on yourself."

"Am I?"

"Yes. You may have made poor choices in the past, but you admit it. You see your foibles. I can't tell you how refreshing that is."

He arched a brow. "Are you by chance thinking of one Mr. Gerald Burn-me? He *is* an overstuffed, high-and-mighty windbag, after all."

She chuckled. "You *are* cruel, Captain Hawke. But I still love you for saying what you feel."

His fingers tangled in her hair. "And you don't love Burn-me?"

She gasped, her show of dismay only partly in jest. "You can ask me that, while I lie here with you?"

He grinned. "I take that as a no."

She frowned, thinking of what might have happened to her if she hadn't found Stone. "If I married him, I fear that I would be pushed into a corset tighter than the one I wore for the ball. Forced to abandon all my projects and resort to basket charity. Allowed to do only what my husband deemed proper and appropriate." She thought of how Stone had come to her aid despite his melancholy. How he had left her a five-page note with suggestions on how she might better help the city's destitute. "I can't imagine Mr. Burnby ever thinking of ways to improve my efforts, as you did."

"Ah, so you found that helpful? You never said."

She leaned back and pillowed her head on her arm. "Your ideas sound so logical, so . . . inspired. I haven't been able to apply any of it yet. Before we left the city, all my energies were taken up with finding you. Perhaps I should tie an anchor to your leg."

He leaned on his elbow and gazed down at her. "I swear, Clara, I never want to hurt you," he said, his voice husky.

"Then stay with me." She hated the plaintive sound underlying her demand, but a thread of fear encircled her heart despite their intimate encounter.

Her fears eased with his next words. "Being here, alone with you, I can't imagine ever leaving your side."

She blinked hard, trying to focus on him through a sudden wash of tears. "Sometimes you're brutally honest, and sometimes . . . sometimes your honesty is so beautiful, it hurts."

He gazed into her eyes, searching, seeing her heart laid bare before him. "I like who I am when you look at me. That's the man I want to be."

Lying back, he urged her on top of him. "Kiss me, Clara. Make me yours."

And she did.

Clara gradually came awake to discover that night had died. She lay content in Stone's arms, their entwined limbs painted in the delicate vermilion of the sunrise. "Stone, it's dawn."

He cracked his eyes open and looked toward the cave entrance, then laid his head back. "A sorry sight."

She stretched, her body feeling warm and delicious. "Do you know the history of this cave?"

"No," he said, twining her hair around his hand as he held her.

"It's called Conrad's Cave. It's named for a magnificent corsair and his wife, Medora. Legend has it they kept a stronghold here."

He smiled at her. "Is that a fact? So we're not the first to . . ."

"Make love here? Not at all." She stroked his cheek. "Perhaps someday we'll come here again."

His eyes darkened slightly. "Perhaps."

She longed to stay here with him, banish the shadows that had crept into his eyes. She knew he was sad at their parting, but they wouldn't be apart for long. "I need to get home, before they discover I'm not in bed." She pulled to her knees and began gathering her clothes.

He lifted himself to his elbows. "Clara, are you . . . comfortable with this? With what we did?"

She smiled and leaned over him, then kissed him hard on the mouth—the kiss of a newly experienced woman. "Yes, my love. Don't worry about me."

"That is hardly possible." He ran his fingers along her arm. "Clara," he said hesitantly. "I want you to know . . ."

At his serious tone, Clara stopped fussing with her petticoat strings and gave him her full attention. "What is it?"

"I really do love you," he said softly. "I always will."

The sadness of his tone disturbed her. She gave him a reassuring smile. "I know, darling. I can't wait to marry you. We'll be able to spend every night together, and—"

"Clara!"

What had sounded like distant sea birds coalesced into understandable language. Someone outside the cave was calling her name. Clara's stomach sank. Her family had discovered that she had run off. Worse, they were about to find her.

"Clara!" Her father's voice, closer now. As close as the Forty Steps. Clara threw on her clothes as fast as she could, knowing already it was too late. No woman could dress in two petticoats, a corset, and a ball gown in the time it would take a man to climb down the Forty Steps. And once her father reached the bottom, it would only take moments to look inside this cave. . . .

"God, I'm so sorry," Stone said. He had already fastened his pants and shrugged on his shirt. "If I thought for one moment—I bloody well wasn't thinking. Bloody hell." Lifting one of his shoes, he shoved it on his foot.

"It's not your fault."

He paused and looked at her. "Clara, you don't understand. Nothing now will help. Nothing at all."

The shadows had returned. Frustrated, Clara took a step toward him, intent on shaking him out of his melancholy.

The light pouring into the cave abruptly vanished. "Clara!" Her father's booming voice echoed harshly against the walls.

Clara turned to find her father silhouetted in the entrance. Her stomach tensed into a painful knot. *I can face this,* she reasoned, trying to keep her head. *As long as Stone is beside me.*

He quivered with rage, his furious gaze jumping

between her and Stone. "By God, Clara, you've been gone all night. And to find you here, looking like—like *that*..." He averted his gaze, as if he couldn't bear to look at her. Clara shoved back her mussed hair, knowing she was a sight in her wrinkled skirts with her dress undone in back.

"Father, it's all right. We—"

"Worse, you're not with a boy of your set, someone you could reasonably marry, but with *him*." He turned on Stone, who stood as silent as a statue at the rear of the cave. "By God, man, we knew you were a cad after that scene last night, but to take it out on Clara—"

"He didn't take revenge with me, Father. He loves me, and I love him."

"Clara," Stone said, stepping toward her. "I'm sorry."

"Sorry?" Her father cried. "That's all you can say? After destroying my daughter's reputation?"

"Father, he and I are going to be—"

"That was not my intent," Stone said, staring at her father.

"You're lucky I don't throw you into the ocean right here and now!" her father cried.

"If you like," Stone said.

Clara stared at him, aghast. "How can you suggest that, Stone? Father? This is ridiculous!"

"What is ridiculous is you having anything to do with this fellow, shaming your family this way." He spun on Stone once more. "If you come anywhere near my daughter again, I swear I will kill you."

"That won't be necessary, despite how satisfying it might feel to you. Excuse me." He cast her a gaze naked with emotion—love, regret, apology all flickered in his eyes. Then he pushed past her father, strode from the cave, and disappeared from sight.

Clara took a step toward the exit, intending to follow him. Her father gripped her arm, bringing her up short. "Don't you dare, Clara."

She tried to tug her arm free. "Let go of me, Father. You don't understand about him. He thinks he's not good enough—"

"He isn't. Damn it, Clara, did you—did you . . ." He stuttered to a stop, then sucked in a breath and tried again. "Did he take advantage of you?"

Clara pulled herself up straight and lifted her chin. "No, Father, he most definitely did not."

Her father looked at her dubiously, his gaze straying over her wrinkled gown, the sagging bodice. "Then your virtue is safe?"

Clara looked away, toward the cave exit. Where would he go? Would she have a chance to find him before he left Newport?

"You won't be seeing him again." Her father's pronouncement sent a chill through her. "Good riddance, I say. He knows he's not worthy of you."

He shook his head, and his expression softened. "Clara, you must stop this nonsense. Your mother and I have always been proud of you. To find you consorting with—with strange men . . ." He shook his head. "I only pray Gerald is still willing to have you."

Clara's eyes filled with tears. She wanted to believe her father had chased Stone away, but the truth pressed into her heart, demanding to be recognized. If Stone had wanted her, truly wanted her, he would have fought for her. Instead, he had run from her, for the last time.

For, she vowed as her heart shattered into a million pieces, she would never pursue him again.

Stone hefted the crate onto his shoulder and turned for what seemed the thousandth time to put it on a waiting delivery cart. Working the docks sunrise to sunset provided enough income to put food in his belly and pay for a bed in Mrs. Drawer's flophouse. That was all he really needed—enough hard work to help him forget.

Sweat dripped between his shoulder blades. The fever nibbled at the edges of his nerves, threatening a return at any time. Once it did, Stone had no idea how he would provide for himself.

At least now he could provide for himself. He no longer waited on the generosity of a certain family on Fifth Avenue. No longer waited on *her* . . .

Don't think about her. Don't do it. Unfortunately, he couldn't turn his thoughts away. No matter what he concerned himself with, Clara lingered there, every moment he was awake. On the rare occasions he had to focus on something else, she danced at the edge of his consciousness, waiting for his full attention, which he invariably gave her. She was his angel, and he knew she would never leave him. He would always think of her.

"Hawke!"

He shoved the crate onto the stack on the flatbed cart and turned to the foreman. A woman in a plain woolen dress stood beside the burly man, looking his way. She waved, then headed toward him, past the line of carts being loaded. The pearly early-morning light glinted off red hair escaping from under her blue plaid scarf.

"There y'are," Lucy said, coming up to him.

"Lucy." He straightened and stared down at her, wondering why she had sought him out. He opened his mouth to ask but suppressed the name that rose to his lips.

"G'on," she coaxed. "You want to ask about 'er."

His jaw tensed. "Why are you here?"

"Not very friendly-like, are you? After I got you this job, 'n' all."

"I already thanked you for that." Lucy hadn't exactly gotten him the work at the docks, but she had pointed him in the right direction. A friend of her cousin's also worked here and put in a good word for him, despite his being "a bloody Limey bastard," as Jake O'Connell indelicately put it.

"Ya see," she said, running the end of her scarf through her fingers. "Her folks—they's pushin' her awful hard to accept that Burnby fella."

He frowned, his chest hitching with possibilities not yet voiced. "How hard?"

"They's practically engaged. I s'pect her to be married to him by Christmas."

"That's only four weeks away!"

She shrugged. "Like I said, they're anxious."

Stop her. The thought flashed through his mind only a second before common sense shoved it away. "It's not my affair." Turning away from her, he strode back to the pallet and lifted another crate onto his shoulder.

"You're just going to walk away?"

"Go home, Lucy."

"Don't you *care?*" Her voice carried to him above the din of the busy wharf. He tried not to hear it, tried not to let his heart answer.

Bloody yes, he cared. He cared so much it stabbed like a knife in his chest. He longed to hail a cab and direct the driver to 675 Fifth Avenue. Pound on the door, dash inside. Find Clara, pull her into his arms, and carry her away with him.

During the lonely hours of the night, he allowed himself to indulge in that sparkling, poignant drift of thought. Allowed himself fantasies of a much more carnal nature, returning again and again to the misty cave by the sea.

His shoulders straining under the weight, he unloaded the crate on the nearly full cart. A pair of dray horses in harness stamped their feet and snorted in the chill morning air. He knew better than to live in an insubstantial dream. He knew better than to interfere. He never deserved her. He didn't deserve anything at all. Clara had never been his. Nothing had changed, and he had been right to leave her.

Or so he kept telling himself.

An overhead crane passed over him, temporarily cloaking him in shadow. He glanced up. A pallet of crates swung overhead, suspended in a net by a hook.

"Another one," said a worker ten feet away. Stone didn't recognize the fellow as one of the regular dockworkers. The man, more nattily dressed than most of them, seemed to be more interested in talking than lifting crates. He had tried to engage Stone in conversation, but Stone had stopped his prying with a single cold glare.

Now, even though the pallet wasn't empty, the fellow wandered across the wharf toward the ship, where a handful of sailors gathered.

Stone turned back to his work. The sound of a whip snapping pierced through the bustle, drawing his attention overhead. A loose cable dangled at the side of the net overhead, and the load swayed.

Stone's gaze lowered to the garrulous worker, standing directly below the load, oblivious to the danger.

Another cable snapped, and the load tilted at a precarious angle, the lack of support putting tremendous strain on the netting. The air filled with the screech and groan of shifting metal and wood, followed by a whip-sharp crack like a warning bell.

"Good God," Stone muttered. Without thinking further, he broke into a run and barreled into the fellow, shoving him hard. The man fell to the ground a few feet away, out of danger. Stone lost his balance and landed hard on the ground behind him.

The sound of grinding wood shattered his ears as boxes landed on the ground right beside him. Before he could catch his breath, much less move, a sharp pain stabbed into his temple.

Then, he knew no more.

Chapter 20

"A Christmas wedding would be quite nice, Clara; you can't deny that."

"I'm not denying it, Mother." Clara sat at the breakfast table in her family's mansion on Fifth Avenue, staring at her untouched plate of ham, eggs, and biscuits that the cook's assistant had insisted on placing before her. Her mother talked of little else but her marriage to Gerald, which would be announced at a gathering in two weeks. After her being caught in a compromising situation with Stone, her family hadn't spoken of the incident, or of him. As far as they were concerned, it had never happened. He had never existed.

Instead, they exhibited their fears for her reputation through their need to marry her off as expeditiously as possible—and with far less fanfare than might be expected of a wealthy society heiress.

Clara found it difficult to care one way or the other. Every moment of the day she fought a secret battle against her heart. She could not push Stone from her mind, no matter how hard she tried. He possessed her, heart, soul, and body, even now, when she knew she would never see him again.

She had vowed never to pursue him. Still, she thought of him, wondered where he might be. Had he gone back to England, or returned here to New York? And, if he remained here, how was he spending his days?

Don't imagine it. Don't imagine seeking him or finding him. Don't think of how sweet it was being his, even for such a brief time.

For even after spending the night in her arms, he could not truly believe she loved him enough. She knew he needed faith in himself, to believe he was worthy of her love. If he never found that faith, that love for himself that enabled him to accept the love of others, there could be no hope for them.

In a handful of weeks, she would belong to another man. Her fantasies of becoming Stone's wife would become nothing more than dreams of what might have been.

Dismayed by her all-too-familiar reverie, she sought a distraction in the day's *Tribune*, left behind by her father. She tugged it toward her. Her eyes skimmed the page, not really reading—until they snagged on a particular name that was always in her thoughts.

Instantly, her dreary existence changed. Her heart began to pound. She sat up straighter, pulling the newspaper closer. Her mother continued to drone on about guests and arrangements, but Clara heard nothing of this, Instead, she read a colorful accounting of a heroic act performed by a dock-worker bearing the unusual name of Stone Hawke.

"Mother, you have to read this." She lurched to her feet, newspaper in hand.

Her mother accepted the newspaper, probably expecting to read some society gossip.

"That item, right there." Clara pointed it out to her, and her mother began to read. "He's been working at the docks all this time. And he threw himself into harm's way to save a stranger! I knew he was a man of honor."

"Hush, Clara. Let me read."

Clara stood behind her mother's chair and read the article again over her shoulder, paying more attention to the details. Stone had saved the author of the piece, a newspaperman who had been reporting on union issues at the docks.

Clara watched her face carefully, and knew when she reached Stone's name. Her eyebrows lifted and her jaw dropped. "My, my. And he was our guest. Ours! I wonder if Mrs. Astor has seen this yet."

Clara smiled. Now that Stone had received public acclaim as a hero, having hosted him would give her family a degree of status among the set.

Mrs. Carrington cleared her throat and began to read aloud. "This heroic figure, this modern-day Galahad, threw himself into the jaws of death to rescue this writer from an untimely and painful death. Dear readers, you would not be reading this column now if not for the quick actions of this simple dockworker, who goes by the picayune and unfitting name, Mr. Stone Hawke. For he is not at all made of stone. His heart is crafted of finer stuff than that which beats in the breasts of most men who walk the streets of this bustling city. He is a true American hero, and this writer is forever in his debt."

Excited to share the article, Clara hadn't read the last paragraph. Her mother continued reading. "Mr. Hawke is presently residing in Bellevue Hospital, having received injuries to his head during his heroic feat. May the good Lord grant him a rapid recovery."

Mrs. Carrington lowered the paper and gave Clara a sympathetic gaze. "Do you want to visit him in hospital? I detest hospitals, but I suppose I could make room in our schedule this afternoon. Now that you're practically engaged to Mr. Burnby, I am willing to allow a brief, fully chaperoned visit."

Her longing to be with him tore like a living thing at her heart. It went against her very nature to refuse. Perhaps she could visit him, her heart reasoned. Just a brief visit, to make certain he was receiving good care, a difficult feat in a public institution known for its crowded, unsanitary conditions. She could sit by his side until he mended. . . .

No. If you see him again, you'll find it impossible to walk away. She had made herself a promise that she would no longer pursue him, no matter what. She had no proof that anything had changed, that he now believed in himself or in his love for her. Still, it pained her deeply to think of him in the hospital, without being able to comfort him. She had never made a more painful decision.

"Clara?" Her mother gave her a puzzled look.

She shook her head. "No, thank you, Mother." She had to be alone, before she began crying in front of her mother. "Why don't you find out if

Mrs. Astor has seen that? I'm going to go . . . to my room. I have things to do."

Turning, she hurried from the room.

At first, Stone knew nothing. He floated in blissful unconsciousness. When he realized he was aware, he found himself dressed in a well-tailored suit—the sort that idiot Burn-me might wear—strolling along a grassy hill toward a cast-iron tea table under an umbrella so white, it burned his eyes.

A lady sat at the table, dressed in glowing white chiffon, her dinner-plate hat cocked at a stylish angle.

Then, as is the way with dreams, he found himself seated and staring into his teacup, without any recollection of having sat down. The thick, dark beverage in his cup looked nothing like tea.

He felt wrapped in cotton, all sounds muffled and distant. No birds twittered; no wind moved the branches of nearby trees.

Even his emotions were muffled. He ought to be angry about his foul-looking tea, but the best he could muster was the observation, "My tea. It's bitter." He knew this without having to taste it. He had already tasted it. Bathed in it.

Finally, he focused on the woman across from him. Though she was dressed as Clara might be, it wasn't her, but her maid, Lucy. "Everyone's tea is bitter," she told him, speaking in an upper-crust English accent that—given her costume—strangely suited her. "That is why we have sugar."

He stared dubiously at the white substance in

the little porcelain container. "I don't remember what it tastes like."

Lucy smiled from under her broad-brimmed hat. "Yes, you do. You've simply forgotten. Here." She pushed the sugar bowl toward him with one gloved finger.

"I'm afraid," he confessed, just like a little boy might. What was wrong with him? Why did the sight of the sugar bowl fill him with such dread? Better to down the noxious beverage as it was than to touch the sweetness. He was staring once more into the thick, bottomless liquid in his teacup. "I'll ruin it."

"Trust yourself."

Using the tiny spoon in the bowl, he scooped up a spoonful of sugar. Carefully, so as not to spill a single precious granule, he lifted it over his cup.

"Do it, Stone. Enjoy the sweetness," Lucy encouraged.

One more second, and he would pour it in. One more second to gather his courage. One more second to question his decision. One more—

The dream ended suddenly, jerking him to consciousness in a single, painful jolt. Stone snapped open his eyes and found himself still in the men's ward in Bellevue Hospital. He had been there close to a week, long enough for his head injury to heal. The doctor intended to keep him there an additional week for observation.

Another week . . . Stone sighed, feeling unusually restless. The strange, otherworldly dream continued to possess him, filling him with an unusual sense of power and wonder. He knew it had meant nothing, yet it made him think of his life in ways he hadn't for a very long time.

He thought about his tumultuous past. He thought about the accident that had put him here instead of taking his life. And he thought about the future that stretched before him.

Most of all, he thought about Clara, how her lovely blue eyes had filled with disappointment and hurt when he failed to stay by her side.

She deserved better from a man who professed to love her.

He missed her dreadfully. In the past, he would have pushed aside such feelings, believing himself unworthy to long for her. Now, he accepted the truth of his loneliness, the lack of "sweetness" that lay in a future without Clara.

And her future without him. He knew in his heart that he loved her more than any other man possibly could. Including Gerald Burn-me, who loved himself and his career more than the lovely sylph he believed it was his right to marry.

She didn't deserve to be wedded to a man who failed to love her for herself. Damn it, she deserved to be loved for the beautiful, kindhearted woman she was, with a love that had nothing to do with who her father happened to be.

He could give her that love.

He, Stone Hawke, former captain in the British Army, now a longshoreman working the New York harbor. Despite his past, despite who he once had been or who he now was, she loved him. Miss Clara Carrington loved him.

Confidence filled him, a welcome friend he had

turned his back on for far too long. His heart surged with possibilities and plans.

All he had to do was convince her of the truth that brimmed inside him, an undeniable force. He could do it, if it wasn't too late. If she would forgive him. If she wasn't already another man's wife . . .

God, no. Don't be late. Don't ruin this, too. He had another chance to do the right thing, for her. For himself. Another chance to prove he was no coward, even when facing the bastions of Fifth Avenue society. Clara deserved a man who could stand on his own damned feet, who would stand by her side, no matter what.

Throwing back the covers, he sat up. His head spun at the sudden change in elevation. He forced himself to wait until his vertigo passed.

"Excuse me, sir." The ward nurse spotted him and hurried over. "You must lie down. Your head injury."

He shook his head, fighting to pretend the action didn't send a shaft of pain through his bandaged temple. "I have to leave. I've been here long enough." He placed his bare feet on the ice-cold floor. "Give me my clothes."

"But, sir. The doctor specifically said—"

"Bloody hell, I don't give a fig what the doctor ordered!" he cried, his booming voice echoing down the ward and drawing the gazes of all the conscious patients. "I'm leaving here. My future depends on it."

"But—"

He glared at the nurse, and she stepped back, her eyes filling with worry. Then she turned and hurried toward the desk, probably to call for brawny orderlies to force him back to bed, perhaps even tie him down.

Stone would have none of it. He found his clothes tucked under the bed. Not stopping to put them on, he bundled them under his arm and charged from the room.

Clara smiled and nodded at her family's guests as they entered the Blue Room, done up for the occasion with vases of white lilies—symbolic of her pristine state, she supposed. Wouldn't these guests be surprised to learn the truth.

Also surprised would be her soon-to-be husband, Gerald Burnby, standing beside her father in a knot of guests. Yet he would accept that fault in her. After all, he wasn't really marrying her but her hefty dowry, while buying himself a secure future with Atlantic-Southern Railroads. He was too smart to make an issue of her virginity.

What surprised her was how little she cared. If Gerald decided he hated her once they were wedded, she would live with it. Her heart had never belonged to him.

Nevertheless, today, with her family and friends in attendance, she would officially become engaged to Mr. Gerald Burnby.

Finally, all the invited guests had entered, and Edgar closed the tall double doors leading to the hall.

Clara left her post by the door and crossed the room to the mullioned window on the room's far side. Despite the party's being held in her honor, she found it difficult to converse with her guests. And they, having heard rumblings about her possible indiscretion in Newport, seemed more interested in gossiping among themselves and casting her curious sideways glances. Clara knew her parents believed that after today, with a well-bred gentleman accepting her hand, these shallow people would consider her "proper" once more.

Proper. . . . She would rather live a thousand days in Stone's arms, even without marriage, than be considered proper by her peers.

Vaguely, the sound of the parlor door opening carried to her across the room. The tenor of the gathering subtly changed—voices stilled, whispers intensified, and someone gasped. Clara turned from the window, and found herself looking at the man who had never left her thoughts. He stood in the center of the gathering, wearing what had to be his finest suit, though it wasn't as well tailored as those worn by the men standing about.

Her father looked as if he had seen a ghost. Before he had a chance to question the uninvited guest, Stone took a step toward her. "Clara, you can't marry that fellow." He pointed toward Gerald, standing ten feet away.

Gerald hurried over to her side. "I say, that's rude of you!"

Clara watched as Stone advanced toward her, despite the rumblings of the guests. Edgar had rushed to her father's side to beg forgiveness for not keeping the interloper out.

Clara ignored them all. She had eyes only for Stone. His gaze locked on hers, and the rest of the room faded away. When he stopped before her, she realized he was carrying a bouquet of simple yellow daisies. "Stone, what—what are you doing?"

"What I should have done before," he said, his jaw set with determination. "Demanding that you be with me and no one else. Especially not a man who doesn't love you."

"Of course I love her!" Burnby looked as if Stone had insulted his very honor.

As if analyzing a bug, Stone cast his eyes on his rival. "Indeed? Do you know what scent she wears? Or the name of the mission where she volunteers her time? Do you know *anything* other than the size of her dowry?"

Gerald frowned. "I don't like your tone."

"Answer the question. Do you know Clara?"

The room had grown deadly silent as the on-lookers waited to see if he would accept the gaunt-let Stone had thrown down. Even her parents waited to see what Gerald Burnby would say. They no doubt believed he could answer the questions easily, and were waiting for him to put Stone in his place before they kicked him out.

Gerald shifted his feet. "Well, yes, of course I know her. Her favorite scent is . . ." He snapped his fingers. "Lilacs!"

Clara sighed, not at all surprised he had found the answer hard to come by.

Realizing he had missed, Gerald tried another flower. "Roses, of course. I knew it; it just took me a moment to recall."

Stone's eyes hardened. "And you would be wrong. You will always be wrong, Burnby, no mat-ter how many times you try. She wears lavender.

And volunteers at the First Episcopalian Mission. I should know. I've been there. Have you?" Without waiting for an answer, he shoved the bouquet he carried at Burnby's chest, forcing him to hold it. His hands free, he scooped up Clara's hands and gazed at her. Her heart tightened with joy as she recognized the light in his eyes.

"I've been all kinds of a fool, Clara," he murmured, his words meant for her alone. Yet the room had fallen so silent, his voice carried to them all. "But something happened to me—something . . . magical. Because of you. We both know we belong together. I was just too addled to believe it was possible to experience such joy in this life."

"Stone, are you sure?" she asked, afraid to believe he had truly put his past to rest. "You trust that I love you? Because I do." She ran her hands up his arms. "Very much. Always."

"Always. Darling Clara, I can't live a day without you." Then his brow furrowed and he shook his head. "No, that's not right. I learned I *can* live on my own, with myself, just as you hoped I would. But I would be awfully miserable, just the same."

"No more demons?"

He shook his head and smiled into her eyes. "No more demons, pet. I'm ready to take sugar with my tea."

"What?"

"Something Lucy said. Somewhere." His eyes grew distant for a moment; then he focused again on her. "It doesn't matter. I found myself again, because you believed in me. That little accident at the docks taught me that helping others means helping yourself, something you do every day. It's a strange feeling, but one I would be happy to grow accustomed to. First, though, you *will* marry me."

His authoritative tone sent a private thrill through her. Other women might be annoyed by his commanding attitude, but she found his arrogance a blessed change from the beaten man who had first set foot on her doorstep. "I thought you would never ask."

He arched an eyebrow. "Was that a question? I didn't think so. There is no question you are going to be my wife." He tempered his words with a teasing grin.

"Oh, Stone, yes!" Clara threw her arms around his neck and hugged him hard. Gasps surrounded her, and conversation resumed, quickly swelling into an uproar.

"Wait just a minute!" Her father stepped over to them, finally giving up on Gerald's ability to lay claim to her. "You can't just waltz in here and get yourself engaged to my daughter. What about Gerald?"

"Gerald can take a flying leap off the Brooklyn Bridge," Stone murmured without looking at him.

"Stone!" Clara said, pretending to be more aghast than she felt.

He turned to her father, his arm securely and possessively around her waist. "We're going to be married, whether or not you approve."

"By God, you have a set on you," her father groused. He stared hard at Stone, and Clara thought she detected a flicker of admiration in his eyes. "I don't recall you standing by my daughter in Newport."

"You're quite right. I didn't. I was a fool and a blackguard. I'm here to rectify that."

His eyes narrowed. "Suppose I cut off Clara without a cent for her disobedience. How do you expect to support her?"

"I believe your own family came from humble stock, or am I wrong?"

"Not wrong."

"I may have little to my name, but I have plans. First, I plan to help you establish and manage Carrington Charitable Homes."

"Carrington *what?*" Mr. Carrington looked at Clara for help. Clara shrugged, as little in the know as he. But the idea sounded wonderful.

"Charity homes," Stone explained. "A philanthropic enterprise that will put your family's name on the map of this city. Clara mentioned that was a goal of yours."

"Did she, now?" He rubbed his mustache.

"What better way to help Clara help people?" Stone said.

"It's a perfect idea, Father," Clara said, knowing he would have accepted it wholeheartedly if she herself had proposed it. "Weren't you trying to think of some philanthropic enterprise to compete with Rockefeller and Vanderbilt?"

"Compete? Well, no. I just felt it was time . . ."

Clara said, "I can't think of a better enterprise than feeding and housing the homeless—"

"Helping them get back on their feet . . ." Stone added.

"Taking in orphans and unwed mothers and injured workers who can't support themselves . . ."

"Managing the homes in an organized, disciplined fashion," Stone finished. He again addressed her father. "You have the money. Clara has the heart. And I have the head."

Mr. Carrington glanced at her mother, who looked as if she was trying to hide a smile. "Brash fella, isn't he? I suppose it's an idea worth considering," he conceded.

"But—but—Mr. Carrington, we had an arrangement," a tentative voice said at his side. "Your daughter. She is supposed to marry *me*."

Mr. Carrington looked at Gerald Burnby, then at his daughter, who was smiling up at the man who had staked his claim on her. He couldn't help noticing that Burnby wasn't complaining about having his heart broken. Nor could he deny that Clara had never looked at Burnby as she was now gazing at her captain.

"It looks like the battle is over, Gerald. After marrying off three daughters, my wife and I have learned not to fight too hard where their hearts are concerned. That way lies madness."

"But—this isn't fair . . ."

"Neither is life. If you plan to succeed in this world, you have to roll with the punches." He slapped Gerald on the shoulder. "Don't take it so hard, Gerald. Look, there's Meryl, my youngest. Isn't she a pretty sight?"

Gerald studied the Carringtons' youngest, who had hurried over to give her older sister a hug of support, along with several of the younger guests. Now that Stone Hawke had received the Carrington stamp of approval—as well as being declared a hero of the city—the set decided to accept him.

"Meryl," Clara said softly, glad for the opportunity to tease her little sister. "Mr. Burnby is looking at you."

Meryl spun around and caught Gerald smoothing his hair into place and straightening his jacket, just before he took a step toward her. "No, thank you. I'm not about to get caught in *that* trap." She quickly slipped through the crowd and disappeared.

Clara laughed. She grasped Stone's hand in her own, anxious to have him to herself. "Please excuse us; we'll be back in a moment," she explained to the debutantes who had come over to meet her new, dashing fiancé.

Taking Stone by the hand, she led him through the gathering and out the door into the hall.

Alone with him there, she looped her arms around his neck. "Thank you for rescuing me."

He shook his head. "Clara, you know you have it backward. You rescued me." Before she could protest, he silenced her with a kiss.

Put a Little Romance in Your Life with
Georgina Gentry

Put a Little Romance in Your Life With
Melanie George